Nothing to Gain

A Blackbridge Novel

Claire Boston

BANTILLY
PUBLISHING

First published by Bantilly Publishing in 2018

Nothing to Gain: The Blackbridge Series

EPUB format: 978-1-925696-17-2
Mobi format: 978-1-925696-18-9
Print: 978-1-925696-19-6

Cover design by Lana Pecherczyk
Edited by Ann Harth
Proofread by Teena Raffa-Mulligan

DEDICATION

To Colleen Browne and Marie Perrier

Two of the best teachers a child could ever hope for.

Thank you for encouraging my writing, teaching me to challenge the world, and to think outside the box.

Chapter 1

The clock on the wall taunted Mai On with its slow-moving
minute hand. Maybe the battery was dead. It was either that, or
the day was dragging as badly as it seemed.

Normally she loved working out the front of the bakery,
catching up with friends and neighbours, and hearing all of the
positive comments about the delicious baked treats in the big
glass cabinets, but normally she'd had a midday siesta to catch
up on sleep. Today she'd been working since one a.m, and
maintaining a friendly and bright façade was becoming more
difficult as the day wore on.

She breathed a sigh of relief as the jingle of the bell above
the door signalled the last of the lunch rush customers had left.

"Thank God," Sylvia said, taking off the powder blue apron
she wore and throwing it on the bench. "I've got to go to the
toilet, I'll be right back."

Mai nodded as her employee dashed out through the kitchen
to the back. She could handle this. She'd done much longer days
when she'd first set up the bakery a couple of years ago. She was
just out of practice.

Mai collected a couple of dirty dishes from one of the small
tables lining the big, glass windows, and wiped the wooden
surface.

Turning back to the counter, she smiled. This was all hers.

She'd designed the bakery to have a nineteen twenties feel,

like the building it was in. The display cabinets had wide, rounded glass with powder blue name tags for each item. Smudged fingerprints at toddler-height marred the perfection, but she didn't mind. It was a joy to see the excited faces of children trying to decide which treat to choose.

She smoothed the tissue paper used to wrap the bread and stacked a couple of small white cardboard boxes neatly on the bench ready for the next customer. They'd almost sold out of bread for the day, so she transferred the remaining loaves to one wicker basket and tipped the crumbs into the bin. The big glass jar containing Florentines was almost empty, as was the shortbread jar. She'd need to make more tomorrow.

Simply reviewing her place, planning for tomorrow, soothed her, lifting some of her fatigue.

She'd worked hard to make it a success, and no one could take it from her now. She would grow; she'd buy the building she was in, then expand into the empty unit next door. More tables meant more customers. *On the Way* would become even more of an icon in Blackbridge.

Mai smiled as she carried the plates back into the kitchen.

The bell over the door rang and she hurried back out. "Hi, Aaron!" She'd left messages for her new landlord over the past couple of weeks, but he hadn't returned her calls. She hadn't seen him since his father's funeral when he'd inherited the building, and he wore the same black suit, still a little too big for his small body, his thinning grey hair combed perfectly in place. She hadn't heard there was a funeral in town today.

He took a step back. "Mai, I, ah, didn't think you'd be here."

"Jodie called in sick. What can I get you?"

"A sour dough loaf and a custard tart, please."

She took the loaf from the shelf and wrapped it. "Any update on when you're putting this building on the market?"

Aaron fumbled through his wallet. "How much?"

Mai frowned. "Did something go wrong with probate?" She boxed up the tart.

"No. It's sold."

It took a second for his words to sink in. "What?"

"I sold the building." Aaron shuffled away from the counter, staring out the window.

"*This* building?" Mai clenched the edge of the counter. "The building you promised to sell to me after probate went through?"

He nodded.

Mai shook her head, refusing to believe him. "Today is not the day to be joking, Aaron. I've been on my feet since one this morning."

"I'm sorry, Mai. I got a better offer." This time he briefly met her eyes, guilt in his expression.

Her breath left her like the air out of a failed soufflé. "Who? There's no one in Blackbridge who's interested."

He cleared his throat. "It's, ah, a Perth company." He swallowed and handed over a twenty dollar note. "Shadbolt Property Developers."

The words made her stomach churn. She stared at him. "You sold out to some money-grubbing city property developer?"

Aaron bristled. "It's not like that, Mai. He offered to buy the building and the land behind it. You only wanted the building."

"Why didn't you tell me, give me the opportunity to bid too?" Her brain couldn't quite process what she had heard, but anger seemed like the right emotion.

"You couldn't afford it."

"How the hell would you know what I can afford?" She shoved his change at him.

"Don't be angry, Mai. It was a business decision."

Mai breathed deeply as the anger in her head snapped and snarled to be let out. This pathetic little man had betrayed her, had sold her livelihood out from under her. Letting out the breath she tried to be rational. Perhaps nothing would change. She had a lease. "When does settlement go through?"

He winced. "Today."

No wonder the slime ball hadn't answered her calls. This is what she got for being patient, for not wanting to be pushy during Aaron and his family's grieving process. She'd waited too long. "All right. Do you have some contact details? I'd like to speak to my new landlord."

"Not on me. I'll email them to you. I'm sure he'll be in touch." He shuffled towards the door. "I gotta go." He fled.

Mai closed her eyes.

"What does that mean?" Sylvia walked out from the kitchen where she'd been waiting and slid the apron back on, tying it around her curvy body.

"I don't know."

"They won't shut the bakery will they?"

She had no idea. Property developers had a bad reputation in the south of Western Australia. "I doubt it," she said with more conviction than she felt. "We have a lease."

"Does it cover the owner dying?" Sylvia asked.

"I'm sure there's a provision, don't worry about it. I'll call the new owner as soon as Aaron sends me his details and get it all sorted out." Mai forced a smile on to her face. "I'm going to whip up some more shortbread biscuits while we're quiet. Give me a yell if you need a hand serving."

Sylvia nodded and Mai escaped to the kitchen.

Her mind whirled as she got the ingredients out of her walk-in storeroom. This could not be happening. She had a plan – she'd received the pre-approval from the bank and was ready to take the next step in her career. Now, she could lose everything she'd worked so hard to build, not to mention her apartment upstairs. She could become jobless and homeless instantly. Her stomach twisted so violently that she dumped the ingredients on the stainless steel bench and closed her eyes, taking a couple of seconds to settle herself.

She shook her head. No need to jump to the worst possible conclusion. Just because a property developer had bought the place didn't mean he would knock it down. The building had history, and yeah, it might need rewiring and the plumbing was occasionally temperamental, but it was still pretty good for a century-old building.

But Aaron had sold the block behind the building as well. It was full of weeds and building rubble and had been empty forever. It also stretched the length of the block. No one bought an empty plot of land without planning to build on it.

She inhaled the sweet scent of the vanilla bean as she added the seed to the mixing bowl and then turned on the mixer. The whir was like meditation music, calming her thoughts. She'd been through troubles before and come through them. The best case scenario would be if the developer only wanted the block and she could buy the building from him.

Or perhaps he'd keep the building and honour her lease.

He couldn't knock it down. This was her home, she'd had her first taste of independence here, it was where she'd pursued her dream, and the place where she'd met Hannah, Kit and Fleur, back when it had been a lolly shop and she'd just moved to town.

It was full of life-changing memories.

Without the bakery she was nothing.

She removed the mixture from the bowl and gently formed it into a ball, the soft, creamy dough almost sensual against her fingers. She rolled it out and used the heart-shaped cutter to make the biscuits before putting them on a tray and in the fridge to cool. After quickly cleaning up, she scanned the shop where Sylvia was serving Gladys and her young grandson. Mai hurried out and offered the boy a melting moment from the jar they kept for children.

"You'll never make any money if you give your biscuits away." Gladys handed over the exact change.

Mai grinned. Gladys said the same thing every time she brought one of her grandchildren in. "Everyone deserves a treat." She waved as they left the bakery.

Sylvia took off her powder blue apron and folded it. "I'm off now."

"All right." If only she'd been able to stay back for an hour to close up. "Have fun on your date tonight."

Sylvia grimaced. "Maybe. Dating at my age is like playing Russian roulette."

Mai chuckled. "Forty-five is not old."

"No, but there aren't any decent eligible men in town." She waved as she walked out the door.

With the last of her staff gone and the bakery thankfully empty, Mai slid into a seat to rest her aching feet. It was never very busy at this time of the day. If she closed early, she could get some more baking done now, because tomorrow would be bedlam.

The idea was way too tempting.

With a groan she forced herself up and then went around the

small eating area, pushing in the chairs and checking the sugar bowls.

Sylvia had already cleaned the sticky fingerprints off the cabinet glass and rearranged the treats so the cabinet didn't look so empty. Mai loved making all of her products, breads, cakes, biscuits and pastries, but tonight would be long and hard as she had additional special orders for New Year's Eve.

Her plan to hire another baker would have to wait until she'd cleared up the mess Aaron had left her in.

With the front of the bakery clean and inviting, Mai headed back to the kitchen. She'd do the Florentines next because she could leave the mixture if she was interrupted by customers.

The bell on the front door rang.

Speak of the devil. "Be right there."

The man standing in her bakery talking on his phone was not her usual clientele. Despite the thirty degrees temperature outside, he wore a dark grey suit that fitted him to perfection. The jacket framed his shoulders, hugged his waist and stopped just short enough to show how his pants defined his butt nicely. Mai took another look just to make sure.

He was probably in his early thirties but flecks of grey shot through the dark brown at his temples. Still he was a nice piece of eye candy and definitely not from around here. She would have heard about a guy this gorgeous by now.

She cleaned the coffee machine as she waited for him to hang up.

His voice was low, but she caught some of the words.

"Let me know if I can do anything to help," he said. "I can be back in Perth in a couple of hours. The project doesn't need me here." He was silent for a moment and then sighed. "All right. I'll talk to you later, Mum."

She liked a guy who called his mother.

As the man hung up he turned to Mai and smiled. "I'm sorry to keep you waiting."

Holy cow. Whoever this guy was, he had a killer smile – friendly and open and a little bit flirty. Be still my heart. She called dibs – she'd spotted him first.

Mai cleared her throat. "Nothing to apologise for. What can I get you?"

"What do you recommend?" That smile again. She willed her pulse rate to slow.

"Do you prefer sweet or savoury?"

"I've always had a bit of a sweet tooth, though I try to control it." He brushed a hand over the front of his suit. "I don't get to exercise as much as I'd like."

His body looked plenty fine to her.

She mentally rolled her eyes. That was the kind of comment Kit would have made. What was wrong with her? She scanned the sparse cabinet. "If you want something small, the jelly cakes are light and fluffy," she said. "Or if you want to be more decadent, then the bee stings are divine."

"The bee sting it is," he said. "And I'd love an espresso as well."

"To have here?"

"Yes, please." He was silent as she set the coffee machine going. "I was actually hoping to catch the owner, if she's available."

Mai put the bee sting onto a plate and slid it in front of him. "What about?" She took the fifty dollar note he handed her.

"I'd prefer to talk directly to the owner."

Everything clicked into place: the suit, the out-of-town vibe, the coyness. Hell. "You're from Shadbolt Property Developers."

He raised his eyebrows and gave a short nod.

Mai counted his change as her brain whirled. "The building's new owner."

"Yes. How did you know?"

"Aaron was just in. He mentioned it." She turned to the coffee machine, brushing at the flour on her apron, then smoothed back the loose strands of hair that had fallen out of her bun. As she reached for the cup, she subtly sniffed at her armpits. Not too bad. Still it wasn't the most powerful position to start from. She handed the man his espresso. "I'm the owner."

"You're Mai On?"

She nodded.

He held out a hand. "Nicholas Shadbolt. It's lovely to meet you." His smile was pure charm, his teeth perfect and white, and a vision of a great white shark baring its teeth popped into her head.

She shook his hand, his skin firm and smooth, the type that used a computer for work. Not like her own that had calluses and burns from years of work in the kitchen.

"Do you have time to talk?"

She hesitated. She wanted to know his plans, but she also wanted to scream at him for daring to buy the building. The irrational, grumpy Mai was running on only a few hours' sleep. She fought back the banshee. It wasn't the kind of first impression she wanted to make. "It's not a great time," she said. "I've had an employee off sick and I've got a lot to finish."

"What about tomorrow?"

She laughed. "New Year's Eve is one of my busiest days." She tucked a stray hair behind her ear. Her brain wouldn't cooperate, wouldn't process all the work she had to do, but this had to be resolved as soon as possible. "If Jodie calls in sick again the only time I'll have free is before work."

"Fine. What time is that?"

"One a.m." The burst of surprise that flashed over his face was intensely satisfying.

"You're the baker as well as the owner?"

"That's right."

"All right. Shall I meet you here at one?"

Mai gaped at him. "Seriously?"

"I'm always serious about business." He smiled.

Annoyance waged a war with respect. She shouldn't have opened her big mouth and challenged him, but she could hardly back down now. She needed to know his plan, had to find out where she stood. Her chest squeezed and she breathed through the stress. "I can give you thirty minutes," she said. "Knock on the front door and I'll let you in. Now if you'll excuse me, I have work to do." Without waiting for his response, she escaped into the kitchen.

The beeping alarm pierced Nicholas's dream full of flames and accusations. He rubbed his face as his pulse rate slowed. It had been two months since the incident and yet it continued to plague his mind in an endless loop of how he could have done things differently.

It was still dark outside, almost pitch black, but his phone gave him enough light to make it to the ensuite bathroom. He flicked the light switch and squinted at the glare from the glazed white tiles. He closed his eyes as he stepped under the warm spray.

He needed to have his wits about him with Mai this morning. And a middle-of-the-night meeting after a largely sleepless night wasn't the best position to start from.

Mai On was nothing like Nicholas had expected. He'd assumed the owner of the bakery would be much older, someone who'd been in the industry for years and was ready for a change. The money on offer for them to vacate the premises should have been snatched up without an issue. But no, Mai was younger than him, and she wasn't happy.

So much for his assumption she was a sales girl. He'd taken in her petite frame, the most gorgeous, almond-shaped brown eyes, and for the first time being exiled to Blackbridge had seemed like a good thing. But she wasn't the sales girl – she had a whole lot more emotionally invested.

Shadbolt normally didn't deal with small fry. 'Go big or go home' was their motto, but Nicholas's father had needed some way to get rid of him and still save face.

Guilt hit him hard. He was lucky he still had a job. If it hadn't been for his mother standing up for him...

He'd fucked up badly. He deserved worse than this.

Nicholas prayed for the pressure in his chest to ease and then twisted off the taps.

He needed to focus on the job at hand. Everyone had a price, and Mai was a small town business owner. He'd charm her, convince her he offered a solid deal that would be good for her business in the long run. And part of the process meant getting up at the witching hour.

The warmth of the night surrounded him as he reviewed his wardrobe. The full suit held little appeal, but he wouldn't give her any excuse to refuse him. He wouldn't fail his father a second time.

The drive from his parents' holiday home to the bakery only took five minutes. The dark hid the flaking paint on the building he'd bought. Instead of looking decrepit, the building had a majesty about it, the façade solid and decorative, a pillar of the community that had seen the town grow.

It would be a shame to see it go.

He parked at the front, noting the bright lights shining at the back in the kitchen and as he walked up to the front door, the shop lights switched on and Mai strode to the coffee machine. She wore white chef's pants and a white T-shirt, with her hair tied back in a tight bun. She appeared a lot more alert than he felt.

Nicholas tapped on the glass and she turned, her eyebrows lifting as if she was surprised to see him there. She'd learn that when he made a promise he kept it.

She held up a hand and went back into the kitchen, returning a minute later with a bunch of keys. As she opened the door, the comforting scent of baking bread floated out. "I didn't think you'd show."

He snorted at her bluntness. At least he knew where he stood with her. She had no faith in him – that club had a lot of members. "You said it was your only free time."

She grunted and locked the door behind him. "Free time is a relative term. I've been here a couple of hours already."

He followed her behind the counter, ignoring the rumble in his stomach at the pastries on display. The bakery had such charm, from the pretty blue product name tags, to the big rounded glass jars filled with biscuits and the bread baskets waiting to be filled.

"Coffee?"

"If you're having one." He didn't need to give her any more excuses to be irritated with him.

She quickly made two cups – his an espresso just the way he liked it.

"Thanks."

"This way." Mai dragged a chair from a tiny office, which was barely big enough for the desk and floor safe, and rolled it over to him. "Take a seat."

He sat as he scanned the kitchen. There was nothing tiny about this space. Two huge ovens billowed heat into the room and through their glass windows he could see bread already beginning to rise. Three big stainless steel tables were in the middle, one already stacked with bread pans and a mixer whirred in the corner. Mai wasn't just alert, she'd been working for hours.

She spread flour liberally over the table and then as if timed to perfection, the mixer stopped and she dragged its dough onto the table, the muscles in her arms bunching as she did so. He'd never realised muscled arms were sexy.

He sipped his drink. "This is great coffee."

"Yes it is." She barely glanced at him. "We've got twenty minutes before Penny starts, so I'd like to get down to business. Did Aaron mention he and I had a verbal agreement for the purchase of this building?"

Shit. His insides clenched. That information hadn't been in the project notes – unless he'd missed something again. "No, he didn't."

"I didn't think so. I've got pre-approval from the bank for the loan. How much do you want for it?"

Nicholas frowned. "For the building?"

"Yes. I'll buy it from you." She stopped kneading and glared at him as if daring him to disagree.

He shook his head. "It's not for sale."

"Look, I know you bought the land behind," she said. "Surely you don't want to have to deal with an old building with its dodgy wiring and plumbing. I'll take it off your hands and you can concentrate on whatever plans you have for the block."

Her tactics were good – acting as if it was a done deal was what he would have done. She really wasn't going to like his response. He shifted in his seat. "That won't work. The building is being demolished."

Mai grabbed the edge of the bench as she swayed. "What?"

Hell. Nicholas leapt to his feet and propelled her into his chair. "Sit down." He didn't need her collapsing.

She sat, leaning forward, her eyes closed, chest heaving.

What a bastard. He should have broken it to her gently.

She needed water, where could he find a glass? He hurried into the cafe area, finding a mug next to the coffee machine and filling it from the tap. After he handed it to her, he gave her a minute to recover.

When the mug stopped shaking in her hand he said, "There's a new development replacing the building."

"But I've still got three years on my lease."

"There's a relocation and demolition clause in it."

She shook her head. "What does that mean?"

He hated the concern in her eyes, but he steeled himself and took an envelope out of his inside jacket pocket and handed it to her. "There are a couple of options," he said. "You can choose to find different premises for your bakery, or you can take one of the shops in the new development when it's completed."

"And what am I supposed to do in the meantime?" she demanded. "Between you demolishing my business and rebuilding?"

"You'll be compensated for it."

Her look of disgust piled an extra foot of guilt onto him. She got to her feet and pushed past him to finish kneading. "Do you know how many businesses that are forced to close down actually reopen?"

"This will be a planned closure."

She shook her head. "Have you got shire permission for the redevelopment?"

"That's just a matter of time." He preferred the business woman to the fragile person she was a second ago.

"You think so?" She chuckled. "You're not from around here, are you?"

He didn't like the confidence with which she said that. "My parents have a holiday home in Blackbridge. I've been coming here for years."

"For what, a week at a time?"

He nodded.

"Then you know squat. What are you planning to do? Knock this beautiful old building down and put up some generic supermarket?" Her gaze pinned him and he fought the urge to squirm.

Why did this woman make him feel guilty about something he did every day of his life? "Didn't you say it had dodgy wiring and plumbing?"

"That's part of its charm." She winked and his heart

stuttered, an uncomfortable sensation.

He couldn't be attracted to her.

Bad things happened when he let his personal feelings influence his business decisions. He'd learnt that the hard way. "The development will contain eight units."

"And be one of those white, soulless concrete monstrosities?"

It wasn't how he would describe it. He nodded.

"Do you really think it will suit a town like Blackbridge?"

"It will provide more opportunities to the town's residents. It's called progress, Miss On. Perhaps you've heard of it?" He regretted the words as soon as they came out. He didn't normally get defensive.

She laughed then, the sound light and rich and it stirred something in his chest. He squashed it.

"Sure I have," she said. "Progress enables me to make as many biscuits, bread and pastries as I do. I'm quite fond of it in fact." She put the dough in a large container and went into another room where he heard the thud of things being moved about. Her voice a little muffled, she said, "I'm also fond of history. Did you know this building was built in 1895 and was the first grocery store in the town?"

He shook his head.

She returned to the room carrying a huge bag of flour. "It was also the only store left standing when the bush fire of twenty-two swept through, destroying half the town. It provided the essentials the town needed to start rebuilding."

As she spoke, Nicholas could see the development falling down around his ears. If the building did indeed have that kind of history, there was no way the shire would let Shadbolt knock it down. Was his father setting him up? Did he want him to fail again? "Be that as it may," he said, "it's my building now."

Mai nodded agreeably. "And since you're the landlord, the back steps need repairing. The safety rail is holding on by a nail – literally – and the toilets keep blocking. I'd appreciate it if you could fix them as soon as possible."

Gritting his teeth, he made a note. "I'll see to it." He didn't need someone falling and hurting themselves. "Do you want to show it to me now?"

"You won't see a lot; the back light over the car park is also broken."

Of course it was.

At that moment a woman in her mid-forties walked in, similarly dressed in white pants and T-shirt. She yawned.

"Morning, Penny," Mai called.

Penny looked at him, her curiosity clear. "Good morning."

"I've got about a dozen special orders for tonight's celebrations so we've got a lot to do," Mai continued.

"Right. I'm on it."

"Before you start, can you let Nicholas out?" She glanced at him. "We were finished here, weren't we?"

Not by a long shot, but he knew when to regroup. "All the information is in the envelope," he said. "Call me when you've read it. I'm sure you'll have questions."

She nodded.

Nicholas followed Penny out the door. He couldn't stuff up another development.

But Mai On was not going to be easy.

Mai's chest was tight, making it hard to breathe, as Nicholas walked out the door. He couldn't take her bakery. She wouldn't let him. She'd worked too damned hard over the past few years to let it all go.

She figured she had a maximum of three days before Nicholas realised she'd been lying about the history of the building, but at least it would give her time to figure out what to do. She couldn't let him knock it down. She'd met the musketeers here and her whole life had changed for the better – she'd discovered hope for the future. It was her home and her refuge.

"Who was that?" Penny asked as she returned to the kitchen.

Mai swallowed hard. "Our new landlord."

"What?" Her eyes widened.

"Aaron sold the building to him, despite our agreement."

"What a bastard!" Penny glanced to the front door. "That explains why he's wearing a suit at this time of the morning."

Yeah, Nicholas hadn't missed a trick. Mai had given him a

fifty-fifty chance of turning up, but the fact that he had and was dressed for business meant he was serious.

Penny got to work and Mai's mind wandered.

Aaron's betrayal had completely blindsided her. He could have hit her over the head with a two by four and she'd have been less shocked.

What on earth was she going to do now?

She'd had plans to expand and suddenly she might lose it all.

Her throat tightened.

No, she couldn't think like that. She needed to plan.

There weren't any empty stores near the main drag. She could hardly be *On the Way* bakery in the middle of nowhere. Besides, she didn't want to leave. This was her place, she'd worked until she was exhausted to build it into an institution.

Moving, even temporarily, felt so much like having to start again.

And that was too depressing to even contemplate.

She'd almost given up several times over the past couple of years — too tired to go on. If it hadn't been for the support of her friends she would have.

The bakery was part of who she was.

Could she really go through it all again?

If she wasn't close to town, she wouldn't get the foot traffic of tourists wandering the town and she'd no longer have the view down the hill to the river. People would get their bread at the local supermarket, rather than from her.

What if it signalled the beginning of the end? What if she couldn't recover? What if she failed?

She bit her lip. She'd put everything on the line to become a baker. She'd disappointed her mother, and endured working odd hours and lack of sleep for the past eight years. The very idea of having to start from scratch made her want to weep. There was simply nothing right about Nicholas's proposal.

She had to convince him that renovating the building was a better business decision than knocking it down.

He was *not* taking her bakery from her.

Chapter 2

The pounding on the door woke Mai. She groaned and pried open her gritty eyes. Light snuck in past the sides of her block-out blinds. What was going on?

"Mai, are you in there?" Fleur. She was picking her up to go to Kit's New Year's Eve party.

Mai had lain down to take a thirty minute power nap after her sixteen-hour day. She shouldn't have bothered. Her body was heavy and her mind was like wool. She threw on her cotton dressing gown and padded through her tiny apartment to let Fleur in.

"Did I miss the memo about it being a pyjama party?" Fleur's normally straight brown hair was a mass of curls, and the blue top she wore brought out the colour in her eyes. Her jeans moulded to her slim frame and she was as gorgeous and put together as always.

Mai rolled her eyes. "I'll be ready in five. Can you feed Calypso?" Mai's rag doll cat jumped down from the couch and ran to greet Fleur with a meow.

"Sure. Long day?"

What an understatement. "Yeah. Jodie called in sick again." Mai went into the bathroom and splashed cold water on her face, immediately feeling better.

"Kit won't mind if you're a no-show," Fleur called.

True, but Mai hadn't been out in ages. A little fatigue

wouldn't ruin her night. She slipped on underwear and took a floaty, baby pink summer dress off its hanger. She loved the way the fabric fell and whirled around her as she walked. She zipped it up as far as she could and then headed into the kitchen. "I need a hand."

Fleur zipped it up the rest of the way. "That's super cute."

Mai grinned. "Thanks." She returned to the bathroom, ran a brush through her hair and quickly applied some makeup. "Who has Kit invited tonight?"

"Your guess is as good as mine." Fleur stood in the doorway. "Gail was at the hospital today with the kids, so she won't be, but she said Gordon was heading out. Aside from that … you know the way word spreads. I wouldn't be surprised if half the town has been invited by someone or other."

"Yeah, Kit loves a good party." She hoped she had the energy for it. Twenty minutes out of town meant loud music and a late night.

She debated briefly between flats and heels, pushing her fire-fighting boots out of the way so she could try both on, but the flats won out. Her feet needed a rest after the day she'd had.

After making sure Calypso had enough water and giving him a treat, Mai grabbed her purse, overnight bag and the cake she'd baked for the party. "Let's go."

She locked her apartment and trotted down the stairs after Fleur to the back door of the bakery. Fleur's small white Hyundai was parked outside and as she sat in it, taking the weight off her feet felt like luxury.

"I saw Sylvia today," Fleur said as she drove out of town. "She said something about your building being sold."

Mai swallowed the lump in her throat and squeezed her eyes shut to banish the tears. She wouldn't cry. "Yeah. Aaron sold the building to someone else."

"I thought she was kidding! How could he sell you out?"

"Money." It was a bitter realisation. "A property developer bought the building and the land behind it."

Fleur frowned. "What's going to happen?"

"He's going to demolish it and build something new." Her chest tightened and she clenched her hands. Fleur slowed the car. "You're joking!"

"If only." Mai stared out of the window at the dense green shrubbery rushing by.

"And what are you supposed to do?"

She shrugged. She hadn't had a chance to assess the proposal he'd given her. "He's given me six months to vacate."

"That's ridiculous. Can he even do that? You've got a lease." Fleur's voice got louder as she spoke.

A fraction of the weight lifted off Mai's shoulders. "I'm not sure."

"What did your mum say? She deals with that kind of law, doesn't she?"

Mai grimaced. "I haven't spoken to her yet." And she didn't want to go running to her mother for help. It was bad enough that Bian had advised her against signing the original lease, had advised her against opening her own bakery.

"I'm sure she'll help you sort it out," Fleur said as she pulled into Kit's drive.

"Yeah." Mai forced a smile.

Tall karri trees lined the dairy farm's gravel drive. In the distance, black and white cows moved away from the large, silver milking shed. Mai wound down her window to listen to the cows mooing to each other and to smell the rich, earthy scent of the land. Some of her fatigue evaporated as she inhaled deeply. Coming out tonight had been the right decision.

They pulled up next to a white 4WD parked outside the low chain-wire fence. Inside the boundary, the farmhouse took centre stage – a beautiful old building with white wooden cladding and a wooden verandah that ran all the way around it. The metal roof curved at the edges, welcoming visitors inside.

They walked up the short gravel path and a huge brindle-coloured bull mastiff ran towards them from the backyard.

"Looks like Hannah's here," Fleur said.

Mai patted Hannah's dog, Joe, before climbing the wooden steps into the house. She found Hannah in the country kitchen balancing on one foot as she mixed up a frozen cocktail, her crutches leaning up against the pantry. The red bows clipping back her short blond hair were cute, matching her knee-length red dress, but the white leg plaster did spoil the look a little.

"Need a hand with that?" Mai asked, opening the fridge to

find a spare shelf for her cake. Rows of salad bowls, meat platters and bottled drinks greeted her. A bit of creative reordering was needed.

Hannah groaned. "It's only been a week and this leg is driving me crazy."

"At least you're alive," Fleur reminded her.

Hannah grimaced. "You're right."

Mai shivered. Hannah had almost died when she was attacked by a stalker. "Are Ryan and Felix coming?"

"They're already here," Hannah said. "Ryan's taken Felix down to the shed to watch the milking. He couldn't stop babbling about it."

Mai could imagine eight-year-old Felix bouncing up and down in excitement. Hannah's boyfriend and his boy were a new fixture in Blackbridge and she liked them both. "What else needs to be done?"

"The ice needs to go into the barrels," Hannah said. "Kit arranged everything else before she left."

Mai lifted the ice bags from the sink and carried them out the back to where two metal barrels sat in the middle of the lawn and tipped them in. Fleur and Hannah were right behind her, Fleur carefully carrying three cocktail glasses full of pink goodness and Hannah cautiously negotiating the grass on her crutches. Mai took a strawberry daiquiri and Fleur motioned towards the two garden sofas which had been moved underneath one of the big gum trees. Kit's garden was like Kit, no fuss and practical – an expanse of lawn with a few trees around the edge and some vegetable beds close to the house.

With a groan, Mai sank into the cushioned seat.

"Hard day?" Hannah asked.

"Long," she replied.

"Plus, her landlord wants her to move out," Fleur added.

"Wait, Aaron wants you to move out?" Hannah asked.

"No, the jerk sold it to someone else," Fleur said.

Hannah gaped at her. "But you had an agreement."

"It was only verbal," Mai told her. She'd been foolish enough to believe he'd keep his word. "If I'd known he would do this I would have put it in writing."

"So who bought it?" Hannah asked.

"Shadbolt Property Developers."

"That doesn't sound good."

Before she responded, Lincoln and Jamie Zanetti walked into the yard. Mai waved a greeting. They were a gorgeous pair. Both brothers reflected their Italian heritage and were tall and dark-haired, but while Lincoln was clean-shaven, Jamie had designer stubble. She'd grown up with them both, and they were like brothers to her.

"Have you got the night off, Sergeant?" Fleur asked.

"Yeah," Lincoln answered.

"That's great," Hannah said. "You should get time in lieu for all the extra work you did helping me before Christmas."

Lincoln shrugged. "That's the life of a small town cop."

"Which is why I became a teacher," Jamie said. "So many school holidays," he joked.

"And still you don't visit us enough," Fleur complained.

"I know." He grimaced and sat next to Mai, giving her a hug. "How's it going, Mayday?"

She inhaled his aftershave, spicy with a hint of citrus. "I could do with some more sleep, but I'll live." She missed his easy smile and good-natured teasing when he was in Perth. They needed to convince him to move back to Blackbridge.

"And some wanker from Perth wants to demolish her bakery," Fleur added.

"What?" Jamie shifted to stare at Mai, mouth gaping.

Mai told the story again, nausea circulating her body. She took a gulp of her drink. "I'll work something out." There had to be something she could do.

"Will you move back home?" he asked.

She cringed. "Not if I can help it." She loved her independence, loved not having to say where she was going, or when she'd be back, loved having space that was just hers.

"Hannah, guess what?" Felix spilled into the backyard, his father not far behind. "Kit let me milk one of the cows and then I got to feed the calves." Breathless, he stopped in front of them, his short, brown hair a little dishevelled with some hay in it.

"Did the calves suck your fingers?" Hannah asked.

He nodded. "Their tongues are so rough." He spotted Joe

lounging on the lawn in the sun and raced off again.

"Is it wrong that I'm jealous of his mobility?" Hannah asked.

Ryan bent down and kissed her. "Not at all. You'll be back to normal in no time."

A stab of wistfulness went through Mai. She'd been so busy building her business that casual flings were all she had time for. Men generally didn't understand why she went to bed so early. She'd been hoping that after she expanded the bakery and hired another baker, she'd be able to take some more time to herself. It was a shame Nicholas had turned out to be a douchebag because he was really easy on the eye.

"Is Kit with you?" Lincoln asked as he slapped Ryan on the shoulder.

"Yeah, she said she'd be right out."

Just then the booming bass of a rock song blared out from the house and Kit walked out dressed in jeans and a low-cut white top, her brown hair loose and flowing. She put a hand on her hip and called, "Let's get this party started!"

Mai grinned as a surge of energy shot through her.

They had great music and all her friends were here.

It would be a fantastic night.

Nicholas glanced down at the mud map he'd been given and then turned off the main highway. This was stupid, going to some random New Year's Eve party where the only person he knew was the cop who'd come out to investigate the break-in at his garden shed last night. But after spending all day researching Blackbridge's history and finding nothing about his building, he needed a drink. It would be good to meet some of the locals, especially if what Mai said about the building was true. The more people he got on his side the better.

Plus being alone on New Year's Eve was kind of tragic.

He'd brought a lot of beer to share and arrived late so the party was well under way. The easier to slip in unnoticed in case the cop, Lincoln, had got it wrong and it wasn't the more the merrier. But he wasn't the only one turning up late because a black van followed him down the driveway.

The line of cars in a nearby paddock soothed his concerns.

One extra person definitely wouldn't be noticed. He shook his head as he followed the home-made sign pointing him towards a paddock for parking. He *definitely* wasn't in Perth anymore, though his BMW navigated the few ruts with ease.

He inhaled deeply, the scent of hay and dirt mixing with the meaty barbecue smell coming from the backyard. The music pumped out loud and was actually decent – Kent Downer's latest song, rather than the country music he'd been expecting. Floodlights and fairy lights lit up the yard, illuminating the large group of people mingling and kids dancing. Adding his drinks to the converted metal oil barrel, he scanned the crowd and zoomed in on a woman in a short, pink dress. Her back was to him, her long black hair shining under the light, and the cut of the dress accentuated her petite curves. That looked like a great place to start networking. Clasping one of his boutique beers he wandered over, spotting Lincoln in the group. Even better.

He raised his bottle to catch Lincoln's attention and the man smiled and waved him over. "Glad you could make it."

"Thanks for the invite," Nicholas said.

"Everyone, this is Nicholas. He's in town for a couple of weeks. Nicholas this is Kit, your hostess, and Fleur, Mai and my brother Jamie."

The woman in the pink dress gasped.

Wow.

It was Mai. The white pants and shirt she'd worn in the bakery really hid her curves. She was beautiful, her dress floaty and feminine, not words he would have associated with her. Without the tight bun, her hair softened her face, although her tight lips and the line between her brows showed she wasn't very happy to see him. "Nice to see you again, Miss On."

"Do you know Mai?" Lincoln said.

"Nicholas is the guy who bought my building," Mai answered.

Lincoln winced. "Oh." He glanced at Nicholas. "Mai just told us about that."

And from the glares from the women, he was public enemy number one. Great. He forced a smile. "Well from what Mai said, the building might be on its way to being heritage listed."

"That old thing?" Jamie scoffed. "I doubt it."

Mai nudged Jamie and he coughed.

That was interesting. "She said it was one of the only surviving buildings after the bush fire of twenty-two."

Fleur nodded, trying to conceal a smile. "Yes, that one. I remember now."

Son of a bitch. Mai had been lying.

He'd wasted the whole day searching for information that didn't exist. He didn't need petty games right now. But at least it was one less thing to worry about.

"Let me introduce you to some more people." Lincoln gestured towards the house.

He definitely had to put some distance between himself and Mai. "Thanks. I'll be in touch next week," he said to Mai.

"I can't wait." She flashed him a fake smile.

When they were out of earshot Nicholas said, "I should go." He wasn't staying where he wasn't welcome.

"Don't worry about it. Looks can't kill and the musketeers won't murder you while I'm around." Lincoln grinned.

Nicholas found himself smiling back. "Musketeers?"

"Mai and her friends, Kit, Fleur and Hannah. They've been friends since primary school and if you argue with one, then you take them all on."

"And I've just become the enemy."

"That's right." Lincoln sipped his beer. "So tell me, what are you planning to do on the site?"

Perhaps Lincoln could talk some sense into Mai and her friends. "It's not quite the shopping centre Mai's expecting," he said. "It's a set of eight units with a central car park."

"So Mai can lease one of the shops when it's done?"

The probing wasn't subtle, but Nicholas had nothing to hide. "Yes, that's part of the agreement."

"So what's the problem?"

"She hasn't told me yet." Sure, it would take six months to build the new complex but she would be compensated for the loss of business.

"Mai's a shrewd business woman, but the bakery is her baby."

Nicholas grimaced. Business and emotion were never a good mix. They needed to stick to the facts, the dollars and cents.

When feelings were involved, when you cared what happened, that's when things got messy.

He wasn't making that mistake again.

Mai's eyes tracked Nicholas as he walked away with Lincoln. He should look completely out of place here in his black pants and a blue dress shirt with its long sleeves rolled halfway up. All the other guys wore jeans and T-shirts, but Nicholas pulled off casual and classy at the same time. What a shame he was a bottom-dwelling, blood-sucking arse.

"You neglected to mention how hot he was," Kit said.

"I already called dibs," Mai told her absently and flushed when her friends laughed. "I didn't mean it. I'm not interested in him."

"Sure you are," Fleur said. "Any single, straight woman would be. Maybe he won't turn out to be so bad after all."

"The man wants to demolish my bakery."

"And if anyone can convince him to change his mind, it's you," Kit said.

Maybe she was right. Perhaps instead of giving him the cold shoulder she should sweet-talk him. But right now she couldn't reconcile that this sexy man would rip her dreams apart. Part of her wanted nothing to do with him, while another purely physical part wanted to have some fun. He *was* very attractive.

"Have you checked out his business?" Jamie asked.

She shook her head. "I've been working non-stop since I found out."

"We should do it tomorrow," Fleur said. "Gather as much intel on him as we can. We might find something we can use as leverage."

Mai knew she could count on her friends. They were behind her one hundred percent, and they would help her make plans. It gave her hope.

Tonight she'd watch Nicholas, see what he did, who he talked to, maybe even chat to him herself.

Know thine enemy.

Wasn't that the first rule of battle?

The night wore on and Mai went through her second, third and fourth wind. She should call it a night, but the music still pumped, the bass a heavy throb, and she doubted she'd sleep through it. She circled around the house heading for the daybed on the front verandah to see if it was any quieter. Only a single porch light pierced the darkness and just out of its reach two people stood close together. Mai stopped at the corner of the house. No way would she interrupt a romantic tryst.

"It's as good as the stuff you'll get in Perth," one guy said, his voice kind of familiar.

"All right. How much have you got?" The other guy held out his hand.

"A couple of grams."

Mai's pulse sped up. Kit would have a fit if she caught anyone doing drugs on her property.

The guy dealing shifted and moved into the light from the front porch, his shaved head reflecting the light, and anger replaced the fear. She stormed forward. "Gordon, what are you doing?"

The men whirled around and Gordon swore, shoving something into his pocket. "Nothing, Mai." He glanced around. "What are you doing out here?"

"That's my question to you," she snapped. "Are you really dealing at Kit's party?"

Gordon fidgeted and the other guy, a blond she didn't recognise, said, "Why don't you fuck off?"

Mai raised her eyebrows. What a lovely member of society. "Why don't you?" She turned back to Gordon. "How could you do this after all that Kit went through with her father? You know what happened. You were dating her."

Guilt flashed across Gordon's face, but he stood tall. "A lot has changed since high school. You wouldn't understand."

Mai shook her head. Gordon had always been a bit of a loser but she hadn't thought he'd sink this low. "You need to leave."

"Don't be like that, Mai," he wheedled. "I've got to make a living. I've got my family to provide for."

Gail would be horrified if she knew. "Either you leave or I'll get Lincoln." She glanced at the blond. "That's Sergeant Zanetti if you don't know him."

Gordon swore. "Fine. I'm leaving."

"You should mind your own business," the blond growled, taking a step forward and bunching his fists.

The hair on Mai's arms stood up, but she stared him down until he followed Gordon out of the yard. Her heart thudded, and she waited until they drove off separately before wrapping her arms around herself. Arseholes.

No longer tired or wanting to be alone, she returned to the backyard where Lincoln had commandeered a spot on the lawn for a bocce game. Gordon probably wouldn't be back, but if he was, he'd see her near the police.

Lincoln and Ryan were teamed up against Jamie and Nicholas. She'd never seen a better looking group of men. It wasn't going to be a hardship to watch them play for a while. Mai settled on the grass.

Good natured insults were flung about as Nicholas tossed his ball and it landed right next to the jack. He flashed a look of pure triumph which lit up his face. "Beat that," he challenged Lincoln. He spotted Mai and winked, and a wave of desire spread through her with a delicious shiver.

Down girl.

"Mate, don't you worry, I will." Lincoln did not like to be beaten. Maybe this would teach him not to invite strangers to parties.

That wasn't fair. Lincoln was inherently nice and always welcoming. Of course he'd invite a guy who was alone. She just wished it hadn't been the guy who would ruin her life.

And he didn't need to be quite so nice to Nicholas. The guys all seemed to like him, which was annoying.

Her gaze drifted from the game to the back of Nicholas's pants. His luscious butt led into his really long legs. He had to be at least a foot taller than her, but if she wore heels when they went out it wouldn't be a problem.

Not that she planned to go out with him.

Her gaze moved to his hands. He cupped the silver bocce ball gently and caressed it absentmindedly with his thumb. He had lovely fingers. Would he caress her skin as gently?

She squeezed her thighs together.

Something about him made her libido go crazy.

Lincoln's shout of glee broke through her musings. She blinked. Lincoln had knocked Nicholas's ball out of contention.

She yawned, her eyes heavy and magnetised by the curve of Nicholas's butt. Jamie said something to him and he laughed, the joyful sound reaching her and making her smile. His laugh was nice.

She lay back on the grass, her head too heavy to keep upright. Maybe she *would* close her eyes for a moment and rest them. She'd had a long day.

By midnight Nicholas had a pleasant tipsy buzzing in his head. It had been a long time since he'd got anywhere near drunk, but Lincoln had convinced him to camp overnight, so he didn't need to worry about driving. He'd decided to be as friendly as possible, make contacts who could help him if Mai chose to be difficult, and found himself having fun. An unfamiliar sensation, particularly in the last few months. His chest squeezed making it hard for him to breathe. He couldn't think about that now, not here. He couldn't change what had happened.

Gulping his beer, he choked as his throat closed up.

"You all right, mate?" Jamie asked, slapping him on the back.

He nodded, coughing and gasping for breath until the air flowed again. The others were looking at him. "Beer went down the wrong hole."

"Well you're up." Jamie motioned for him to step up to the line.

The game. Of course. He could do this.

He and Jamie won the game, much to Lincoln's disgust. He scanned the yard for Mai and found her lying on the grass fast asleep. His heart tugged. She looked young and sweet with her hands tucked under her head and her hair falling partially across her face.

No, he couldn't afford to get involved, to get emotional. If he got soft, he'd make the same bad decisions that had led to him being down here, the decisions that had almost ruined Shadbolt.

"Should someone wake her?" he asked Jamie.

Jamie chuckled. "She must be tuckered out to sleep through this racket."

He wanted to know more about Mai. "Does she always start early?"

"Yeah. Normally she takes a nap before coming out at night." Jamie crouched down next to Mai and brushed her hair off her face. "Mayday, it's time to wake up."

Part of him wanted to pull Jamie away, stop him from touching her. Not good. His interest in Mai was strictly business. But he would have to be a moron not to notice her beauty.

Mai opened her eyes. "Did I drift off?" She sat up and stretched, her breasts rising a little further out of her dress. He hardened.

"You sure did." Jamie stood back up.

"Your game must have been particularly boring." Mai grinned at him and then caught sight of Nicholas. She stared at him for a long moment.

"We won." Though it went against everything his brain yelled at him, Nicholas offered her a hand and she took it, her small hand in his. With only the smallest tug, she was on her feet, swaying a little. He steadied her, his hands against her soft icy skin. She had to be freezing. He pulled her closer, rubbing her arms, trying to get some warmth into her. His nose filled with her citrusy scent.

"What the hell?" She shoved him hard and he let go.

What had he just done? He didn't touch people without their permission and here he was practically fondling her. He stepped back. "Sorry. You were cold."

"Here, Mai, take my jacket," Jamie said, handing it to her.

Nicholas needed to get out of there. He'd obviously had too much to drink. His fingers still tingled from the softness of her skin. "I'm going to get some water."

Inside the much warmer kitchen, he found a glass in one of the wall cupboards and filled it with water. He skulled it and then closed his eyes.

He shouldn't have come.

Being here connected him to the community, forming

relationships like he had with Lincoln and his mates. Not a good thing. They'd turn on him if he hurt Mai's business and it would all end badly, he knew that. He'd failed his best friend in Perth because he'd trusted him too much. He couldn't make the same mistake again.

A woman on crutches came into the room, wobbling slightly as she came to a stop. She scowled. "You're Nicholas Shadbolt."

He nodded. She had to be one of Mai's friends.

As she reached into a high cupboard to get a glass, one of her crutches slipped with a crash to the floor and the woman wobbled.

"Need a hand?" he asked, holding her arm to steady her.

She hesitated. "Please." She handed him the glass.

"I broke my leg in primary school," he said as he turned on the tap. "It was cool for about a week getting people to sign the cast and then I couldn't wait to get it off."

The woman nodded. "Tell me about it. It's driving me crazy." She took a sip. "I'm Hannah."

"Ryan's girlfriend."

Hannah beamed and blushed. "Yeah."

At that moment the man himself walked in. "There you are." Ryan drew Hannah into his arms and kissed her.

That was his cue to leave. Nicholas wandered back outside onto the verandah.

Around him people started the countdown. "Ten, nine, eight…"

Thank God the year was over. The new year couldn't possibly be as bad as the past one.

He shook his head. He needed to be positive. He would successfully complete the development in Blackbridge and prove his capability to his father.

"Happy New Year!" The shout went up all around the yard.

People were hugging and kissing, wishing each other a happy new year. Someone bumped into him and he found himself looking down at Mai.

His breath caught as her espresso brown eyes captured him.

"I don't like you," she stated, "but happy new year anyway." Before he could prepare himself, she threw her arms around his neck and kissed him soundly on the mouth. It wasn't more than a second-long kiss, with a hint of strawberry, but desire shot straight through him. Mai took a hasty step back, her eyes wide with shock. "Crap." She turned and walked away.

He couldn't agree more, but he took a step after her before he managed to catch himself. That would not end well. Mai was upset he'd bought her building. Taking advantage of the situation would not help.

No matter how much he wanted to stop her, draw her into his arms and kiss her senseless, it wasn't going to happen.

Business and pleasure didn't mix.

Ever.

Chapter 3

The dull throb in Mai's head woke her the next morning. With a groan she cracked open one eye and sunlight stabbed her. She squeezed her eyes shut. She hadn't drunk *that* much last night, however a large glass of water and a couple of painkillers would go down a treat right about now.

In the bed next to hers, Fleur snored quietly. Mai would have preferred to be sound asleep as well.

A glance at her phone told her it was nine o'clock. Not as late as she'd hoped, but later than she'd slept in ages. Her tight bladder added to her discomfort and she crept out of bed. She stopped in the bathroom, doing her best to keep quiet. The house was fairly silent, but somewhere voices were murmuring softly.

Next stop water and some painkillers.

Walking past Kit's bedroom, she nearly bumped into Jamie coming out. She gasped. He shouldn't be in there.

He grinned. "It's not what you think."

"And what's that?"

"That Kit and I slept together."

They walked through the living area where Lincoln was curled up asleep on one of the sofas and into the kitchen. "Aren't you still dating Sandra?"

"Yeah."

Mai put the kettle on. "Then there's no way." Neither Jamie

nor Kit were like that.

"You're right – we shared a bed. So what about you?"

She frowned. "What do you mean?" She raided Kit's first aid kit for some painkillers and swallowed two.

"You kissed Nicholas."

She froze at the memory. Midnight, wishing everyone a happy new year. Feeling so happy she kissed everyone, including Nicholas. Though it couldn't really be called a kiss – more like an electric shock of desire. "I don't like him. I was caught up in the celebration."

Except that wasn't a hundred percent correct. She wouldn't start the new year by lying to herself. She'd kissed Nicholas because she'd wanted to get it out of her system and she'd figured being tipsy gave her a fall back excuse. That had backfired. If anything she wanted to kiss him again.

Jamie raised his eyebrows. She ignored him. "Coffee?"

"Yes, please."

There was a knock at the kitchen door and speak of the devil, Nicholas stuck his head in. "Did someone say coffee?"

He wore what he'd worn last night, but his clothes weren't rumpled like he'd slept in them. He looked put together and fresh, sexy with that hint of stubble. Why was he still here?

"Yeah, Mai's making. Come in, mate." Jamie gestured him in.

"There's only instant coffee."

"Fine by me," Nicholas replied. "As long as it's strong and black, it'll work."

Mai dumped three spoons of instant coffee into his cup and poured in the hot water. "Here you go."

Nicholas took a sip and his eyebrows raised, but he swallowed. "Lovely. Thank you." He smiled as if amused.

What was it about him that made her act like she was in kindergarten? She prided herself on being calm in every situation and she realised things didn't always work out the way she planned.

But him buying the building had really thrown her, had tossed up all her fears in her face and made her feel like she was scrabbling to keep a hold. She hated it, wanted to hate him. But she couldn't. Maybe it was the way Jamie and the others had welcomed him into the fold that made him seem trustworthy.

She took her coffee and her phone and went out the back onto the verandah.

The paddock to the right of her contained a sea of swags and tents. Dozens of people had chosen to camp overnight. Some were already up and cooking bacon on the barbecues, the smell carrying in the air, making Mai's stomach rumble. Felix ran around with a friend, and Joe begged for Hannah to sling him a piece of meat by the barbecue. Mai wandered over.

"I hope we didn't wake you," Hannah said.

"You didn't." Mai stole a piece of bacon from the plate where Hannah piled it.

"Good. Felix woke up at the crack of dawn. Kit took him to milk the cows and let us sleep for a bit longer."

Of course Kit had been up early, despite the late night. The cows waited for no one. "She must be shattered."

"She said something about going back to bed afterwards," Hannah said.

Lincoln came outside with a backpack slung over his shoulder, and trotted down the steps, his face grim. "Can I get some bacon to go?"

Mai's phone beeped and she read the message. Her heart raced. Not what she needed on her one day off.

"What is it?" Hannah asked.

"Fire call out." She didn't have a car to get back to town and as second-in-command she needed to be there.

As Hannah handed Lincoln a bacon butty, Mai asked, "You heading back to town?"

"Yeah. Got a call about some vandalism. Thought I'd see to it straight away so I could enjoy the rest of the day." His eyes were sad.

"Can I get a lift?"

"Sure."

"Give me a minute." She dashed inside to grab her bag. Nicholas was no longer in the kitchen with Jamie – not that she cared.

In the car, she called to get details of the fire. Not many of her team were likely to be sober enough to deal with a fire this morning. She'd stopped drinking as soon as she'd kissed

Nicholas. It was enough to make anyone sober.

When she hung up Lincoln asked, "What's the call?"

"Smoke was spotted out near Greenfish Bay. Some idiot probably had a campfire last night." Another brigade was mobilising but it was a slow start all around.

"You take care of yourself."

"Always do." Lincoln knew more about what she did as a volunteer fire-fighter than the others. As the local emergency coordinator he understood the dangers.

He dropped her at the fire station, where only Lawrence's car was parked. Not a good start.

The fire captain had the fast attack vehicle primed and ready to go, as she headed for her spare gear. "Is it just you and me?"

"No, we've got a new recruit." Lawrence ran his hand through his salt and pepper hair. He seemed weary today. "Which is just as well because I got no other responses. I'm going to call around now."

Mai dressed quickly and returned to Lawrence as Nicholas entered the fire station.

Mai frowned as her pulse sped up. "What are you doing here?"

Nicholas stopped walking. "Mai."

Lawrence smiled. "Have you met Nicholas? He's transferred down from a city branch."

He had to be kidding. Mai didn't move while Lawrence showed Nicholas the gear. She didn't want to be stuck in a car with this man for the next hour or so. Not after she'd been stupid enough to kiss him.

And what did a city boy know about a bush fire? If this was more than smoke, she had to know what skills the person fighting next to her had.

She slid behind the wheel of the fast attack. No way was he driving.

As Nicholas got in, Mai told Lawrence, "I'll radio when we get there."

"We'll follow when I can get more volunteers, but the other brigade is mobilising too."

She nodded and was silent as she drove out of town, lights flashing, siren on. Nicholas's presence pervaded the cab, the bulk of his yellow fire-fighting gear taking up a lot of space, making her aware of how masculine and sexy he was. She shouldn't have kissed him last night. But she didn't have time to think about it now. She needed to find out if he knew what he was doing. "How long have you been a volunteer?"

"Six months."

Great, he was green. "Been to many fires?"

"This will be my first non-drill."

Crap. "Have you done the full training?" Please let him have done that at least.

"Yeah."

That was something, but a real fire was a whole other ball game to the drills. "OK. When we get out there, I'm in charge. You do what I say, when I say it – got it?"

"Yes, ma'am."

He was entirely too agreeable. She didn't trust it. The male fire-fighters generally didn't like to be told what to do by a woman – at least not at first. Not until they realised she could save their arses.

Nicholas stared straight ahead, tugging on his earlobe, his foot tapping a rapid beat.

Was he nervous?

She remembered how scared she'd been on her first call out. "It's probably just a campfire smoking," she said. "People forget there's a total fire ban in summer on nights like New Year's Eve."

"Have you been doing this long?" Nicholas asked.

"Six years."

His eyes widened. "You must have been young when you started."

"I was twenty. That summer there'd been quite a few bush fires and the bakery I worked at provided food for the volunteers. I wanted to help."

"Have you lived in Blackbridge your whole life?"

"Since I was twelve." Maybe some generic conversation would keep his mind off where they were going. "What about you? Why did you become a volunteer?"

He was silent for a moment. "There was a fire in the hills last summer. My brother lost his house and afterwards he joined the volunteer brigade and convinced me to as well." He glanced out of the window.

She'd seen the devastation first hand, knew how horrified people were to have lost everything. Most people focused on rebuilding, not helping others. It made Mai warm to him a little more. "So how long are you staying in the area?" It was odd for him to transfer if he was only staying a week or two.

"I'm working down here for the next six months until the development is completed. I figured since it's fire season it made sense to transfer."

The development that would destroy her business, her career and her home. Mai scowled. She slowed to turn onto the gravel road leading out to Greenfish Bay. Smoke rose above the low coastal scrub, a long thin white cloud. It hadn't taken hold yet. She pointed it out to Nicholas. "It's good there's no wind this morning."

"How far away are we?"

"Another five minutes." She hadn't been out here in years, not since Fleur's father had taken them both fishing. It wasn't a pleasant memory. She'd discovered her aversion to blood when Fleur's father had sliced open his finger when he was filleting a fish. She shuddered. There had been blood everywhere and she had been sure he would bleed to death out here in the middle of nowhere.

The bay wasn't popular amongst families, which probably explained the abysmal state of the road. She slowed as the corrugated ruts jarred the vehicle and her teeth. A dark blue sedan slid around the corner in front of them, fish-tailing as it did so, a cloud of dust in its wake as it headed straight towards them.

Heart in her throat, she slammed down the horn and took her foot off the accelerator, as the car corrected itself and narrowly missed the fast attack vehicle. Mai caught a glimpse of the driver – Gordon.

Had he come out here after last night? Had he lit the fire?

Nicholas swore as Mai slowed, glancing in her side mirror. Nothing but dust. Gordon hadn't run off the road or stopped. The idiot. She would have a few choice words to say to him when she saw him next.

"Are you all right?" Nicholas asked.

"Yeah." She accelerated as her heart rate slowed. "You?"

"Yep. If I wasn't awake before, I am now."

Mai smiled. "Distracted you from the fire for a minute."

"I could have done without the distraction," Nicholas said. "It doesn't look too bad though."

"No. Hopefully whoever lit it was sensible enough to contain it." Though if it had been Gordon, they probably weren't that lucky.

A few minutes later, she saw for herself. In the middle of the gravel car park were the remains of a massive bonfire about two metres in diameter. Whoever had built it had piled log after log on it and they were now charcoaled remains. It must have been planned as there were no trees that size in the area. When they'd left they'd thrown a bit of dirt on it and some green tree branches, maybe with the hope of smothering it. Instead it had made the whole thing smoke and flames were flickering around the edges. If today had been windier a spark could have carried into the bush only a few metres away.

Gordon definitely deserved a visit.

The car park wasn't more than a cleared gravel area, cordoned off from the surrounding scrub by some long, round wooden posts. It was empty except for the smoking pile of wood and leaves in the very middle of the area – a bonfire only, not the bush fire Nicholas had feared. He let out a deep breath and his shoulders relaxed. Mai had been right – it was nothing serious.

He hadn't realised how unprepared he felt until he was in the fast attack vehicle racing towards the fire with only Mai next to him. The thought of facing a wall of flames – even prepared – was damned frightening.

It was another way he'd failed. This shouldn't have been the first fire he attended – he'd had other opportunities but work had always come first.

Hell, the real reason he'd signed up as a volunteer was because Shadbolt had introduced a requirement that all staff had to do volunteer work – his mother's idea. He'd attended the training sessions with his brother, but was always too busy to go to an actual fire.

And that had come back to bite him after his last development in Baldivis burned to the ground. The police had suspected arson and he'd been chief suspect with both motive and knowledge.

So when the text had come in this morning, it had seemed like a way of proving himself and the perfect excuse to get away from Mai and the attraction that pulsed between them.

That had backfired.

Mai picked up the radio. "Control, this is Blackbridge Fast Attack One, over."

"Go ahead, Fast Attack One. What's the status?"

"Some idiots have built a bonfire in the carpark. It's contained, just smoking. We'll put it out, remove the hazard and come back. No backup necessary."

"Roger that."

They both got out of the truck and Nicholas waited for instructions. He had no idea what he should do.

Mai circled the fire and scowled. "Someone's been getting high." She pointed out the empty syringes in the coals and sighed. "Grab the hose. Turn it on slowly and keep it directed at the base of the fire. It's got a lot of pressure and you don't want to spray the coals out of the fire."

Yeah, the last thing he needed was to cause a real emergency.

At least he remembered how to connect the hose and turn it on. The water on the coals sent a cloud of steam into the air and the fire hissed in protest. He slowly worked his way around the bonfire while Mai patrolled the area, searching for stray coal or ash. She was focused and seemed confident in his ability to follow instructions. He appreciated that.

She returned to the fire and nodded at the soaking puddle. "We need to move the ashes out of the centre of the car park. We don't want anyone running over it and melting their tyres."

He shut off the hose and took the shovel she handed him. They worked together in silence, spreading the ashes over the car park, breaking up the couple of small logs of wood that were still intact and then wetting it all down again to make sure no embers remained. Next to him Mai shovelled hard, not the least bit concerned about the work. She was strong and competent, whereas his breath came in short pants and his back ached. He grimaced and kept working, trying to keep up with Mai's pace. No way would he show her how unfit he was.

He would start a new fitness regime tomorrow.

By the time Mai was satisfied, they'd been working for over an hour and the sun beat down, its harsh rays sucking the moisture from the air. Mai stripped off her yellow jacket and a line of sweat on her white T-shirt between her breasts drew Nicholas's eye. The T-shirt was too thick for it to be transparent but tight enough to accentuate her small perky breasts. He shouldn't be looking.

He cleared his throat. "Are we done?" He took off his own jacket before rolling up the hose.

"Yeah." She checked everything was packed away properly and then radioed control. "We're all clear."

Nicholas subtly stretched his back and shoulders. He'd be lucky if he'd be able to move tomorrow.

They got into the cab and the silence between them grew. He wanted to clear the air, to talk about the development and get things square with her.

Perhaps now was the perfect opportunity. He had the whole drive back to town with Mai as a captive audience.

He might as well take advantage of it.

As Mai drove out of the car park she asked, "How'd you like your first call out?" No question about it, he'd followed her instructions to the letter and he'd worked hard clearing the debris too. He'd been struggling to keep up with her, panting quietly and sweat pouring down his face, so she'd slowed her pace, not wanting to be responsible for him injuring himself. He would be sore enough tomorrow.

He smiled. "It was a lot better than I expected."

Meaning it wasn't terrifying. Those fires would come. "Most of what we get called out to are structural fires or minor blazes."

"Not like the bush fire of twenty-two?"

Mai grimaced. OK, she deserved that. "There was a big bush fire in nineteen twenty-two and part of the town was burnt."

"But your bakery wasn't the last building standing?"

"No," she admitted. "It was built from the ashes, which still makes it almost a hundred years old."

"I would have uncovered the truth eventually."

She nodded. "I was running on only a few hours' sleep, and it seemed like a good way to put you off."

"Why are you so against my development?"

She glanced at him, surprised. "You're destroying my business."

He shook his head. "I'm asking you to relocate it temporarily."

She snorted. As if it was so simple. A disruption like this could be terminal.

"The additional shops will bring more opportunities into town and get rid of the eyesore of an empty block."

"Yeah, your white monstrosity will be so much better." She clenched the steering wheel, her shoulders tense. "Those types of concrete units don't fit the aesthetic of the town."

He chuckled. "You mean the architecture that has an old beach shack next to a modern mansion? That has buildings from the twenties next to brick buildings of the seventies and eighties?"

"My part of the town has heritage buildings," Mai argued. "The least you could do is build something that fits in." She was grasping at straws.

"So you've taken a look at the proposal?"

She didn't want to admit she hadn't. "I haven't read it all." Or done more than scan through the document. She'd been too tired to face it.

"Then why are you so against it?"

She'd thought he'd be smarter than this. "Because you want to close down my business."

"No I don't. I'm offering you a place at the new premises with discounted rent."

She shook her head. He didn't get it. "What am I supposed to do for six months while you build?"

"I can give you a reasonable payment for loss of business, or help with relocation."

"There are some things money can't buy. *On the Way* is an institution, people travel from neighbouring towns to get my products. I can't just close one day and reopen six months later and expect they'll pick up where they left off. They'll find somewhere else to go." She'd worked her butt off *every* day for the past two years to make her bakery a success. She'd survived on little sleep and very little money in those first few months until word had spread. The thought of having to start again devastated her. But Nicholas didn't need to know that. She wouldn't show her weakness in front of him. "I have staff who need their jobs."

"I'm sure we can work out something. Perhaps you can work from home for a while."

She laughed, loud and disbelieving. "That would be the home you're knocking down?"

"What?" His impression of a gaping fish gave her a certain amount of satisfaction.

"I live above the bakery." Nicholas hadn't done his research. Just her luck.

"Isn't there storage space above?"

Mai shook her head. "When they were built, they were designed to have living quarters upstairs. I've lived there for two years. Makes the commute to work short."

"I was told they were empty, that only two shops were leased and one lease was about to run out."

She would definitely ban Aaron from the bakery. He could buy his bread elsewhere, the rat. "It sounds as if Aaron played us both." It didn't matter now. It all boiled down to one cold hard truth. "I'm the only person throwing a spanner in your works." Her palms were sweaty. The florist next door had already told Mai she wasn't renewing her lease.

"Yes."

She didn't stand a chance. Why would a developer of his reputation care about a single small business owner? How could she make him care?

Did he have a soft side?

"I'm sure when you read the proposal, you'll find it an adequate arrangement." His tone was all charm and confidence.

Mai felt ill.

There was nothing adequate about the situation. She would have to start again from scratch, she'd have to tell her staff that they were out of work and some of them were sole-providers for their families.

She breathed deeply to control the anger and fear, but as she drove into the fire station, she knew one thing for certain.

She was so screwed.

Chapter 4

After Mai had cleaned up from the call out, she drove to Gordon's house. She wanted answers about the fire, and was worried about what he'd got himself into. He'd been in her class all through high school and while they hadn't been particularly close, she wanted to help him. His old blue sedan was out the front of the modest brick and tile house so Mai pulled in. The garden was tidy, lawns had been mowed and roses were blooming in the garden beds. It was an average suburban house with no hint the occupant was breaking the law.

Gordon's wife answered her knock.

Crap. She hadn't thought this through, hadn't considered she might not be able to talk to Gordon alone. "Hi, Gail, is Gordon home?"

"No, he's taken the kids to the park. Can I help you with anything?"

"Ah, no." What excuse could she give her?

"You're not going to ask him to volunteer are you?" Gail demanded. "That's way too dangerous."

Relief filled her. "Ah, well, I heard he didn't have a lot of work at the moment."

"He's fine. You better not ask him, Mai. His family needs him." The glare could have baked bread.

"I won't," Mai assured her. "Nice seeing you." Quickly she returned to her car and drove to the park a couple of blocks away. Gordon sat on a park bench watching his four-year-old daughter play on the slide while pushing his baby son in a red pram. No one else was around. Most people headed for the park by the river with the larger playground and barbecue facilities, instead of this small area that was usually used by people doing early morning boot camp.

His daughter squealed in delight as she slid down the slide. Gordon had a beautiful young family. Why was he getting mixed up in drugs? Surely there had to be some kind of legal work available to him. She wasn't sure what qualifications he had, but maybe Kit could get him some work at her farm. But she had to get through to him, had to speak up rather than ignore the situation.

She strode over to him and sat down. "Morning, Gordon."

Gordon winced. "Mai."

"You want to tell me what you were doing out at Greenfish Bay?"

"Sorry about that." He didn't look at her.

"Sorry about what – nearly crashing into us, or starting the fire that we were called to put out?"

"The fire wasn't me." He held up his hands as if that was the worst of his crimes.

She raised her eyebrows. "Really? So it was a coincidence that yours was the only car leaving the area when we drove out?"

"Honest, Mai. It was already lit when I got out there last night."

"Delivering drugs."

"I don't need to explain myself to you." He folded his arms across his chest.

This wasn't getting her anywhere. "No. You could explain yourself to Lincoln." She didn't want to get him into trouble, she wanted to help.

He scowled at her. "It's no big deal. I'm offering a product same as you do."

How dare he compare the two! Anger simmered in her belly. "My product isn't illegal. It doesn't ruin people's lives."

"Haven't you heard of the sugar epidemic?" He smirked at her. "Besides, people choose to take it, I don't force it on them."

She took a long, slow breath to control her anger. "You give them access." How could he be justifying it? He'd seen how it had affected Kit.

"I have to support my family." His son shifted in the pram.

"By ruining other families."

"Don't get all high and mighty on me, Mai. Not all of us have rich parents to buy them shops."

He had some nerve. "My parents didn't buy me my bakery," Mai growled. "I worked my butt off to build it up, to make it what it is."

Gordon snorted. "Whatever. Are we done here?"

She wasn't going to convince him, she could tell by the stiffness of his posture, his refusal to look at her, but still she tried one last time. "Meth could kill you, or one of your clients."

"That's why I don't take it – I'm not stupid."

That was debatable. "If I catch you dealing again, I will tell the police."

"You do what you need to do."

Frustration hummed along Mai's skin as she strode back to her car. Gordon wasn't her business. She should turn him in and let Lincoln deal with him.

She couldn't though. Not with his family relying on him. She had to hope he would consider what she'd said and make some changes.

But she wasn't quite naive enough to actually think he would.

Mai got back into her car and sighed. Today was not going well. First Nicholas and now this. She'd hoped Gordon would tell her it was a once-off deal, a New Year's job.

But no.

He still sat on the bench, gently pushing the pram. Anyone looking would think him the perfect father, taking his kids out to play. A short, weedy guy walked his Rottweiler into the park, the dog heeling next to him perfectly. He wasn't anyone Mai recognised, so probably a tourist down for the summer holidays. The guy's clothes hung off him like he'd lost twenty kilograms lately, and his dark hair was dishevelled. As Mai watched he strolled over and sat next to Gordon, saying something to him.

No way.

Gordon had taken his kids to the park to do a deal.

Mai reached for the door handle ready to give them both a serve, but Gordon snapped to attention, tension in his every muscle.

The guy's gaze roamed the playground, his arms along the back of the bench. Gordon kept glancing at him and it was obvious they were having a conversation that Gordon wasn't happy about.

Should she call the police? But what could she say? By the time they got here the guy could be gone.

The man took something out of his jeans back pocket and slid it across to Gordon who took it and stuffed it in his shorts. Then the guy got up and headed towards the car park.

Their eyes met and the irritation in his froze Mai for a second, her heart pounding. Crap. What if he came over and said something to her? She seized her phone off the seat next to her and hit call on the first person in her recently called list.

"Are you back from the fire already?" Fleur asked.

Relief flooded her. "Yeah." She let her gaze roam over the park as if she was searching for someone as the guy came closer, still looking at her. Her skin crawled. He had the intensity of a snake about to strike. "Weren't we meeting at the park for lunch?"

"Not that I recall, but last night is a little hazy in places." She laughed.

The guy was right outside her window now. Her skin prickled.

"We agreed to meet to go over the proposal." She put her hand to her head, glad the guy couldn't hear Fleur's end of the conversation.

"We still can if you like. Shall I ring the others and you can come to my place this afternoon?"

"Sounds great." The guy was still there, waiting. Did he want to say something to her? She couldn't hang up yet. "How about two?"

"Perfect. I'll see you then."

"Wait!" What could she say to keep Fleur on the phone? She couldn't exactly ignore the man standing right next to her and drive off. It would be confirmation that she'd seen him and Gordon, that she was scared.

"Yeah?"

The guy moved away and Mai watched him in her rear view mirror until he crossed the car park and continued up the street. She slumped down in relief. "Nothing. Don't worry about it."

"Are you all right?"

"Yeah, I'll tell you about it later." She hung up and started her car. She wanted to get out of here.

The guy gave her the creeps. Who just stood outside a car waiting like that? He had to be involved with the drugs Gordon was dealing. Unless Gordon did other shady stuff Mai didn't know about.

She groaned.

She shouldn't get involved.

It was none of her business.

But if she saw him around again, she'd definitely let Lincoln know.

The itching feeling in Mai's skin faded as she shut the door to her apartment and greeted Calypso. She let out a breath. She wasn't likely to see the creepy guy again.

She made herself some Vietnamese rolls for lunch and sat at her kitchen table with Nicholas's proposal.

It was time for her to think strategically.

The document included dates she had to vacate the building, the proposed schedule for the development build and the date for her to move into the new premises.

The six-month timeline seemed optimistic, but she had no experience with the building trade. Hannah's cabins had taken a couple of months to build, but the shell of the cabins had been done in a week — a lot of it was prefabricated. Perhaps concrete slabs were similar.

There was a decent lump sum payment for her inconvenience if she chose to take a shop in the new building, and nothing if she didn't.

The carrot or the stick.

Included in the proposal was an artist's rendition of the final building. It wasn't quite as hideous as she'd been expecting, but it wasn't pretty either. There was nothing charming about it and *On the Way* oozed charm. It was part of her brand, to make people's visits an experience rather than just a shopping expedition.

So what were her options?

Take the offer and shut for six months hoping people wouldn't forget her.

Take the offer and find a temporary premise for six months and hope it didn't completely exhaust and ruin her.

Fight the proposal at the shire. If Nicholas didn't have planning permission yet, she could stop it before it started – though that was no guarantee he wouldn't kick her out anyway.

Find another building and start again.

Her heart ached. She couldn't give up *On the Way*, but the mountain of work in front of her seemed insurmountable. She'd already spent thousands of hours building her business. She'd thought she'd put those eighteen-hour days behind her when she'd been able to afford to hire Penny. The idea of going through it again made her want to curl up in a ball and cry.

She had to consider her staff as well. They relied on her for an income, they *needed* the jobs she provided – there weren't many employment options in Blackbridge.

She closed her eyes as Calypso jumped onto her lap and she ran her hand over his soft fur, drawing comfort from it.

This shouldn't be happening. Aaron had agreed to the sale. The building was supposed to be *hers*.

Mai shook her head. It didn't matter now. Aaron had sold her out and she had to deal with the consequences. And next time she wouldn't let her compassion stop her from getting the agreement in writing.

Her first step had to be finding out what real estate was available, both for her bakery and herself. The new development didn't have apartments above the shops and so she needed to find somewhere to live. She picked up her laptop and did a quick search. Only two potential buildings in Blackbridge and neither was great, but she had to inspect them.

She reviewed houses next, but there were no rentals in her price range in the area. She would have to find a roommate. She cringed. Finding a place to live would be step two. First she needed to find a home for her bakery.

And there was no time like the present.

She grabbed her keys and headed out.

By the time Mai drove to Fleur's house she was thoroughly depressed. She'd inspected her options and peered through the grimy windows which revealed both buildings would require a lot of time and money to get them into shape.

She got out of the car and took a deep breath, trying to shake off her mood before she went inside.

Plenty of bees buzzed in the cottage garden, Fleur's mother's roses were in full bloom and a mass of different colours and Mai took a moment to appreciate the beauty before following the path up the steps and into the old miller's cottage.

"Fleur?" she called.

"In the kitchen!"

Mai put Calypso on the wooden floor to explore and walked through the living area into the light, airy kitchen at the back. Sunlight shone through the window looking out over the yard and Fleur filled the kettle at the kitchen sink.

"I'm sorry about earlier," Fleur said. "I have no recollection about meeting at the park."

Mai grimaced as she put her notes and the bakery box on the table. "That's because I lied." She told Fleur about Gordon and the creepy guy.

"You need to go to Lincoln."

"I will next time. Gordon might change his mind."

Fleur scowled. "I doubt it."

So did Mai, but she wasn't ready to give up on him yet.

"The musketeers reporting for duty." Kit grinned, saluting as she walked into Fleur's kitchen, with Hannah hobbling behind her.

Mai smiled. She could always count on her friends to cheer her up, to help her when she needed it. "Thanks for coming."

Fleur handed Kit and Hannah coffees and Hannah said, "Give us the full rundown. What has Nicholas proposed?"

Mai updated them. "If it's all legit, I'm going to have to move out while the new premises are built." She sighed. "I hate the idea of that beautiful building being demolished."

Hannah smiled. "You're always complaining about something breaking."

"But I love it. It was where we met."

Fleur put her hand on Mai's. "Yeah, but it didn't make us who we are. It's just a place, we carry our memories with us."

"And a new building has to have advantages, doesn't it?" Kit asked.

"You're right." Mai huffed out a breath. She'd been so focused on the negative, on the fear, that she hadn't looked at the potential positives. A brand new building where she might be able to customise the interior. She'd need to consider that a little more. But for now she needed to work out what to do in the interim. "I checked out the two potential properties today — the old cafe on Mortimer Road or the warehouse down by the river."

"Is that it?" Hannah asked.

Mai nodded. "The warehouse is massive and smells like fish, and the old cafe needs a face-lift, plus the kitchen is tiny. Penny and I will get in each other's way."

"Let's do a pro and con list for each," Fleur said.

They worked quickly, bouncing ideas off each other as they came up with a list for both properties. When they were done Mai reviewed the list. "It comes down to cutting my production and having a nice venue, or keeping my current production and having a crappy location."

"It doesn't have to be crappy," Hannah said. "I'm sure we can do something nice with the warehouse space."

"What about the fish smell?" Fleur asked. "That won't be appealing."

"I don't think it's worth spending a lot of money on a place I'll only be in for six months."

"So you're definitely going to take a lease in the new development?" Kit asked.

"I don't know." The thought of working with Nicholas didn't thrill her, but the location was perfect.

"The cafe has a lot of potential," Fleur said. "It won't be as pretty as your current place, but there'll be space for more tables."

"I agree," Hannah said. "People will drive the extra distance for you, Mai."

"Those that know about me might," Mai said. But when it came down to it, people went with the easiest option. "But the move will damage my reputation."

"No, it won't," Kit told her. "You'll get the word out that you're expanding to meet the demands of your customers and ask people to support you through the transition."

It wouldn't be quite that easy, but Mai could spin it to her advantage, and use the customer list she'd built to give updates on the project.

If she took the cafe, she'd have to review her processes, maybe do more of the prep work in the evening so they didn't need to do it when there were two of them in the kitchen. She should take Penny by the place and see what they could work out.

Which meant she had to tell the rest of her staff about the demolition. They were going to be devastated and she had no good news for them.

"Nicholas is paying for the relocation, right?" Kit asked.

"If I take a unit in his development." It really was the best option, but she still felt manipulated, as if the whole situation was out of her control. She rubbed her eyes. "I'll get some quotes and find out how much Nicholas is willing to cough up."

"Can your mum negotiate something for you?" Kit asked.

She'd been waiting for it to come up. Mai took a sip of her drink. "I haven't told her yet."

"Why not?" Hannah asked.

"I wanted to put a plan together first."

Kit stared her down.

Crap. The musketeers always knew when she wasn't telling the truth. "She never wanted me to be a baker. She'll tell me to cut my losses, and I'm not doing that. I don't have the energy to fight her at the moment."

"*Or* she might give you some sound legal advice," Kit argued. "Sure Bian was a pain when you first started, but that was years ago. She's always bragging about you now."

Mai didn't comment. How could she explain that she still felt like she'd let her mother down, still thought she was less than her sisters who were all at university?

Losing her bakery would mean she'd failed, that her mother had been right.

Hannah tapped her pen on the paper in front of her. "Has Nicholas got planning permission yet?"

"No."

She smiled. "We need to find out when the council meeting is."

"Why?" Mai asked.

"If enough people protest, the planning permission will get knocked back, or revised. Perhaps we can get him to leave your building and build around it."

Kit grinned. "I like the way you think."

Mai hesitated. "It might make things worse. He could refuse me any place in the new development and then I'll be left with nothing."

"He wouldn't do that. He likes you, Mai," Fleur said.

Mai shook her head. She couldn't think of him in that way. This was business.

"He kissed you last night," Hannah said.

Mai's face burned. "It was nothing."

All three of her friends just looked at her.

"It *was* nothing," she insisted. "I'm not getting involved with a guy who could destroy my life."

"It's not that bad, is it?" Kit asked. "It's a temporary adjustment."

"Most small businesses don't survive more than three years." Mai sighed. "I'm scared of losing everything, having to start from scratch again."

Fleur hugged her. "We won't let that happen, Mai. We'll help you through this."

The others nodded and her heart swelled. She wasn't alone.

"Though, you really should talk to your mum," Kit said.

Mai huffed out a breath. "Fine. I'll visit her tomorrow and we'll go from there."

It wasn't the best plan, but it was something.

"What about your apartment? Are you going to move back home?" Hannah asked.

"I don't know. I can't afford any rentals in town."

"You can always move in with me," Fleur said. "I've got plenty of space and could do with help paying the mortgage."

Mai hadn't even considered Fleur's place. "I thought you liked your own space."

"I do, and I wouldn't offer to just anyone. But we wouldn't get into each other's hair. Calypso has never been a problem and I know the importance of being quiet while you're sleeping."

Fleur worked a variable shift pattern at the local hospital. It was the perfect solution, but Mai didn't want to take advantage of her friend. "Are you sure?"

"Of course. We'll have fun."

They would, and it didn't have to be permanent. She smiled. Finally something good to come out of her day. "All right. That would be great."

With her shoulders already feeling a little lighter, she turned to her friends. "Enough about me. What are your new year's resolutions?" She wanted to forget about her problems for the rest of the day.

Mai looked up at the modern, two-storey, architecturally designed house she'd grown up in, her muscles clenching. She'd never really liked the building, despite the gorgeous views over the town from its perch on the hill. It reminded her too much of when they'd lived in Perth and she'd had to take care of her siblings with her grandmother while her parents worked endlessly in their high-powered corporate jobs. It reminded her that money couldn't buy happiness.

She'd never had any privacy here, her younger sisters always coming into her room, borrowing her things, or waking her up when she was sleeping so they could talk about their latest teenage drama.

She'd chosen to be a baker, to do a job she loved, even if the pay wasn't the best because she'd wanted to be happy. And she'd been ecstatic when she'd discovered she could convert the area above her bakery into an apartment and finally move out of home.

At least with Fleur's offer, she wouldn't have to go back.

She couldn't stand here all day procrastinating. She needed answers.

She walked in to find her three younger sisters lounging in the TV room on the big cushy red couches, watching a movie with the air conditioning blasting. She'd rarely spent those gloriously long summer holidays when she'd been at high school at home, had always been off with the musketeers, and she'd never had the even longer breaks that her sisters enjoyed now they were at university.

"Hi, Mai," Eden called. She held out her hands for Calypso and Mai handed him over.

"Is Mum home?"

"In the garden."

Mai continued down the long, high-ceilinged hallway and out the back door. Both of her parents were weeding the garden, her father in his lush vegetable garden close to the back door, and her mother across the lawn under the shade of a magnolia tree.

"Hi, baby," her dad called, straightening up and stretching his back, his hands covered in dirt. Taller than her by only a couple of inches, he always had a presence, a way of being, that couldn't be ignored. Today he wore black shorts and an AC/DC T-shirt that had faded to grey from years of use.

"Hi." She kissed his cheek, her heart warming.

"What have you got there?" he asked, indicating the papers she held.

"Something I wanted to get Mum's advice on."

Her mother walked over, her large floppy cotton hat shading her expression. The old T-shirt and shorts she wore were a far cry from the power suits that were her costume of Mai's youth, but still she commanded attention, and could cause a person to wither with one look. "Legal advice?"

Mai nodded, the nerves churning in her stomach like a mixer on high. She couldn't get emotional, she had to stick with the facts. "The bakery building has been sold."

"Weren't you buying it?" her father asked.

"Aaron sold it to a property developer." She was pleased her voice was steady.

He reached out and squeezed her arm.

"Do they want to renegotiate the lease?" Her mother took off her gardening gloves and wiped her hands on her shorts.

"No. I've been given six months to vacate the premises."

Both her parents gaped at her.

"Can they do that?" Anh glanced at his wife.

Her mother snapped to attention. "I need to read your lease. Let me clean up."

This was it. She'd discover exactly where she stood. Following her mother inside, she sat at the kitchen table and placed the paperwork in front of her.

"Tell me what happened."

After Mai explained, Bian read through the lease, her frown becoming more pronounced as she did so. "This is a terrible contract. Why didn't you show it to me before you signed it?"

Mai clenched her hands together. "Because you didn't want me to go into business for myself."

"That's not right."

Mai didn't want to argue about it now. "Can we focus on the proposal, please?"

Her mother looked at her for a long moment, her gaze piercing, before she turned her attention to the proposal.

"This could work out for you." Her mother tapped the end of a pen against the paper as she read through it. "It's a decent offer."

"I'm not giving up my bakery," Mai snapped. She'd known this was coming.

Her mother held up a hand. "I'm not telling you to. How much will it cost to relocate twice?" Her mother was calm as always, no emotion on her face.

Mai had to be as emotionless as her mother. "The problem is where to move to. I've got a choice of somewhere too small or too big."

"It's temporary. You'll make do." Bian waved away her concerns. "His offer is low, but it's a starting bid. He'll expect to have to increase it." She jotted down some notes. "Have you got a copy of the development plans?"

Mai held her anger in as she handed them over. Her mother had no idea how much work was involved, how hard it had been to set up, to make her name, to become a success. How could she be so flippant?

"This is a nice place. Maybe I'll look at moving in – my office is getting kind of shabby."

Mai stared at her mother in disbelief, the sting of hurt sharp. She supported the development, supported the man who was hurting her daughter?

"I'm going to have to leave?" Mai asked.

Her mother glanced at her. "Has the planning permission gone through?"

"Not yet."

"You could make a fuss and protest the development, but the most that will get you is a delay and a pissed off developer," she said. "The shire doesn't have a good reason to deny the application, particularly as it's encouraging growth in the town."

Mai unclenched her hands. "Could I use this to my advantage?"

"How do you mean?"

"I want more cafe space," she said. "If I propose to take two of the units do you think he'll let me put in all the things I need: extraction fans, extra power points, that kind of thing?"

"Within reason."

Perhaps she could turn it into an opportunity.

"A guy like Nicholas Shadbolt doesn't want fuss, he wants to make money. When you put in your list of demands make it more than you want and then negotiate down to what you really need. That way they'll feel like they're getting something as well."

Mai smiled.

The musketeers were right. She would use this situation to launch the next stage of her business, one that put her on the map.

She could do this.

She would succeed.

Chapter 5

Nicholas swore as he hung up the phone. Didn't anyone work during the week after New Year? He scanned the list in front of him: he'd left a message at a demolition company for a quote, and the company in Albany that would fabricate the concrete slabs was closed for another week.

He couldn't get a thing done.

He hated not being productive.

Especially when his father wanted an update at the end of the week.

Anxiety gripped his chest and he prowled around the huge holiday house, unable to settle. Everything here reminded him of the business and how he'd failed his family. The sleek charcoal grey sofas in the living room were where he and his father had sat with Shane and his father to discuss the Baldivis project, the glossy red cabinets in the kitchen had been there since the successful Joondalup project, and the outdoor deck with the built-in barbecue had been added when Shadbolt were wining and dining a prospective client.

The wall of photographs was the worst. Each one represented a family holiday, usually taken after the successful completion of another development.

There would never be a photo for the Baldivis project.

He rubbed at the burning sensation in his chest and popped an antacid.

Focus on the here and now, not on the past – which meant he needed to progress with the new development.

Mai had barely spoken to him when they'd returned to the fire station the other day, not that he blamed her.

It was his own fault. If Shadbolt hadn't been in such a rush to get rid of him they never would have bought the place. Guilt had been his constant companion since the Baldivis incident, since he'd discovered he didn't really know his best friend, but now it suffocated him. He couldn't stay in here, surrounded by these memories.

Slamming through the back door, he strode down the steps of the back deck onto the lawn and took big, deep gulps of fresh air.

He had to get a grip, had to get the business with Mai resolved as soon as possible, had to fill the remaining units.

The intense pressure in his chest made him grit his teeth. It wasn't a heart attack, it just felt like one. Forcing his feet forward, he breathed like his doctor had taught him, focusing on the blue wrens flitting through the grevilleas bordering the yard, and then walked towards the swing hanging from the ghost gum at the back that his brother had erected for his children the last time he was down here.

Focus on the positive.

In the long term, the new building would be a better structure for Mai; she wouldn't need to worry about dodgy wiring and plumbing. The whole development would attract more people to that part of town and therefore more customers for her.

The tension in his chest eased.

He needed to arrange another meeting with Mai and make some enquiries about prospective tenants. There wasn't much else he could do until businesses reopened next week.

It was as if the universe wanted him to fail.

He squeezed his eyes shut. His wandering took him over to the beige garden shed that was big enough to store a decent-sized boat. The lock needed to be fixed after the break-in, but there wasn't much in there to steal – only a few holiday toys: a badminton net, some deflated water tubes, a cricket set and some boogie boards. His old yellow surfboard tied to the ceiling caught his eye. It used to hang side-by-side with Shane's white board, but at some stage Shane must have taken his home.

He grimaced. Shane wouldn't be surfing any time soon, but perhaps when he got out of rehab Nicholas would suggest they go again.

Shane had always had an excess of energy and hated to sit around the house with their parents and siblings. He always had to be doing something, living life to the fullest. He'd kept Nicholas amused and on his toes. When had things gone so wrong?

Defeated, he turned away and latched the shed shut. He shouldn't be thinking about Shane or surfing now. It was a work day and he should be working. Forcing himself back inside, he stood by the kitchen table and flicked through the artist's sketch of the development. It was a functional design, easy to manufacture and build. He wouldn't call it the white monstrosity that Mai had, but he'd admit it wasn't pretty – not that it needed to be.

But what if the design was instrumental in getting the project approved by the shire? Maybe he should do some more research just in case.

Nicholas drove into town, finding a parking spot down by the slow-moving river. A number of families were having picnics on the grassed area between the road and the river, and lots of kids squealed and yelled as they played at the playground. Young and carefree. It had been a long time since he'd been either.

Turning away from the happy scene he surveyed the buildings. The two-storey colonial-style pub on the corner had verandahs all the way around both storeys. The deep burgundy of the brickwork was both calming and classy. Next to it was a cafe in a building of a similar era, this time single storey with a cream render, and next to that ... Nicholas winced. A hideous drab brown building from the seventies that took the scene from charming to blah.

Maybe Mai had a point.

He bought an ice cream from the shop in the blah building and continued to wander. The several small boutique clothing shops were quirky and cute and the souvenir store sold locally made wares. A definite mix-match of styles, but the older buildings, those that combined design with function were by far the most attractive.

He'd never paid attention to aesthetics before. It wasn't part of the Shadbolt brief. But then again, most of Shadbolt's developments were in new areas and shopping centres or business units didn't need pizazz. He turned down the street towards *On the Way*. The building was a focal point in spite of the peeling paint. It had a charm about it with the curved pediments on the upstairs windows and the decorative moulding on the frieze.

He continued walking and stood across the road from the empty block of land, trying to visualise how the new development would look.

Soulless.

It wouldn't be as hideous as the seventies building by the river, but it would be nowhere as lovely as the existing building.

Did it matter? They'd already sold two units based on the current plans. Plus it would cost a lot more to add some flair. Concrete slab was cheap because it was simple and easy. Any extra decoration would add to the price.

He was being tested on this project. If he didn't make the required profit he could be without a job. Not that he deserved to still have one.

He shook his head. Not going back down that rabbit hole again today. He needed to concentrate on *this* development. Which meant he needed to sell more units. The tourist centre would be his next stop to find out when the local markets were held.

The back of the bakery wasn't as pretty as the front. The rendered walls were plain and the small car park had enough parking for the shops. A short flight of wooden stairs had been added to the middle door and the railing hung away from the posts. Mai had said it needed fixing. He could repair it now before someone was hurt. A couple of nails wouldn't cost much.

And while he was here, he'd fix the light that wasn't working. Blackbridge was a safe town, but he'd hate it if Mai worried about going out to her car at night. His gaze lifted to the upper storey of the building. The middle window contained a beige, fluffy rag doll cat sitting in front of a lacy curtain, surveying the view.

Just like the cat he'd had as a kid.

Drawn towards the building, he examined the steps and light, made a list of what he needed and then headed back to his car, relieved to have something to do.

Mai might be angry at him about the development, but perhaps fixing the step and light would earn him some Brownie points.

And even if it didn't, it gave him an excuse to call her again.

Someone was making a God awful noise outside. Mai squeezed her eyes shut and pulled the pillow over her ears, trying to ignore the incessant banging that had woken her from her siesta.

It didn't help. She was awake now.

And had only been asleep an hour.

She scowled as she got up, slipping on a black singlet and denim shorts before peering out her bedroom window to check what was going on. The noise was definitely coming from below but she couldn't see anyone.

Annoyed, she padded down the interior stairs and flung open the back door. "What the hell ... Nicholas?"

Face flushed, dressed in suit pants and a white shirt rolled up at the sleeves, he was wielding a hammer and looked oddly out of place. Did the man not have any casual clothing?

"I fixed the step." Nicholas glanced up and the smile on his face faded. "Did I wake you?"

Mai ran a hand through her hair and encountered a tangle of knots. What kind of hot mess did she look like? She should have at least put a bra on. Crossing her arms over her chest, she said, "I always take a siesta at this time."

"Shit. I'm sorry." He tugged his earlobe. "I didn't think. I was in the area and remembered your complaints. The light is working now."

Mai picked Calypso up as he brushed past her ankles, before focusing on the stair rail. It appeared sturdy now and it was nice of him to do it considering the place wouldn't be there much longer. "Thanks."

He lifted his eyes from her chest, the intensity of his gaze making her body flush. She must have flashed him when she'd bent over. Great.

He cleared his throat. "I'm done now, so you can go back to sleep. Sorry about disturbing you."

She wasn't sleepy any more. That hungry stare had woken her all the way up. "I won't go back to sleep now. Do you want to come up for a coffee?" What was she thinking? She shouldn't be inviting him up to her tiny apartment. It was her private space and she hadn't done her hair. That didn't matter, she could still talk business.

Yeah, like that's why you invited him up.

He paused only a split second. "Sure. Let me put these things in my car."

Too late to withdraw the invitation. "Come up the stairs when you're done." She hurried upstairs to put her apartment to rights.

Luckily the space wasn't large and she kept it tidy by default. She dropped Calypso on the couch before slipping on a bra and quickly brushing her hair, closing the door on her bedroom as she came out. By the time he knocked she was in the kitchen filling the kettle.

"Come in."

He entered and her apartment seemed even smaller with him inside, the musky scent of his aftershave wafting towards her.

"You've done an amazing job up here."

"Thanks." Her heart hurt. She loved her little apartment, loved that she had a space of her own after years of sharing with her sisters and brother, and now she would lose it. How was she going to afford a place of her own? She couldn't live with Fleur indefinitely.

He stood there, waiting, and she remembered her manners. "Have a seat." She indicated the small four-seat dining table. "Do you want a Vietnamese iced coffee?"

"Is that different from regular iced coffee?"

She nodded. "It's made with condensed milk, ice and black coffee." But he drank his coffee espresso style. "It might be too sweet for you."

"I'll give it a try. Is that your heritage?"

She liked the way he phrased the question. Normally people simply said, *Is that where you're from?* and she'd answer no. "Yes. My parents immigrated here with their families in the eighties." She made the drinks and sat opposite him, but it was still too close for comfort.

"Have you had a chance to read my proposal?" Nicholas asked.

Business. Good idea. She needed to focus on that rather than the very attractive man in front of her. "Yes. I took it to my lawyer yesterday."

Nicholas's eyebrows raised. "Lawyer?"

"A good business woman always gets advice when she needs it." There was no need for him to know her lawyer was her mother. "I need a couple of days to put my costs together."

"All right." His phone beeped. "Excuse me a second."

Even though his hairline had a thin strip of sweat on it making his brown hair look darker, he was still refined and put together, not like he'd spent time in the sun fixing the stairs. Everything about him said money, from his clothes, to his Rolex watch, to his phone. Even his nails were manicured. He really was a different creature from what Mai was used to.

"Sorry about that." Nicholas slipped his phone back into his pocket.

Mai took a sip of her drink, enjoying the cool sweetness of it. "No problem."

"Have you found new premises yet?" Nicholas asked.

As if it was that easy. "No. There's nothing suitable."

"There must be."

She laughed at his disbelief. "Blackbridge is a small town. Most of the shops are occupied."

Calypso jumped down from the couch and padded over, meowing up at Nicholas. He picked him up, placing him on his lap in an unconscious gesture. It was kind of sweet. "That's Calypso."

Nicholas smiled as he stroked the cat's head and Calypso purred his approval.

Mai shifted in her seat. She shouldn't be jealous of her cat. Keep this visit about business. "There's a warehouse that smells like fish, or a place out on Mortimer Road which isn't big enough."

Nicholas tugged on his ear. "I'm sure we can work something out."

Mai ignored the surge of warmth at the word 'we'. "It's not really your problem is it?"

"Not directly," he agreed. "But I've tasted your products and I don't want you to go out of business."

"Neither do I." Speaking of food, she got to her feet and took a jar of shortbread from the cupboard. She took one and then offered the jar to Nicholas.

"Thanks. That wasn't a hint." He smiled.

This smile was genuine — it reached his eyes — and revealed a tiny dimple on the right side of his cheek. It was so different from the salesman charm when they'd first met at the bakery and made him even more appealing.

Damn it.

Their eyes locked and Mai recognised the attraction in his forest green eyes. This wasn't good.

At that moment, both of their phones beeped. Relieved, Mai got to her feet to get hers as Nicholas said, "There's a shed fire at Foley's farm."

Close to Kit's place.

She responded to the text. "Are you going?"

"Yeah, I might as well. I'll give you a lift."

Mai nodded. "Let me get changed. Can you put some food in Calypso's bowl? It's in the cupboard on the left and his bowl is on the floor." She didn't wait for his response.

They needed to be fast so the fire didn't spread. Quickly she changed into her fire-fighting gear, slinging the thick yellow jacket over her shoulder, and headed back into the living area.

"Ready?" she asked Nicholas.

He nodded, though he looked a little pale.

"Don't worry. I'll keep you out of trouble." She slapped him on the back and followed him down the stairs to his car.

❦

Saved by the bell.

They had definitely been having a moment — an unwanted

one – when their phones had beeped. Nicholas couldn't mix business with pleasure. Not now, not ever.

He needed to get her to sign up to the development and then avoid her like a union rep on a construction site.

He pulled into the fire station and reality hit him. He was going out to a real structure fire. Something definitely bigger than the bonfire.

The hairs on his arm stood up.

Mai unlocked the shed as another car pulled into the car park. "Get dressed and then you can help me inspect the vehicles."

He nodded though she wasn't looking at him, was already striding over to the big tanker. The vehicle dwarfed her, but there was no denying she knew what she was doing as she unplugged a cable and made sure the compartments were closed tight.

As he dressed in the fire-retardant gear and picked up his helmet and gloves, Lawrence walked in with three other men.

"Foley called it in," Lawrence explained as they gathered around a table. "He's got an old shed at the back of his property and near as he can tell, the fire's over there. Might have been some kids mucking about. The wind is blowing it away from the bush towards the paddock, but we're due for a wind change in a couple of hours. We want it under control before then."

"Where's the nearest water stand?" Mai asked.

"Foley said we can use his dam. There's also a stand on the road on the way in." Lawrence pointed at the map in front of him. "The bush brigade is mobilising now and Foley's got his own equipment. Any other questions?" He looked at Nicholas.

Nicholas shook his head. He needed to have some idea of what he was doing to ask any questions. What was he doing here?

"Let's go."

Mai gestured for Nicholas to follow her and she got into the fast attack vehicle. "How are you feeling?"

"Fine." He could fake it. "What do you expect to see when we get there?"

"Foley's farm is mostly sheep," she said. "That means the paddocks won't have a lot of fuel in them, which is good." She sped up as she left town. "If we're lucky the shed will be far enough away from any trees, so they don't light up."

"And if they do?"

"Let's hope they don't." She pulled into a drive and raced along the bumpy ground.

Nicholas clung on to the hand hold above the door. She was so incredibly calm, while the jolts of the car were shaking up the nerves in his stomach, like a martini shaken not stirred.

A man on a motorbike waited near the farmhouse, and gestured for them to follow.

Mai smiled. "They've got all the gates open for us."

"Don't they always?"

She shook her head. "No. Sometimes they're more worried about their livestock escaping than making it easy for us to access the fire."

In the distance a dark cloud of smoke billowed up into the sky. They were heading right towards it. His hands shook and he pressed his palms onto his thighs. Heading into danger wasn't something he was used to.

Smoke and flames poured out of the open side of the silver corrugated iron shed and the gaps between the roof and the walls. The paddock in front of it also burned. The low lake of flames was spreading quickly. A couple of men were already there using a homemade water tanker to hose down the paddock.

"What do we do?" Nicholas asked.

"We're on spotter duty." Mai drove over to one of the men. She wound down the window. "What's in the shed, Foley?"

"Nothing but old bits and pieces."

"I'm going to do a loop."

The tanker pulled up and people jumped out getting the hoses ready. Mai drove down the fire edge towards the shed. "Keep an eye out for spot fires," she said. "I want to scan the other side, see if there's anything that will make it spread in the other direction."

"Like what?"

"Old oil barrels for starters." She snatched up the radio. "This is Blackbridge Fast Attack One. We've got chemicals back here. Ask Foley what they are, over."

Around the back of the rusted shed were six plastic drums on a pallet, but they didn't look all that old. He squinted. His chemistry was a little rusty, but if he was correct, they were full of hydrochloric acid.

"He says there shouldn't be any," came the response. "He's heading over now."

Mai parked. "Get the hose."

Nicholas jumped out, his hands shaking as he did as she asked. The fire radiated out, a wall of heat, and the thick, black smoke smelled sharply of chemicals. He screwed up his nose and breathed through his mouth.

"Aim for the barrels." Mai watched him carefully.

Don't let him mess up. He sprayed the drums and steam clouded the wall of the shed.

Foley roared up on a motorcycle. He spoke to Mai, shaking his head, but Nicholas couldn't hear them over the crackle of the fire and the engine.

Mai joined him as Foley departed. "He doesn't know what they are." She glanced over to the tanker that had already put out much of the paddock fire and now focused on the structure.

There was worry in her eyes. "Is the acid flammable?"

"No, but the ones at the back might be something else. There's a chance they could go boom."

Nicholas's heart stopped for a split second. Should they evacuate? No, they couldn't. They were the emergency team, the line of defence.

"We need to get this section of the shed doused first." She went back to the vehicle and a minute later the tanker moved towards them. It moved far too slowly for Nicholas's liking. Who the hell left random barrels of chemicals at the back of someone's property?

Another brigade arrived.

"Move the vehicle over there," Mai pointed, "and then inspect the area for spot fires. I'll join you in a minute." She strode over to where Lawrence spoke to the captain of the other brigade.

Was that her way of telling him he was doing something wrong?

He did as she asked, moving upwind far enough away from

the shed that the heat wasn't quite so bad and the smell was a little more tolerable.

The other fire-fighters wore breathing apparatus and worked together to put out the fire. And he was kicking through dirt to make sure no sparks ignited.

Not what he'd expected.

Mai strode over and handed him a drink from the esky in the vehicle. "You need to stay hydrated." She didn't wait for his response, just went back to the car, grabbed the radio from inside and clipped it on her jacket and then took the opposite side of the paddock to check.

Shit, should he have got the radio? He had a vague memory of something he'd learned at training but it wouldn't stick.

Had he messed up again?

It was another two hours before the fire was out. Nicholas's clothing was heavy and hot, and his legs ached. He slumped against the fast attack bonnet while Mai and Lawrence went to chat to Foley and the other brigade captain.

"We're on watch duty," Mai said when she returned.

Nicholas frowned. "Watch duty?" Did that mean he couldn't go home yet?

"We need to keep an eye on the shed to make sure it doesn't reignite," she said. "It'll only be for a couple of hours, but if you've got things to do, I can get one of the others to stay."

Nicholas shook his head. "I can stay."

"Great. We'll make sure Lincoln doesn't get into trouble when he gets out here. The shed's not that stable."

"Lincoln?"

"Foley's calling the police because the barrels weren't his." She wrinkled her forehead and glanced back at the shed.

What else could they be for?

When the tankers and the farmers had left, Mai handed him another bottle of water. "How did you like your first real fire?"

"I didn't do much."

"Sure you did. You teamed with me to secure the perimeter."

"Wandering around kicking dirt isn't particularly important." He winced at the sulk in his tone.

"It's vital," she said. "Everyone else is focused on the main fire, so if a new one sparks up they could get caught in the middle." Her eyes flashed in annoyance.

Nicholas ducked his head. "I didn't realise."

"I gathered." She rolled her eyes. "Don't worry, you're not the first to believe you've been put in the naughty corner. Everyone wants the glamour of holding the hose – although maybe it's a guy thing."

He flushed. He'd behaved like a prat, let his insecurity get the best of him. "What do we do while we wait?"

"We rehydrate." She sipped her water. "And we keep a look-out." She took off her jacket and threw it into the car, then reattached the portable radio. Her hair was tied back in a pony-tail but she had loose strands over her face which she brushed back and tucked under her helmet. "Come on."

He followed her over to the shed. The metal sides were bowed and the whole building steamed. The acrid stench filled his nostrils making him screw up his nose.

Mai stood at the entrance of the blackened shell. "All the beams will be weakened," she said. "It's swaying a little in the wind."

"Will Foley knock it down?"

"He'll have to, but not until Lincoln's taken a look. I guess he'll call in the arson investigators from Albany."

"Why does he even have a shed out here?" It was nowhere near the farm house.

"It used to be a shearing shed," Mai said. "Foley said he hasn't used it since he built the one closer to the farm house a couple of years ago."

"Odd place for a shed."

Mai shook her head. "Apparently there's a road through there." She pointed towards the bush. "It goes out onto the highway, but the way we came was quicker from Blackbridge. Kit's farm is on the other side."

Nicholas tried to get his bearings. He could have sworn they were nowhere near Kit's place.

She continued walking around the structure, kicking at smoking dirt and scanning the area. Her competence and authority made him more confident. If it flared up, she'd know what to do. And that was kind of a turn on. He'd worked with plenty of women before, but none had given him the same buzz as Mai.

Every so often the blackened ground around him gave off little puffs of smoke so he examined them.

The silence between them was heavy, but what could he talk about – the development? That wasn't a great topic of conversation. Not if she couldn't find temporary accommodation for herself and the bakery.

And he knew nothing else about her, except she was a volunteer fire-fighter.

But he couldn't help being intrigued by her. She was confident, feisty and kind. She looked as if she'd blow over in a strong wind and yet she lugged around trays of baked goods as if they weighed nothing, and held a fire hose as if it was a garden hose.

He wanted to get to know her.

No, he couldn't. Mixing business with personal relationships was a quick path to hell. He had to ignore the pull to speak, to hold her hand, to be with her. They circled back to the ute.

"Blackbridge Police to Blackbridge Fast Attack One," the radio blared.

Mai smiled. "This is Blackbridge Fast Attack One, go ahead, Slinky."

"We're on our way out now."

"Roger that."

Nicholas didn't like the twinge of jealousy at Mai's obvious affection for whoever was on the radio. "Slinky?"

She grinned. "It's the musketeers' nickname for Lincoln."

Her grin was something else. It lit up her face and the wickedness sent a shot of lust to his groin. He had it bad for her.

He turned on his heel and headed in the opposite direction.

He needed the distance.

<h1 style="text-align:center">Chapter 6</h1>

The crackle of burnt grass signalled Nicholas walking away and Mai breathed a sigh of relief. He looked damned fine in the uniform, the pants sitting nicely on his hips and the tight white T-shirt showing off his broad chest. Even his petty concerns about not being allowed into the thick of things didn't put her off. She'd heard similar comments too many times to be fazed by them.

She swallowed. There was nothing to gain from lusting after him.

Not when he was tearing down her home.

But he had impressed her today. He'd learned quickly and followed her instructions, and that was important. If she couldn't trust the people she worked with, she wouldn't be able to do her job effectively.

Which she should be doing now instead of staring after Nicholas like a fool.

She circled the shed in the opposite direction to Nicholas to make sure the paddock was clear of embers. The ground and building were still radiating heat, but the sea breeze had kicked in giving a breath of somewhat cooler and much fresher air.

She wandered over to the chemical containers that had given them all cause for concern. The dozen or so plastic containers had melted into a large deformed lump.

They must have been empty.

What were they doing there? Foley had seemed disturbed to see them. Something weird was going on.

She turned as the sounds of an engine reached her, and spotted the police car. When it pulled up, Lincoln, Ryan and Foley got out.

Foley knew where to go and what not to touch, but Mai kept an eye on them as she continued her rounds. Their voices carried in the breeze.

"Are you sure none of your farmhands would store stuff here?" Lincoln asked Foley.

"Mate, I know how chemicals are meant to be stored and it's not like this. I don't need pure acid on the farm."

"We definitely need to call Albany." Lincoln walked past Mai to get to the squad car, giving her a pointed look. She shouldn't be eavesdropping, but if Lincoln was calling in backup, then there was definitely more to those barrels.

Hannah had had some drain cleaner stolen from the holiday park last month. Maybe it was related, but surely Lincoln wouldn't need to call Albany for a simple theft.

"What's wrong?"

She jumped at Nicholas's voice. He was right next to her, his sexy presence distracting her. "Lincoln's calling in Albany," she said. "He only does that when it's serious."

"Think it's drug-related?"

Mai froze. "What makes you say that?"

"I, ah, saw a documentary on meth amphetamine recently and it mentioned meth was made with large quantities of chemicals – brake fluid, drain cleaner, acids and stuff."

Could Gordon be making his own supply? But why store the chemicals all the way out here?

Maybe it was the creepy guy she'd seen him with.

She shook her head. Talk about paranoia. She had no idea what Gordon and the creepy guy had been discussing – he might have been offering Gordon a job.

Still her skin felt tight. If she mentioned it to Lincoln now, he'd tell her off for not telling him sooner and she was too tired to deal with that today. She'd call him tomorrow.

Walking back to the fast attack vehicle, she slid into the passenger seat with a sigh.

Her shorter than usual midday nap was wearing on her. The sun had sunk below the tree line, which shaded them from its harsh glare, but it would still be a couple of hours before dark. They should be finished long before then.

"Are you all right?" Nicholas asked.

"Just tired." She rubbed her hands over her face and dumped her helmet on the seat beside her.

"What time did you get up this morning?"

"I started work at one."

"And I interrupted your siesta. I'm sorry."

"Don't worry about it. I'm used to it." Or had been when she'd been the only baker.

"How much longer do we need to stay out here?"

She checked the time. "About ten minutes as long as nothing flares up. Do you want to double check everything is stowed?" She already had, but it would be good practice for him and meant he wasn't standing less than a metre away from her, looking refreshingly dishevelled with his mussed up hair and light film of sweat on his body.

Mai closed her eyes.

Lincoln wandered over. "Ryan and I are going to stay here until the Albany detectives arrive."

"How long will that be?"

"At least an hour."

"Need me to send someone out with pizza?" she asked.

He chuckled. "You do not need to feed the world, Mai. We'll be fine, but thanks for the offer."

Mai couldn't help it. It was why she loved baking. Her grandmother had taught her to always make sure there was food on the table.

"Are you good to go?" Lincoln asked as Nicholas came back.

"Yeah, we're done here," she said.

"I'll drive," Nicholas said. "You look dead on your feet."

She scowled. "I'm fine." This was nothing compared to what she'd endured in the early days of her bakery, but he could drive if it made him feel better. She said her goodbyes and then settled back in the seat and closed her eyes.

They bumped through the paddock and Nicholas was silent

until they reached the bitumen road. "Are you hungry?"

"Starving."

"Do you want to get something to eat on the way home?"

Was he asking her out? She clamped down on the little thrill. She wanted to work out her negotiation strategy before she spent any more time with him. It needed to be resolved before things went any further. "Not tonight. I'm going straight to bed."

She shouldn't have said that. Now she had images of Nicholas in bed with her.

Not a great idea – at least not yet.

But after the contract was signed was another thing entirely.

Nicholas hung up from his father and gasped for breath as the familiar panic flooded him. It wasn't possible to have a conversation with him without feeling like he was a failure. He lurched out of his father's leather office chair as the anxiety gripped him in its clutches. He couldn't work in here anymore. It was too much his father's space, large commanding desk, harsh leather furniture and the masculinity dialled up to eleven. The room reminded him of how far he'd fallen.

He grabbed his laptop and the plans and stumbled into the kitchen, dumping them on the table and sinking into one of the chairs. He focused on breathing slowly, counting back from twenty, and the panic receded until he could breathe normally again.

He couldn't keep living like this.

His anxiety was unmanageable.

He had to do something about it, had to get back to a life where he didn't second-guess everything he did, where he wasn't afraid to make the big decisions.

How had one event turned him into such a mess?

A photo across the room caught his eye. Shadbolt's very first development. His father stood out the front with Nicholas – all of six – on his shoulders. Both were beaming.

He couldn't remember a time when he wasn't expected to take over the company. Couldn't ever remember questioning the assumption. But he also couldn't remember the last time he'd enjoyed going to work. It was all paperwork and figures, playing hardball with contractors and arguing over minor contract issues.

He closed his eyes, thought back.

There was one summer, back during university when he'd worked for Jameson Construction. It had been a Shadbolt development and he and Shane were in training even then to take over their respective companies from their fathers. He'd loved building something with his own hands, feeling as if he'd actually achieved something. Being literally hands-on had given him a sense of satisfaction that pushing paper never had, whereas Shane much preferred to be in the air-conditioned office overseeing the details.

And look where it had led.

With accusations of arson, fraud and his friend in a rehab facility.

He shook his head. Plenty of people didn't like their work, and at least he was paid well for his.

Still, part of him envied Mai's passion. She worked as hard as he did, possibly harder, and she probably earned much less money, but she loved every minute of it.

Was that why he'd dropped the ball on the Baldivis project? Because he didn't like the work, because he didn't care?

No, that wasn't the reason.

He'd cared too much, he'd believed in Shane, had trusted him despite what his gut told him. He should have pushed harder, got to the bottom of it. He might have discovered Shane's meth addiction sooner and been able to do something to help. He'd let it go too far.

With a sigh he flicked through the plans. He'd had enough for today. He was over all of it; work, the tension in his chest, the guilt. He needed a break, needed to take some time for himself.

Through the front window the ocean called to him. He wandered closer. It was a beautiful day, the sun shone bright and warm, and the swell was just right. A couple of surfers were out there taking advantage of the conditions.

A deep yearning to feel the cool spray of the water filled him. His doctor had said he should find something that would help him relax and surfing had always done that for him. And it held a lot more appeal than working.

Could he really do it?

He was already heading for the stairs when he realised he'd made his decision.

Not long afterwards, he crossed the road to the surf beach and wandered down the sandy path. To his right was a pile of towels and shoes, and to his left, a family with two young primary school-aged kids played with boogie boards. He dumped his towel where he stood and strode into the water with his board, sucking in his breath at the cold. He'd forgotten how icy the southern ocean was. He'd need to get a wetsuit if he kept this up.

His arms were burning by the time he got past the break. Relieved he'd made it this far, he sat up on the board and scanned the swell.

"Hey, Nic!"

The surfer paddled towards him, fully decked out in a wrist to ankle black wetsuit. Lucky bastard. He smiled. "Jamie."

"Mate, aren't you cold?" Jamie asked.

Nicholas laughed, a sound that was almost foreign to his ears. "Freezing. It was a spur of the moment decision."

"Well you can take the next wave." Jamie gestured.

He wasn't quite ready, wanted time to psych himself up, but he could hardly say no. That was probably completely against the surfers' code. So he paddled as a wave came towards him.

Then instinct kicked in and he stood on the board, surfing the wave, wobbling a little as he got the balance right. His chest filled. He'd forgotten the exhilaration of riding the wave, feeling the spray of the water against his face and listening to the shush of the wave as he sliced along it.

Just what he needed.

He briefly closed his eyes to savour the freedom and when he opened them again he was heading straight towards another surfer.

Shit.

Mai.

He turned sharply and overcompensated, losing his footing

and hitting the water hard. The leg line of his board snapped straight and the swell pulled him down.

Finding the sand, he pushed up, surfacing and gasping for breath. Where was Mai?

Nicholas hauled himself onto his board. She wasn't far from him, straddling her board, holding her head, her hand red.

She was bleeding. He'd hurt her. His heart raced.

He paddled over. "Mai, are you all right?"

She scowled. "Your board hit me in the head."

"I'm so sorry." He reached out to touch her and thought better of it. "It's bleeding pretty badly. You should probably get it checked."

Mai's face went pale as she pulled her bloodied hand away from her head and she swayed.

Jamie paddled up and swore. "That looks bad, Mayday. Let's get you to shore before you become shark bait."

Nicholas froze. He hadn't thought about sharks.

"Come on, Mai. Here's a good wave." Jamie gave her board a shove and Mai paddled lying down, managing to catch it to shore.

"What happened?" Jamie asked as they followed her.

"I didn't see her in time. I fell off and my board hit her."

Jamie shook his head. "This isn't the way to endear yourself to her, mate."

Yeah, no kidding.

He waded out of the surf and jogged over to where Mai sat on the sand, a towel pressed against her head. "Let me take a look."

She shook her head, holding up a hand, her eyes closed. "Not yet." She breathed deeply.

What was wrong with her?

"Mayday, we need to see how bad it is. You won't see anything." Jamie pried the towel away.

Mai squeezed her eyes tighter.

A gash about a centimetre long just above her eye was bleeding profusely. His shoulders sagged. "You might need stitches."

"Figures," she muttered.

Jamie replaced the towel. "Hold it tight, Mai."

He needed to fix this. "I live across the road," he said. "We'll clean you up there, put a Band-Aid over it and see if that's all that's needed."

"All right." Mai's voice was subdued and her eyes stayed shut.

"You're going to need to lead her across, mate," Jamie said. "Mai faints at the sight of blood and there's a lot of it."

Mai groaned. "Shut up, Jamie."

That explained her swaying on the board. Nicholas helped Mai to her feet and then led her up the beach path to his place, leaving Jamie to bring the boards. At the laundry door, Mai stripped her wetsuit down to her waist revealing the very brief bikini top she had on underneath.

She had beautiful breasts.

It was lucky she still had her eyes closed, so she couldn't see him ogling her. He snatched a towel off the washing machine and thrust it at her. "Here."

"Thanks."

While Jamie hosed off the surfboards, Nicholas found the first aid kit and directed Mai to sit at the kitchen table. "I'm so sorry."

She cracked open one eye to look at him. "You didn't do it on purpose."

She didn't seem mad. He breathed a sigh of relief. "It's been a while since I surfed."

"I gathered," she said dryly.

He deserved that. Carefully removing the towel from Mai's forehead showed the bleeding had slowed and it wasn't as bad as it first had appeared. He sighed as he cleaned and dried it, then applied a Band-Aid as Jamie came in. He'd stripped off his wetsuit and wore a towel wrapped around his waist.

"All fixed, Mayday?" Jamie asked.

"I think so." She glanced up at Nicholas.

"Yeah, it's not too deep. It shouldn't need stitches." He packed up the first aid kit. "How does it feel?"

"Sore." She prodded the Band-Aid gingerly and winced.

Guilt gripped him again. "I'm really sorry."

"Don't sweat it."

He couldn't help it. There had to be something he could do

to make it up to her. "Can I get you a drink?"

"No—"

"I could do with a cuppa tea," Jamie said.

Mai sighed. "A coffee would be great."

She didn't seem keen to stay so perhaps he'd imagined the moment the other day. That was good. He put the kettle on and went to clear the documents off the kitchen table.

"Are these your development plans?" Jamie asked.

"Yeah."

"Can I take a look?"

"If you want to." He left them where they were, the nerves that had disappeared now prickling at the edge of his consciousness as he prepared the drinks. Mai had made her feelings about the development abundantly clear, but Jamie might be a little more unbiased. Should he even discuss it with Mai in the room? "What do you think?" he asked as he handed Jamie a mug of tea.

"It's kind of boring." Jamie winced. "Sorry, mate, what I mean is it's not as pretty as what's there now."

Mai raised her eyebrows in an I-told-you-so look. He glanced away. She was too distracting wearing nothing but a bikini top and towel. His eyes wanted to look lower, feast on her breasts and that was not a good idea.

He focused on Jamie instead. "What would you suggest?"

"What do you mean?"

"If you could change the appearance of the building, what would you change it to?"

"It doesn't fit what's already there." Jamie sat down and pulled the plans closer. "All the buildings are older, more twenties architecture like Mai's building. Which unit are you having, Mayday?"

"We haven't negotiated it yet," she said, "but I'd like these two."

Nicholas stepped forward to see what she was pointing at. "Two?" That was the best news he'd had all day.

"Yeah. I was going to expand into the empty shop when I bought the building."

"I could definitely do you a deal." His phone rang. His father. Not what he needed right now. "Excuse me, I have to get this." He took a couple of steps away as he answered.

"I forgot to tell you that I leased one of the units," his father said.

Nicholas froze. "What? Which one?" He walked over to the table to review the plan.

"On the corner."

Please don't let it be the one Mai wants. "Which corner?"

"Give me a sec." There was a rustle of papers. "Number eight."

Nicholas glanced at Mai. "Our existing tenant wanted that one."

Mai's eyes widened. He turned away.

"Tell her it's too late. It's gone. That's why paperwork is so vital."

Nicholas's chest tightened at the dig. "Dad, please don't lease any more units without talking to me first."

His father laughed. "Don't be ridiculous, if I've got a fish on the line, I'm going to hook it. Be sure you keep the online files up to date."

Nicholas held on to his temper. "I'm in negotiations with people down here. I don't want you to sell something I'm negotiating."

"Tell them it's a possibility. It'll make them sign it faster." He was unrepentant.

There was nothing Nicholas could do. He needed to go into damage control, which meant he needed to get his father off the phone. "Do you want me to give a summary at the management meeting on Monday?"

"God, no. It's best if you keep a really low profile. Send me your update and I'll present it."

He should be used to the backlash by now, but he wasn't. It hurt every damned time. "Fine. I'll talk to you later." He hung up and took several long, slow breaths.

"Which unit is gone?" Mai asked.

He needed to put on his game face. Turning he pointed at the plans. "This one."

She squared her shoulders. "Right, in that case I want units six and seven."

Relief filled him. "I'll fill out the paperwork for you right now."

"We need to negotiate first."

"OK. What do you want?"

She shook her head and held up a hand. "Slow down. I need to put my terms together first."

"Mai, I can't guarantee you those spots unless you sign."

Anger flashed in her eyes. "You can't bully me into signing an unfair contract. Your proposal clearly states there are reparations available for my inconvenience and we need to discuss those before I sign anything."

Damn. He needed to make her understand that she couldn't delay for long. "That's fine, but I can't stop my father leasing any more units."

"Tell him we're in negotiations."

"He doesn't care if there's not a signed contract."

Mai stood up, tension in her every muscle as she glared at him. "Are you telling me Shadbolt Property Developers' word isn't good enough? How would that affect your reputation if word got out?"

This was rapidly spiralling out of control. All of a sudden he saw another train wreck on the horizon, another way he'd completely messed up. He lashed out. "Are you threatening to go public?"

"Hey guys, chill for a second." Jamie held up a both hands in a placating gesture. "It sounds like Nicholas's father is being a douchebag, but it's not Nic's fault. Why don't you set a time to negotiate?"

Mai glared at both of them, her displeasure clear. "Fine. Come to my apartment tomorrow at two. We'll negotiate then."

Relief coursed through him, releasing the tension. "I'll be there."

"Great, I'm sure you two are going to have a fantastic partnership," Jamie said. "I'd better go. I promised Dad I'd help in the cheese factory this afternoon." He got to his feet. "Do you want a lift home, Mai?"

"Yes. I might drop by Fleur's and get her to examine this cut." She put a hand to her forehead.

"Good idea."

Nicholas had forgotten about her injury. Just another way he was hurting her. He sighed and walked them out.

"Thanks for the drink, mate." Jamie shook his hand. "We'll have to catch up later in the week."

The pleasure that swept through him surprised him. At least someone was pleased about him being here. "That'd be great."

When he returned to the kitchen, the development plans didn't give him the sense of dread they usually did. More than half the units were almost signed. He could do the rest. After he had a shower, he'd go into town and see if he could interest anyone else.

He would succeed.

He had to.

Chapter 7

It was already dark when Mai pulled up outside the bakery but the light Nicholas had replaced shone brightly above her door.

Shutting her car door, she heard a soft tap. The street was empty, this part of town quiet. She was far enough away from the restaurants and pub not to have to worry about the noise of people out and about late at night.

As she climbed the steps, the tap came again, like a door left open in a breeze. Her skin prickled. Her door was closed, so she checked the florist shop next door, but it was shut as well.

Mai stood listening. Perhaps it was a can rolling over the pavement. A light breeze rustled leaves, a few birds chattered to each other and the occasional car on the main highway rumbled past. And then the tap.

Her chest tightened. It was coming from the corner, from the empty unit next to hers. Her light didn't reach that far and the shadows were dark.

The creepy guy's image flitted through her mind. She shook herself. There was no reason for him to be here. Still she had to check it out; she couldn't call Lincoln without some proof something was wrong. She switched on the torch app on her phone and slowly walked into the corner, her car key gripped between her fingers as a makeshift weapon just in case.

Her light pierced the darkness. She gasped. The door to the vacant unit tapped against the splintered wooden frame. The faint smell of wet paint reached her.

Was someone still inside?

She glanced over her shoulder, but the car park was empty. The tap again had her whirling back around.

She wasn't safe.

Backing away, she called Lincoln.

"What's up, Mayday?"

His voice had her relaxing her grip on her phone. "Someone's broken into the unit next to the bakery. I can smell wet paint."

"I'll be right there. Wait for me inside," he commanded.

Her skin tightened. "Why?"

"Just do it."

The silence as he hung up was like a safety rope snapping. Hands shaking, she finally managed to unlock the door to her bakery and opened it wide, then flicked on the hallway light.

The scent of bread that always permeated the bakery swept away some of her fear.

She stepped inside, but didn't close the door.

If someone was still in the unit, she wanted to get a photo of them coming out. She was far enough away that she could duck inside before they reached her.

Slowly she sat on the step.

The bright lights above and behind her should have been comforting, but instead felt like a targeted spotlight.

Should she switch them off?

No, the darkness would be worse.

The time dragged as she scanned the car park for movement. Checking the time again, she breathed out a sigh of relief as Lincoln finally pulled into the car park with Sue, one of his senior constables not far behind.

"Did you go in?" he asked.

"No."

"Good. Wait here."

Lincoln and Sue cautiously entered the building and a minute later Lincoln returned, a frown deep on his forehead.

"Anyone in there?"

"No, but I need you to look at something and I need Nicholas's number."

Of course. It was Nicholas's building. She gave him the number and waited while he called Nicholas to tell him about the break in. When he was finished, he said, "Come with me."

The unit had last been used as a clothing shop so the back storage area was smaller than Mai's kitchen. Lincoln shone his torch into the room. The doors of the little kitchenette had been ripped off and broken up, stacked on the floor in a tee-pee shape as if someone was building a campfire. Underneath them were the blackened remains of whatever had been used as kindling and a ripped T-shirt running from the fire to underneath the nearby cabinets.

Mai's chest tightened. It was crude. "Someone tried to light a fire." Tried to burn down the building. Why would they do that?

Lincoln nodded. "That's what I thought."

Anger rose up in Mai. Some bastard had tried to burn down her home, her business. She clenched her fists. "Did they leave any evidence?"

He took her arm and led her back outside. "I can't tell you, Mai, but I'll need to ask you some questions later."

"Lincoln!" He couldn't possibly leave her in the dark. This affected her life.

He shook his head, his expression grim. "I'm investigating."

Nicholas pulled into the car park and she held on to her temper, gritting her teeth. He didn't need to see her lose it.

"Why don't you go upstairs and Sue and I will drop by later?" His frown deepened as Nicholas walked over.

He wasn't telling her something, but now wasn't the time to argue with him. He needed to let Nicholas know about the extent of the break in.

She nodded a greeting and went into her building, locking the door behind her. With the sound of the bolt clicking into place, the anger and fear left her. Why would anyone want to burn down a building that would be demolished in a couple of months? It made no sense.

It would do nothing except hurt her. The florist was already wrapping up her business, so soon it would only be Mai in the building.

But she couldn't think of a single person who would do this to her.

She needed to get answers – if not from Lincoln, from Nicholas.

She'd make sure of it.

The sense of dread built as Nicholas walked towards Lincoln and Mai. Lincoln had said there'd been a break in. This was the second time he'd had to meet the police at one of his sites. At least this time, the building still stood.

But the reality didn't stop his lungs from constricting. Whatever had happened, his father would be pissed. He barely acknowledged Mai leaving as he focused on Lincoln. "What happened?"

"We're still working it out. When was the last time you were here?" Lincoln was direct, to the point with no friendly greeting. He was in cop mode.

"Friday, after I spoke to Mai I took a quick look inside to check if anything needed cleaning out."

"Nothing was out of place?"

"No. The water and electricity were off because it's been empty a while and there was a layer of dust on everything, but whoever had been in there last had cleared it out before leaving."

"So nothing was broken?"

"No." Nicholas braced himself. He wasn't going to like what was coming next.

Lincoln gestured for him to follow. "There are a couple of things you need to see."

He entered the building and the strong light from Lincoln's torch illuminated the small storage area cum kitchenette. As the light panned down nausea rose in Nicholas's stomach.

No.

Not again.

The pile of broken wood in the middle of the small floor was the remains of a campfire.

But the cloth would spread the flames to the cabinets.

Not a campfire. An attempt to start a fire.

His stomach heaved and he clamped down on his teeth, refusing to let the nausea out.

Fuck.

This was bad, really bad.

"This wasn't here on Friday?" Lincoln asked, his question mild.

He shook his head, unable to speak. What did Lincoln think, that he'd leave something like this here, that he wouldn't call the police?

"You need to see this as well." Lincoln walked out towards the shop front and Nicholas followed mutely. What else was there?

The smell of wet paint hit him first and he screwed up his nose. A female police officer was in the room taking pictures, a torch set up to illuminate the wall. The large, scrawled black letters that ran the length of the entire room captured Nicholas's attention.

Will this one burn too?

Nicholas took a step back, his throat squeezing shut. No.

"Do you know what that means?"

He didn't want this. *Really* didn't need this now. But it answered the question that had been haunting him.

The fire in Baldivis hadn't been an accident.

"Nicholas?"

He let out a deep breath and nodded once.

"Care to explain?"

Nicholas swallowed, hoping it would ease the tension in his throat. He had to get a grip, had to explain to Lincoln. "It's going to take some time."

"All right. Why don't you wait outside and I'll be out in a minute?" It wasn't a request.

It was starting again. The police, the explanations, the suspicion. He'd hoped it was all over.

In a slight daze, Nicholas walked out of the building. He noticed Mai's car and glanced up at her darkened window. Had she seen what was inside? Would she refuse to do business with him?

Everything was unravelling.

And he could do nothing to stop it.

By the time Lincoln came out, Nicholas's nerves were wound tight. He followed Lincoln over to the steps outside the bakery's back door and sat down.

He needed to take charge of the discussion, needed to lead it where it had to go. "Did you find any evidence as to who broke in?"

"We have a few leads." Lincoln took out his notepad. "We suspect that attempting to light a fire was an afterthought, otherwise the person would have brought the necessary tools."

Nicholas nodded. It made sense, but it didn't make him feel any better.

"Do you want to explain what the words on the wall meant?"

He didn't want to go over it again. He'd lost count of how many times he'd repeated himself. Taking a deep breath, he straightened his posture. "There was a fire at the last development I worked on," he said. "A shopping complex in Baldivis burnt to the ground and the police suspected arson." He had to tell Lincoln the whole truth. "I was the main suspect for a while."

Lincoln raised his eyebrows. "Why?"

"The development was going badly, we had unions protesting and I discovered a partner had made some bad business decisions." That was putting it mildly. If he'd kept a closer eye on what Shane was up to ... "The police thought we'd burnt it down so we could claim insurance and start again."

"Did you?" Lincoln's expression was impassive, a far different person from the cheerful, friendly man he'd been on New Year's Eve.

Lincoln was doing his job, but it still hurt. "No." He swallowed hard. "If it had been me, I would have made sure the insurance was paid."

"It wasn't?"

Nicholas shook his head, the familiar nausea clouding his stomach whenever he thought about it. "It was overdue, but I'd been so busy I hadn't approved the payment." That single fact had moved the suspicion away from him and turned his father and his colleagues against him. They had lost everything in the fire, millions of dollars because he'd not clicked authorise on a single payment. He'd tried to negotiate with the insurance company but they hadn't listened. He hadn't paid so they weren't insured – simple as that.

He'd almost ruined the company.

Lincoln's attitude softened slightly, his tone more questioning than accusatory. "Who knew that you'd bought the bakery building?"

He wasn't sure. Settlement had only just gone through. "Shadbolt of course, Aaron who sold it to me, as well as the tenants Mai and Janet. I've got a planning application with the council so whoever has access to that, and I guess anyone those people have told."

"Who stood to lose from the Baldivis fire?"

He answered on rote, the questions so familiar to him. "Shadbolt Property Developers and Jameson Construction."

"Anyone from Jameson's know about the development down here?"

"I don't know. I was on a leave of absence while the police investigated and then I was sent down here." The Jamesons weren't talking to his parents yet and Shane was in rehab.

"Has anyone asked you about your development here?"

"Jamie and the musketeers."

Lincoln scowled. "Where were you this afternoon?"

And there it was, the insinuation he had something to do with this. "I was working at home. After lunch I went surfing where I ran into Jamie and Mai and they came to my place afterwards for a drink."

"Can you think of anyone who might hold a grudge against Shadbolt?"

Nicholas hesitated. Shane had been pretty mad about the whole Baldivis incident, but he didn't need the police asking questions of him again. "No."

"All right. If you think of anything that might be useful, give me a call." Lincoln handed him a card and shook his hand.

"Thanks. Let me know if you find anything else."

He walked back to his car. It was dark and late, but there was one thing he had to do.

He had to call his father.

Chapter 8

Nicholas's ultimatum switched Mai into business mode. She wouldn't get emotional, but she *would* get what she wanted. After she'd left his house, she'd calmed down and realised Jamie had been right. Nicholas couldn't control what his father did, which meant she needed to be quick. She'd been to view the cafe out on Mortimer Road and while it wasn't perfect, it would do for the interim. She'd started the paperwork for leasing it straight away. Step one was complete.

Now it was time for step two.

Scanning her living area to make sure it was tidy, she cleared the table of everything aside from her paperwork. Calypso was flaked out on the couch as if he owned it and the espresso machine was on.

When Nicholas knocked on the door, she ran her hands over the lapels of the one business suit she owned, rolled her shoulders back and down and opened the door. She'd show him she was a business woman who knew what she wanted.

He was all business as well, dressed in a black suit with clean lines that accentuated his lean frame and a green tie that made his eyes look even greener. His leather laptop bag was draped over one shoulder like a stylish accessory. Why couldn't he look awkward or have a badly fitted suit? Why did he need to look so delicious that she wished he was here for other matters? She stepped back and gestured him inside. "Come in. Would you like a coffee?"

"If you're having one." He stood stiff as if waiting for an attack.

That was her fault. She'd lashed out at him. "Take a seat." She gave him a small smile, made him an espresso and poured herself some ice water with mint leaves in it, before sitting down with her notes.

"Do you still want the two units you indicated?" Nicholas asked, pulling out the plans.

The stiff, impersonal vibe wasn't going to work. She could do business and still be friendly, relaxed even. She needed to crack the tension, needed to get him back on side. The negotiations had to go well. If they didn't, she'd lose everything. "Yes." She got up again and took the biscuit jar from the bench. Food always helped. "Help yourself."

He took a melting moment. "Are you trying to butter me up?" His smile thawed the freeze in the room.

"Will it work?"

"Maybe."

Some of the tension in her shoulders melted away. "This is what I had in mind." She handed him the floor plan sketch she'd worked on. The designated kitchen and cafe areas were clearly marked, as were the modifications she wanted.

He examined it carefully. "What are these?"

"Power points and an extraction fan."

He frowned. "All right. I'll need to talk to my builder."

She was happy with that. "Some of the interior modelling will be able to be carried over from the existing cafe. Will the flooring and painting be included in the lease?"

"To a certain value – you should be fine as long as you don't want diamond-encrusted paint."

She smiled. "No. It's all fairly standard." She passed him the sheet with the costs, pleased her hand didn't shake. She couldn't show him how much this meant to her.

He perused the list and nodded. "What else have you got for me?"

This would be trickier. He didn't have to agree to any of it, above what he'd already offered. "I'm happy to sign a ten-year lease." Perhaps it would make him more amenable. She sipped her water and braced herself. "The cafe on Mortimer Road will require the least amount of modification to be ready as a temporary location," she said. "The issue with it is kitchen space. I'm going to have to purchase a large enough freezer to allow me to do some of the prep during the day and freeze it." If she had the ovens working during the day, she could keep up her production schedule. Penny could work daylight hours and they'd partially cook some of the goods, which would mean they would only need a short time to bake in the morning.

"How much?"

Mai handed him another document. "The freezer would of course then move to your development."

He nodded. "What about the numbers for outfitting the cafe?"

"Here." She couldn't read his expression. He'd make a brilliant poker player. She clenched the glass in front of her. She wasn't sure the bank would give her the money for the freezer if he refused, not when it was a temporary solution.

Nicholas read through the figures and jotted down some notes. The silence hurt her ears and she barely dared to breathe. Finally he looked up. "Is there anything else you need?"

She shook her head.

"When would you vacate this building?"

"After the school holidays – the beginning of February. It will take at least that much time to outfit the cafe." But it meant he could start on the demolition sooner.

"All right."

Her heart leapt as she stared at him. "Were you agreeing with my last statement, or to the whole proposal?"

He smiled. "The whole proposal." He held out his hand. "You've got yourself a deal. I'll do up the paperwork tomorrow."

Relief coursed through her and she leapt out of her chair. "Thank you." Mai shook his hand. She was shaking. She hadn't thought he would actually agree to everything. She squeezed her eyes closed, trying to prevent the flow of overjoyed tears.

"Hey, what's wrong?" Nicholas stood up. "I said yes and you're trembling." He pulled her into his arms and she wrapped hers around him. He felt so good; warm, strong and comforting, and she was too emotional to care whether this was a good idea.

"I'm happy," she mumbled against his chest.

"What?" He drew her away and looked down at her.

"I'm happy," she repeated. "Really, Nicholas. Thank you."

"It's my pleasure. You're not asking for much in the scheme of things, not when I'm disrupting your business so much. A world without *On the Way* would be a much sadder place."

His expression was intense, those green eyes the colour of her Christmas biscuits and all of a sudden she was aware of being in his arms, his firm hands holding her hips. It wouldn't take more than her rising up onto her toes to have her lips meet his. She stepped back, breaking the hold and cleared her throat. "For a sweet comment like that you can have one of my secret stash." She took a container out of the fridge and placed one of the pastries on a plate, handing it to him.

He glanced down at it and then back at her. "What is it?"

"It doesn't have a name as yet." She kept her distance from him, hoping her hormones would stop dancing around.

"You developed it?"

"Yeah." It took an age to make so it wouldn't be a regular item on her menu, but she was considering making it as part of her special orders list.

He took a bite and his eyes rolled back in his head. "Oh my God." His groan sent her hormones into a frenzy.

Damn.

"This is *amazing*. It's tart and creamy, and the outside is crisp and …" He took another bite and groaned again.

Her whole body tingled. She liked the sound of him being pleasured. Maybe after she'd signed the contract she could explore where this attraction could go. She cleared her throat. "I take it you like it?"

"It might be addictive. You should call it Mai's Delight, or Mai's Challenge, because you won't be able to stop at one. I want another one."

"Help yourself." She gestured to the container on the table, liking the warm glow at his praise.

Calypso jumped onto one of the dining chairs and Nicholas grabbed the container, holding it out of the cat's reach. "You're not getting any."

"He gets his own cat treats," Mai said.

"You bake for pets as well?"

"Just for my friends. I'm not licenced for pet food so I do it at home."

"Is there anything you can't do?" He laughed, but his eyes captured hers and there was earnestness in them. His respect and admiration were clear. It was a heady combination that boosted his appeal.

She blinked and moved away. "I can't paint."

"Sorry?"

"I can't paint – like walls and stuff. Well it's more like it doesn't interest me. I should be able to twist Jamie or the musketeers' arms to help me with the Mortimer Road cafe." She collected their cups and put them in the sink.

"I'll help."

Surprise and then pleasure coursed through her. "Thank you. That would be great." She could do with all the help she could get and it would give her a chance to get to know Nicholas better.

He glanced at his watch. "I need to go. The council meeting starts shortly and they're discussing the planning permission today."

"Good luck." Her mother had been right. There was no point fighting the development, not now she had everything she wanted. She walked him to the door. "Does Lincoln know who broke in downstairs?"

The good humour vanished from Nicholas's face and his body tensed. Mai wished she hadn't asked.

"Not yet."

She'd ask Lincoln for more details because it was obviously a sore point for Nicholas. She wasn't happy about the situation either. Changing the subject, she asked, "Are you going to the training session at the fire station tomorrow night?"

"Yeah."

"I'll see you then."

Nicholas shook his head as if shaking something off and then smiled. "I'll look forward to it."

Heat rushed through her at his smile.

"Me too."

Nicholas shoved the thought of the break-in out of his head. There wasn't anything he could do about it. He needed to focus on the positives and that was the meeting with Mai. It had gone far better than he'd expected, and after she'd signed the contract he'd have only three more units to sell.

But he never should have offered to help her.

It had been an automatic reaction to comfort her when she'd teared up inside, and she'd felt so good in his arms, soft and warm, and she fit him perfectly. He'd wanted to cheer her up, to hold her, to make her feel better.

He scowled.

He wasn't going to be here for long, and was too messed up right now to deal with the stress of a new relationship.

He needed to think about something else.

With only half an hour before the council meeting, he drove over to the shire building where he met with the planning manager.

"Glad you could make it." Floyd shook his hand. "It's always easier when the petitioner is at the meeting so questions can be answered immediately."

"Of course." He followed Floyd into the large meeting hall where a number of people were already seated on the rows of plastic chairs. His item was further down the agenda, so he took his seat and slid his laptop out of its case. He would work on the details of Mai's contract while he waited for his turn.

When the meeting began he tuned in so he didn't miss his turn. The first item was public question time and started an hour of debate about whether a certain tree in the community park should be cut down. Thank goodness he had his laptop.

As the group voted, he looked up. It was the planning department's turn so he saved his work and shut his laptop as Floyd stood. "We've received a petition to demolish the building on Jackson Street and replace it with an eight unit building with a central car park," he said. "We've had no detractors from this proposal and recommend it goes ahead."

A man behind him said, "I lodged a complaint today."

Nicholas's stomach clenched as he turned. The man was

younger than him and everything about him said bogan, from his blue plaid shirt to his shaved head and the packet of cigarettes tucked into his top pocket. "Shadbolt is a dodgy company. Their last development burned down and the police thought it was deliberately lit. We don't want them bringing their troubles here."

His pulse raced. What the hell? How did he know about Baldivis? Only Lincoln knew as far as he was aware.

"Gordon's right. The development will be an eyesore – it's modern and ugly, and doesn't fit the architecture of the area." Another voice, female this time. Nicholas shifted to see Kit standing. She stared at him as if daring him to contradict her. Her words echoed those of Jamie's the day before.

It hurt – a sharp, twisting pain in his gut. Had he been set up?

He'd trusted the meeting with Mai had been genuine, but maybe she'd been playing him.

Lincoln had said if you take on one musketeer you take them all on, and Kit wouldn't be here if Mai hadn't asked her to be.

Mai was a hell of an actress. He'd really believed her.

"It probably should be heritage listed," Kit continued.

"The development encourages economic growth in the area," Floyd said.

Gordon spoke. "If we let these Perth blokes in, they'll take all the money and run back to the city. They don't give a shit about the town."

"It should be someone local doing the development," another man piped up.

Nicholas closed his eyes for a second as his heartburn flared. This was going south fast. He shouldn't have got involved in the community, should have kept to himself. His father would see this as another example of how he'd completely fucked up.

Floyd held up a hand to stop the murmuring that had broken out in the crowd. "We have Nicholas Shadbolt from Shadbolt Property Developers here today. Nicholas, do you want to say something?"

Nicholas buttoned his jacket as he stood. He would convince them this was the best deal. He had to. "If anything is an eyesore, it's the empty block behind the building. The existing building is dangerous. The wiring and plumbing are not up to standard and it would cost a significant amount to repair. The new units will fix these problems, and additionally provide more parking in the centre of town. I've just come from negotiating with one of my tenants and she is happy with the proposal I have offered her." He stared directly at Kit.

Kit grimaced.

Perhaps she hadn't known about his discussions with Mai. "Five of the units have already been leased or sold and I don't anticipate it will take long to fill the rest. The development will give local business owners more choice as I believe there are limited options available in Blackbridge at this time."

An older Asian woman stood. Unlike the others who wore jeans and T-shirts, she wore a white blouse and knee-length pencil skirt. "I'd be interested in one of those units," she said. "I'm tired of my landlord refusing to fix the air-conditioning." She raised an eyebrow at the man who'd piped up.

The man grimaced. "It's not that bad, Bian."

A grey-haired man got to his feet. "Kit is right. The development will ruin the aesthetics of the town. People love the quaintness of Blackbridge. That modern monstrosity will destroy the look. Maybe we *should* look at applying for heritage listing."

Fuck. That was the last thing he needed. His chest squeezed tighter as the crowd discussed the history of the building and what the town planning guidelines technically allowed. He had a wild card he could use, though he didn't want to. Not when it would affect Mai.

When it was clear they were getting nowhere, he pulled it out. "If you want to get technical, the whole area is zoned as a retail area. I have a tenant who lives above her bakery, which is *technically* not allowed by the zoning laws." He let it sit for a moment as people exchanged glances. They all knew who he was talking about. "Should I tell her to vacate immediately?"

He allowed them to backpedal for a few minutes before he continued. "It seems your biggest concern is the appearance of the building." There were a few nods. "If we changed the façade to suit the surrounding architecture, would that be suitable?"

No one said anything, so he looked directly at Kit.

She squirmed, then nodded.

Floyd took over. "So the vote is to approve the planning proposal on the condition that an updated design is submitted and approved by the council?"

The vote took place and the proposal was approved.

Nicholas kept his expression bland as relief washed through him. He excused himself and walked out.

He had more work to do.

But at least he'd salvaged the situation.

The day couldn't have gone better. Mai's negotiations with Nicholas had been successful, she'd sourced the extra supplies she needed for the new cafe and the takings at the cafe had been an all-time high.

She pulled down her block-out blinds as her phone rang. Her friends and family knew not to call her after eight unless it was urgent. She frowned at Kit's name on the display and answered.

"I may have made a big mistake," Kit said.

She suppressed a smile as she threw back her bed covers. "What did you do?"

"Don't get mad, OK? I was trying to help."

She chuckled. Kit had always tried to negotiate before admitting what she'd done. "Did you buy bread from the supermarket?"

"Worse. I went to the council meeting tonight."

Mai switched on her bedside lamp. "What for?"

"They were discussing Nicholas's development."

Dread filled Mai and she sank down on to her bed giving Kit her full attention. "What *did* you do?"

Kit cleared her throat. "I thought you didn't want to move. I thought you'd want someone to fight for you."

She closed her eyes, trying not to imagine the worst. Kit always believed she knew what was best. "Spit it out."

"I protested the development."

"*Kit!*" Mai groaned. "Nicholas and I came to an agreement today." Which was yet to be signed. Was this going to ruin their negotiations?

"Well you didn't tell me you'd changed your mind," Kit defended herself.

It hadn't occurred to her. "What happened?"

"Gordon spoke up first, which was weird."

It was. Was he trying to get into her good books so she didn't turn him in to the police?

"He said Shadbolt were dodgy and burnt down their last building. Do you know anything about that?"

Mai's skin flushed hot and then cold. The attempted fire next door. Could Nicholas have been behind it? She didn't want to believe it. "No."

"You should check it out," Kit told her. "Then a couple of the usual suspects got behind my call for it to be heritage listed."

She reached for her tablet and turned it on. "What was the outcome?" How mad would Nicholas be?

"The development has been approved on the condition Nicholas makes the outside look more like the surrounding buildings."

That didn't sound too bad, but she didn't know how much it would cost. "How did Nicholas react?"

"He was pretty calm and collected through the debate," Kit said. "But he looked pissed when he walked out. Then your mother read me the riot act after the meeting."

"Mum?"

"Yeah, she was there. Told me I shouldn't have interfered."

Mai sighed. "She was right." But why had she been there in the first place? Her mother didn't attend council meetings unless it affected something she was working on.

"Yeah, I know. I was worried you were going to lose the bakery and I wanted to do something to help."

She couldn't be mad. Kit's heart was in the right place. "I'm not going to lose it, as long as Nicholas doesn't back out of the agreement we made today. He still needs to draw up the paperwork."

Kit swore. "I'm sorry. I'll apologise to him tomorrow, tell him you had nothing to do with it. Have you got his number?"

Mai gave it to her. "I'm sure it will be fine," she said with more optimism than she felt. "Listen, I'm going to sleep. I'll talk to you later."

"All right. Sorry, Mayday."

Mai hung up and dumped her phone on the bedside table, squeezing her eyes shut. Damn it. Would Nicholas think she'd asked Kit to attend the meeting? She hoped not, but she needed to make sure, she couldn't let this mess up their negotiations. She dialled his number.

He didn't answer.

When the voicemail message came on she hung up. She wasn't sure what to say, how to explain Kit had acted on her own without sounding defensive. Besides, she'd see him tomorrow at the training session and be able to explain everything in person.

She typed a search criteria into her tablet and yawned, rolling her shoulders. She should be going to sleep, but Kit's mention of arson had her concerned.

The results highlighted a number of newspaper articles from a couple of months ago and she read them quickly. A Shadbolt development in Baldivis had burned to the ground and Nicholas had been suspected for a while. There was no mention of a final outcome or charges being laid.

The idea he was guilty didn't sit well with her, but was that because she liked him? She needed to detach herself from her attraction and think critically. He'd seemed upfront in his discussions with her.

But why would anyone else want to light a fire in her building?

She put her tablet aside and switched off the light, but her brain wouldn't switch off as easily. Tomorrow she'd call Lincoln and make sure he knew about this.

And hope Nicholas really was innocent.

Chapter 9

Nicholas was running a little late for the fire training on Friday night. He'd spent the day on the phone to his architect and to the concrete slab manufacturer trying to figure out the easiest and cheapest way he could meet the new conditions on the development.

He'd also endured an awkward conversation with his father when he'd explained what had happened. Another mark in the bad son column. Not that it was his fault this time.

Besides he really liked the new design the architect had come up with for the façade. It was a nice call back to the twenties, not dissimilar to the building that now stood there. Unfortunately it would take some extra finessing to achieve the look, which of course added to the cost.

He was tempted to take some of the expense out of the offer he'd negotiated with Mai. The more he'd thought about it, the clearer it had become. Kit wouldn't have turned up at the meeting if Mai hadn't asked her to.

And if she hadn't sent Kit to the meeting, the development would have been approved.

He'd made a rookie mistake trusting her.

Bitterness was a bad taste in his mouth. He sighed. He was being melodramatic. It was business, he shouldn't take it personally – this was exactly why business and pleasure didn't mix.

He shook his head.

He'd actually thought Mai had been upfront, had accepted the development. She'd seemed enthusiastic about it yesterday, had cried when he'd accepted her terms.

It stung that he'd been fooled.

He got out of his car and acknowledged the people standing around talking. Training hadn't started yet. Scanning the faces he found Mai behind the wheel of the tanker, moving it to the empty space next to the fire station. She waved and he nodded, but he wasn't going to be friendly. Fool me once and all that crap.

He headed into the station greeting Lawrence and Jeremy who he'd met earlier in the week.

Lawrence clapped his hands as Mai came back in. "Tonight we're doing a full audit on the tanker, the fast attack vehicle and trailer, as well as a stocktake of the equipment room."

Around him people groaned.

Lawrence shook his head. "We need to make sure everything is in place and working. If we have time when it's done, we'll do hose drills." He turned to Mai. "You and Nicholas do the fast attack since you've used it most recently."

Damn it. He didn't want to be stuck with Mai, having to make small talk. Nicholas walked over to the vehicle without saying a word.

Mai picked up a checklist and joined him. "Kit told me about the council meeting last night."

He raised an eyebrow, surprised she'd mentioned it.

She grimaced. "I'm sorry. I had no idea what she'd planned."

Yeah, right. "So it's a coincidence her words mirrored Jamie's?"

"Jamie?" She frowned. "What's he got to do with it?"

Like she didn't know. "He said the design didn't fit when he saw the plans the other day."

"It's true, *I* told you that. But this wasn't a set up." She placed a hand on his arm, her eyes concerned. "I promise you. I spoke to Kit when I first found out, when I was still upset about the development, but I never asked her to do this." She sighed. "Kit has a habit of going off half-cocked when she believes in something or is trying to protect someone. When Hannah was being stalked, Kit went to Lincoln about … something Hannah didn't want him to know. She means well."

Hannah had been stalked? No, he couldn't be distracted. "That's convenient for you." Her hand was warm on his arm and he wanted to believe her.

Mai's eyes narrowed. "No it's not. She's made the development harder for you and now you're mad at me – how is that convenient?"

He didn't respond.

"I might have fibbed to you about the building's history in a moment of panic, but I would never do something so backhanded." Her gaze focused on his. "I'm happy with what we agreed yesterday. My reaction was real."

Though he wasn't sure if he should, he did believe her. "All right." Maybe he had overreacted, been overly sensitive. After the Baldivis incident, that wasn't surprising.

"I really am sorry." She glanced at the list she held. "We'd better get started."

He nodded.

He'd still be more careful from now on.

He couldn't afford to fail.

They worked through the checklist quickly, Mai calling out the items and Nicholas checking them. It enabled him to familiarise himself with the vehicle, which was invaluable.

When they finished, they went to help in the equipment room.

"How do you find Blackbridge compared to your other brigade?" Jeremy asked.

"It's a lot busier," Nicholas said. Not that he'd ever attended a call.

"He's a newbie," Mai said. "Just off his Ps. The Foley fire was his first real blaze."

"You did good," Jeremy said. "I wouldn't have picked you as a noob."

Pleasure warmed him. "Thanks. Do you know what caused the fire?"

Jeremy shrugged and looked around. "Hey, Foley. What caused the fire?"

Everyone in the room stopped to listen.

Foley frowned. "Some bastard had been storing chemicals inside the shed and it looks like he stopped for a smoke."

"What would they do that for?" Jeremy asked.

"The cops wouldn't say, but they got pretty excited. I reckon it was drug-making chemicals – for meth or something."

Nicholas raised his eyebrows. There had been some big quantities of chemicals there – more than your backyard meth lab.

"They found a lock on the gate that leads to the back road," Foley continued. "And the hinges have been repaired. It used to be a bitch to open."

"You didn't notice?" Jeremy asked.

"Don't start questioning me." Foley scowled. "I got the third degree from those Albany detectives. I haven't been in the back paddock since I stopped using the shed. One of my guys checked the fences about six months ago when we moved the sheep in, but they didn't mention the gate. They all got questioned too."

"Someone's not going to be happy about losing all that stuff," Mai said.

"Yeah, my heart bleeds," Foley said. "Insurance aren't going to pay up because they consider it an abandoned structure. Bastards."

"Are you guys finished in there yet?" Lawrence boomed from the doorway.

"Just about," Jeremy reported.

"Good because we're going to do some hose drills."

Nicholas followed the others out of the room. Hard drugs were not something he would have associated with the sleepy town of Blackbridge. But what the hell did he know? He hadn't known Shane was using either.

Not until it was too late.

By the time they were done with the drills, Mai was tired. Usually she enjoyed the camaraderie, the teasing, and working through different exercises, but the stress of the last week had finally caught up with her and all she wanted to do was sleep.

She had a staff meeting tomorrow to tell everyone what was happening and wanted to be alert for it. She grabbed a slice of pizza to go, wishing she hadn't walked down to the fire station this evening. "I'll see you guys next week."

"Off so soon?" Jeremy called.

"Yeah, it's past my bedtime and I'm walking home."

"I'll give you a lift." Nicholas placed a hand on her arm to stop her. "I've got some work I need to finish."

Her heart jumped. Maybe he wasn't mad at her any longer. "That would be great." She walked out to his BMW and he opened the boot so she could put her kit bag in with his.

She sank into the soft, leather seats, her whole body heavy. Her eyelids closed and she forced them back open, straightening her spine. "How long will it take you to get some updated designs?"

"My architect sent it through today. I'll get the revised quotes for the concrete before I resubmit them to council."

Meaning it was likely to cost him more. She winced. "I'd love to see it."

He pulled up at the back of the bakery and turned to her. He was silent for a moment as he studied her. "Do you want to come over tomorrow? I have the paperwork ready for you to sign and I can show you then."

Tomorrow was Saturday. Didn't he take the weekend off? Or was this more of a social invitation? No, she was hoping for too much. Besides, she still needed to ask him about the arson thing before she decided if she wanted to pursue anything further with him. "Sure. What time?"

"I'm free all day."

"How about two?"

"Great. Feel free to bring Calypso."

Her heart warmed that he'd remembered her cat. "Thanks." She got out of the car and remembered her kit bag. "Do you want to pop the boot?"

He got out, opened the boot and lifted out her bag. "Good night, Mai." His fingers brushed hers as he handed it over and a spark ran up her arm. They were standing close, and all she would have to do is take a small step forward to kiss him goodnight. She clearly remembered the kiss they'd shared on

New Year's, the zing that had flooded her body. But he might not be interested, not after the fiasco with Kit. And she hadn't signed the paperwork yet.

One thing at a time.

"Good night." She walked up the steps and opened her door. She glanced back at him.

"Sweet dreams." He gave her a half smile, his expression unreadable.

"You too." She closed the door behind her, cutting off the sensation.

Business first.

Then they could explore where this thing could go.

Mai took her time getting ready the next afternoon. She needed the boost of confidence after the staff meeting she'd just had. Jodie had gone into panic mode even though there would be no change to her working hours, and Sylvia and Penny had peppered her with questions. The only one not worried about the move was Trent, who would be going back to part-time hours when school started back.

Flicking through her wardrobe she paused at her business suit for a moment before settling on her emerald green halter-neck dress which finished just above her knees. She wanted this to be more of a social occasion, and to see if anything more could come of their relationship. Slipping on her cute black flats, she then headed for the kitchen to where she'd packaged up a fresh batch of Mai's Delights. Was it too much? She straightened the bow and called Calypso.

Only one way to find out.

Nerves prickled her skin on the drive over and her heart beat a little faster as she knocked on his door.

Nicholas opened it, his phone to his ear, his expression apologetic. Despite the temperature being in the low thirties, he wore black pants and a white business shirt, though he'd rolled the sleeves up. Maybe he was treating today like a business meeting. She should have gone with something less flirty. He motioned her inside as he said, "The changes are required to get planning permission." His tone was stern, no-nonsense.

She walked into the living area where the dining table was covered with plans and his laptop was on.

"I know," he said. "Listen Dad, I've got a client here to sign some paperwork. Can we discuss this more tomorrow?"

Client? Well that cleared up that question. Her face flushed as disappointment swirled through her. She should have worn her suit.

He frowned and turned his back on her to shuffle some of the papers on the table. "I'll be at least an hour." Finally he sighed. "I'll call you back." He hung up and clutched the back of the dining chair, his knuckles white and body tense. Mai's heart went out to him.

"Is everything all right?"

He stiffened and then turned to Mai, his eyes a little distant. "I'm sorry. Can I get you a drink?"

"A tea would be great, but we can reschedule if you're busy."

"No, I'd like to get the paperwork signed." He gestured to the table. "Take a seat. The contract's on the table."

His words were clipped, but he picked up Calypso who was rubbing against his pants and stroked him, nuzzling his fur before handing him to Mai. As he put the kettle on, his movements were fast and a little jerky.

She recognised his agitation. She put Calypso down and walked over to him. "I'm sorry Kit made your life more difficult."

He sighed. "It wouldn't be a big deal if there hadn't been issues with the last development." He winced. "Forget I said anything."

This was her chance to ask. "Are you talking about the fire?"

He stared at her. "You know about that?"

"Kit mentioned something about it, so I googled it."

He continued making the tea. "I guess you've got questions."

She nodded.

"Fire away."

"Did the police ever find out what happened?"

"No, they're still investigating."

"Did you tell Lincoln about it after the break in?"

He handed her the tea. "Why do you ask?"

He was avoiding the question. That was odd. "Someone

tried to light a fire in the empty unit. I called Lincoln."

"It wasn't me." The words were flat, definite.

"I didn't think it was." Not after she'd had time to think about it.

"Really?" The disbelief was clear on his face.

She sipped her drink. "You strike me as an intelligent man," she said. "You wouldn't light a fire at your new development if the police still had you on their suspect list for the earlier blaze."

"No, I wouldn't."

"So who have you annoyed lately?"

"Huh?" He blinked at her.

"First the Baldivis project and then this one. If someone was angry at the company, they'd hardly drive for four hours to break in and set a badly prepared fire – they'd target one of your Perth developments."

Nicholas stared at her for a long moment and then nodded. "You're right. I hadn't thought about it like that." His phone rang, and he swore and hit cancel. Almost immediately the phone rang again.

"Do you need to get that?"

Nicholas hesitated. "No. It's my father. He can wait."

"How did he take the arson accusations?" What kind of relationship did he have with his father?

"He didn't believe them."

"That's good." The phone continued to ring. "So the reason he keeps calling you on a Saturday afternoon is because he's a workaholic?"

"He's micro-managing."

Why was Nicholas so tense? "Because he doesn't think you're capable?"

"Not after the fire."

She frowned. "But you said he didn't believe it was you."

"He didn't, but he did blame me for not paying the insurance." Nicholas almost spat out the words.

Mai sat back. "You had no insurance when the development burned down?"

He ran a hand through his hair. "It was two days overdue. I'd barely been in the office over the past week. We'd had issues with the construction company ..."

She placed a hand on his arm. He obviously blamed himself. "It could have happened to anyone."

"Not according to my father."

She hated seeing him so stressed. "That's rubbish. It was an oversight that normally wouldn't have mattered. You didn't do it on purpose."

"No, I didn't." He stood up and walked to the window, looking out over the backyard, his posture stiff.

Mai wasn't sure what to say. She watched him for a moment, and then turned her attention to the paperwork in front of her. "Is this my contract?"

"Do you really want to sign now you know about the fire?"

She met his dark expression. He was hurting. "I imagine you've already double-checked the insurance details." She kept her voice light. "The new design is lovely." They hadn't changed the layout of the building, but the façade had flourishes, extra detail on the walls and across the roof that were reminiscent of an earlier era.

He walked back to her, his shoulders relaxing. "Thanks. I like the changes as well."

Mai examined the floor plan next and discovered he'd made the adjustments she'd asked for.

Turning to the paperwork, she carefully read through the agreement. It seemed to have everything, but she should run it past her mother first. "Can you email this to me? I should send it to my lawyer."

"Sure." He pressed a couple of buttons on the laptop. "Your mother?"

"Yes, how did you know?"

"She contacted me yesterday about a unit. She's going to lease one."

"So you've only got a couple left to lease?"

"Yeah and I talked to a co-op this morning who might be interested."

Mai opened her email on her phone and forwarded the proposal to her mother. Then she sent a text asking her to review it.

Nicholas was still focused on his screen, and her stomach rumbled. She took the bakery box from the kitchen bench and offered it to Nicholas. "Mai's Delight?"

His whole face lit up. "You didn't need to do that." He stood and got a couple of plates out, handing her one.

At least she'd managed to cheer him up.

"Have you leased the new place yet?" he asked.

"I signed the agreement yesterday and it's effective immediately."

"I'm glad." His laptop dinged with the sound of an email message. He groaned. "I need to answer this."

"Go ahead." She sipped her tea and then bit into the pastry. It really was one of her best creations.

About ten minutes later, Nicholas was still typing on his computer and her phone rang. Nerves sprang to her skin. Her mother.

"The agreement looks good," Bian said.

Relief swept through her. "Nothing I need to worry about?"

"No, he's agreed to everything you wanted, hasn't he?"

"Yeah."

"Then feel free to sign it. I'm going to lease one of the units myself."

"Nicholas just told me that."

"It's the weekend. Is he working?"

Mai's face flushed. "You know me, Mum. I work strange hours so I have to fit things in when I can. I'll drop by tomorrow to chat." She hung up.

Nicholas watched her. "Everything OK?"

"Yes. Have you got a pen?"

He handed her a silver pen with a satisfying weightiness to it as if to symbolise the importance of the task it was about to do. She tested it, drawing a line on the back of the plan and it was smooth, the colour a rich blue.

She smoothed down the signing page. This was it.

Breathing in deeply, she signed her name and then dated first one and then the second contract.

She passed them over to Nicholas who quickly countersigned them.

It was done.

She had taken the next step in her career. She would be a success.

Smiling at Nicholas, she said, "I'm glad we've got it sorted." Now maybe they could explore the attraction between them.

"Me too."

"How long are you planning to stay in Blackbridge?"

"At least until the development is finished." He hesitated and then added, "I'm meant to be doing penance for my mistake, but I'm enjoying it down here."

His father sounded like a complete douchebag. "That's good, and I'm sure the development will be a success."

"I hope so. I don't like the message that was left at the building."

"Message?"

"You didn't see the graffiti on the wall?"

"No."

"It said, Will this one burn too?"

Her teeth clenched. She didn't like the sound of that. "Maybe you should put a smoke detector in there just in case."

"That's a good idea."

Perhaps she should move to Fleur's sooner than she planned. Though if she stayed in her apartment she'd be able to keep an eye out for anyone skulking about.

"I'm glad you found a temporary solution for the bakery."

It took her a second to catch up with the change of topic. "Me too. It's going to be a busy few weeks."

"I meant it when I said I'll help," Nicholas said. "I'd like to."

And she'd like to have him around. "Don't worry," Mai assured him. "I could do with all the free labour I can get."

He chuckled. "All right."

They stood there looking at each other. The crinkle in his forehead wasn't there now, as if the weight that had caused it had been lifted. His smile drew her in and she leaned forward just a little. What was she doing? "Do you want to go out to dinner with me?" she blurted.

Nicholas hesitated. "I don't think that's a good idea."

She stepped back, the rejection sharp, and her face flushed. She could have sworn the attraction was mutual. "Why not?"

"We have a business relationship — anything else could get messy."

He hadn't actually denied he was interested. "The contract is signed and I can keep business and pleasure separate." She moved closer and he eyed her warily. "Why shouldn't we explore this attraction between us?"

"Because it could end badly."

"All relationships could. It's not a reason not to try." She smiled at him. "There's a lovely winery out of town. Let's have dinner to celebrate."

The indecision was clear on his face, but his eyes didn't leave hers.

Slowly she stepped forward. "We both need to eat."

His eyes darkened.

Mai rose up onto her toes and brought his head down to hers. Their lips met and there was that spark again, a thrill that raced straight down her spine and tingled her skin. She gasped as he took control, pulling her closer and deepening the kiss.

He was good at this.

He tasted sweet like the pastry he'd just eaten and his hands, firm on her back, made her feel secure. His lips teased, tasted and heat shot through her.

She wanted this passion. Craved the desire, the connection. She needed to be closer to him. She dug her fingers into his hair as something warm and soft rubbed against her leg. She jerked back. "What the ...?" She looked down, catching her breath.

Calypso.

Damn.

Nicholas cleared his throat. "So, dinner tonight?"

She grinned. "Absolutely. How about I pick you up at five-thirty? I tend to eat early because of getting up so early."

"Five-thirty is great, but I'll pick you up." He ran his hand through his hair.

"I'll be waiting." She gathered up the paperwork and her cat, and left before he had a chance to change his mind.

She couldn't wait for tonight.

Chapter 10

What had he just agreed to? Nicholas shook his head as he closed the door behind Mai and then wandered back into the living area. Dating Mai would only end up with him hurting her when he returned to Perth. And his father would see it as a conflict of interest.

But damn if he wasn't aroused by the way she'd taken charge. It took a much stronger man than him to say no.

He tugged on his earlobe as his phone rang. His father was incessant, but there was no way Nicholas could ignore it this time. "Hi, Dad."

"You've finally decided to answer your phone?"

He rolled his eyes. "I was still in my meeting."

His father harrumphed. "Is it signed? I don't see the contract in the folder."

"I've just walked the client out. I'll scan and upload it now."

"I'll wait."

Nicholas reached for his antacid and then stopped. He hadn't needed them at all while talking to Mai, only needed them with his father. He touched his lips, still warm and singing from her kiss. She made him feel good, whereas his father just stressed him out. With a sigh, he went into the study to scan and email the document. "I should have the contract on another one of the units signed by the end of next week."

"Which leaves how many?"

"Two."

"What about the changes to the design those hippies demanded? How much are they going to cost?"

He breathed out, ignoring the way his chest tightened. "I'm still getting quotes," he said. "But the design is good and it should be approved."

"You thought the last design would be approved as well," his father reminded him.

He wouldn't be allowed to make a single mistake ever again. Not with his father. He'd destroyed that trust forever. "I didn't understand the community then," Nicholas said. "Mai likes the new design."

"Who's Mai?"

Nicholas winced. "She's the tenant in the current building, the baker. She saw the plans today when she came to sign the contract."

"You shouldn't go showing them to just anyone. It gives them time to come up with arguments against it."

"Mai wouldn't do that," Nicholas said.

"How would you know? You've only been there for a week."

There was no way he would mention how much time he'd already spent with Mai. "You're right. Is there anything else I can help you with?"

By the time he hung up, Nicholas's head throbbed and the antacid wasn't touching the stabbing pain in his stomach. How had he lived with this stress and tension all of the time? It was ridiculous that he hadn't noticed it, hadn't done something about it. The massive anxiety attack after the Baldivis fire had him thinking he was having a heart attack, but still he hadn't recognised it had been the boiling point of all the stress he constantly lived with. Work was slowly destroying him.

He hated it.

There was no joy, no sense of satisfaction, just day after day of trying to live up to his father's unrealistic expectations. He didn't have the passion that Mai had for her bakery, about the food she baked.

What would it be like to wake up and actually look forward to going to work?

He couldn't imagine it. Work had been an expectation, a responsibility for so long.

But what would he do instead?

A few months ago his father would have gone mental at the suggestion Nicholas wanted to leave the company. Now though … he might welcome the move.

He stood up and stretched, the time on the oven catching his attention. Shit, he had to get ready for his date with Mai.

His skin prickled with nervous anticipation. If he was honest with himself, the only thing he really wanted right now was to get to know Mai better, find out what made her tick, surround himself with her optimism.

He needed some of that in his life.

Work could get stuffed. And if he quit, he wouldn't have to worry about a conflict of interest, or mixing business with pleasure.

He swallowed a couple of headache pills and got ready.

Tonight he would forget about everything going on in his life and would focus on what he wanted.

Mai.

Mai fluffed around her apartment waiting for Nicholas to arrive. She couldn't sit still, the nerves flitting around her stomach like a deranged butterfly, so she straightened the remote on the coffee table, brushed Calypso's hair off the couch and reviewed her supply of treats to see if she needed to do more baking. She'd dressed up a little and had enough time to second-guess the decision. The Vale winery was kind of posh, so she'd curled her hair and wore a floral, fifties-style dress, with a big skirt and petticoat that always made her feel feminine and in charge, and a killer pair of black heels.

When the doorbell finally rang, she picked up her bag and hurried down the steps to the back door. Nicholas had dressed down from his usual business suits. The rolled-up sleeves of his black shirt accentuated his long arms and the slim fit of his beige chinos made Mai consider taking his hand and dragging him upstairs to her apartment.

"You look beautiful, Mai." He kissed the back of her hand.

Heat rushed to her cheeks. "Thanks. You look pretty good yourself." She kept her hand in his as she walked down the steps to his car.

As Nicholas opened the door for her, a white hatchback pulled into the car park. Mai groaned as her sister Leanne got out.

"Hi, Mai." She gave Nicholas a once over and smiled before focusing back on Mai. "We've run out of bread at home and I was supposed to come and get some earlier."

Mai raised her eyebrows. "The bakery is closed." And she was busy.

"Well, duh, that's why I came around the back to you." She waved at Nicholas. "Hi, I'm Leanne, Mai's sister. You don't mind if she lets me in for a second, right?" Leanne ignored the daggers Mai sent her and walked over to the steps.

"Not at all. We've got time," Nicholas said.

Damn it. "I won't be a minute," Mai told him and unlocked the door again. Once inside Leanne said, "Who's the hunk?"

Mai's face heated as she moved down the corridor out of Nicholas's hearing. "That's Nicholas Shadbolt. He's new in town."

"The property developer? The guy who's shutting you down?" Leanne gaped at her.

"Yes and no, he's not shutting me down." She greeted Sylvia who was counting the till. "Have we got any loaves left?"

"Just the rye. I was just going to pack it up for the CWA."

Mai grabbed a loaf and handed it to Leanne.

Leanne screwed up her nose. "I don't like rye."

"Then you should have come in earlier." Mai shepherded her back towards the door.

"Can I get some pastries too?"

Was she kidding? "No." At Leanne's pout, she said, "They're going to charity and you've interrupted my date enough."

"Oh, so it is a date?"

"Yes."

"Is it serious?"

They were at the door and Mai shot her sister a shut-up-now look. "We'll talk later."

Leanne laughed. "We'd better." She waved at Nicholas who

leaned against his car, arms crossed over his chest, stance relaxed. "Thanks. I'll let you two get back to your date now. You be good to my sister, all right?"

Mai closed her eyes, asking for patience.

"I will. Nice meeting you, Leanne." Nicholas smiled.

Mai waited until Leanne had left before moving down the stairs and climbing into the car. "Sorry about that."

"It's not a problem. It's not every day I get called a hunk."

"You heard that?"

He chuckled. "Yeah. She seems nice."

"She is when she's not in annoying little sister mode." Mai smiled. "How was the rest of your day?"

"Fine." He frowned.

"Want to talk about it?"

He was silent for so long that she wasn't sure he would answer. Finally he sighed. "How did you know you wanted to be a baker?"

Mai glanced at him. It was an odd question. "When we had to choose our subjects for the final two years in high school, there wasn't anything that interested me. I've always loved to cook, loved providing food for people." Did that sound stupid? "The school counsellor provided me with some options and the moment I saw baker I knew it was what I wanted to do."

"Did you finish high school?"

"Yeah. There was no way Mum would have let me drop out, but I got a part-time job at a bakery, a kind of unofficial apprenticeship, and I fell in love with it."

"You don't mind the hours?"

"It was hard getting up so early at first, but I'm used to it now." They drove along Mortimer Road and Mai pointed out the cafe. "That's the place I've leased."

Nicholas slowed down. "It looks nice."

Mai shrugged. "It will do in the interim. The owners have given me permission to put in a ramp up to the door to make it more accessible." A couple of her regulars were in wheelchairs.

"Word will spread pretty quickly, especially if you put up a notice in the bakery now."

"I hope so." It wouldn't be quite that easy, but it was a worry for another night. "So what about you? Have you always wanted to be a property developer?"

His hands tightened on the steering wheel. "I don't remember a time when it wasn't expected of me."

"That's not what I asked."

He blew out a breath. "I don't know."

The admission surprised her. He'd seemed so confident when she'd first met him. "Do you enjoy it?"

"No." He barked out a surprised laugh. "Wow, I didn't mean to say that."

"Is it true?"

"Yes." He tugged on his ear. "I shouldn't be telling you this. You're going to regret signing the contract with me."

Mai shook her head. "I signed the contract with the company you work for. Even if you weren't there, I'm sure they'd get the development finished." She shifted in her seat to better see him. "What do you want to do?"

He shrugged. "I have no idea."

They arrived at the winery and Nicholas got out of the car, ending the conversation.

She wanted to talk to him about it, he was clearly upset, but she didn't want to push him. As Mai opened her door she took a deep breath in. The eucalyptus trees bordering the car park had a sharp, fresh scent. Row upon row of grapevines rose up the hill away from the pretty wooden restaurant on stilts. It was a little like a tree house surrounded as it was by the eucalyptus, and underneath the building there were tables and chairs where guests could sit.

Together they walked across the almost empty gravel car park and up the steps into the restaurant where they were shown to a table with a view of the vineyard.

Polished jarrah floorboards and the rows of tables set with glassware, shining silverware and crisp white linen tablecloths gave it an air of respectability, but every so often a statue of a quirky fantasy creature peeked out of various spots of the restaurant – in the rafters, behind a pot plant, on a post. "I love the feel of this place," Mai said. "It's classy but quirky."

Nicholas smiled. "Your place has a similar vibe."

Pleasure swept through her. "Thank you. I wanted it to be a place of good food and friendly people."

"You succeeded."

His praise meant a lot to her and she didn't want to stop and question why. She opened her menu. "The food here is fantastic."

"What would you recommend?"

She glanced at him over the menu. "What do you like?"

He smiled at her. "You."

Such a cheesy line and yet it sent a thrill through her. She was glad they were on the same page. "I was all set to dislike you when I found out who you were, but it turns out I like you too." But he was only here for a few months and she needed to remember that.

His gaze was steady. "I'm glad." He broke the connection by looking at his menu. "I like seafood."

She turned up her nose. "That's not my favourite, but Kit raves about the chilli mussels."

The waiter came over and they ordered their food and wine.

It probably wasn't the right time to continue their conversation from the car — too heavy for a first date. "How long has your family had a house down here?"

"Since I was a kid. We used to come down here a few times a year."

"Did you enjoy getting away from the city?"

"Yeah. My friend Shane and I would go surfing every day." His smile faded.

She touched the wound above her eye. "But you don't surf much now?"

"No. There's never any time."

She hesitated. She didn't want to ruin their date by talking about things which made Nicholas uncomfortable but they kept coming back to it. "Do you work a lot?"

"Too much." He sighed. "Have you ever done something every day and then suddenly asked yourself why?"

She took her time with the answer. "I spent the first part of my childhood watching my parents working constantly. I barely saw them and it was my responsibility, as the oldest child, to help my grandmother with the younger kids. I decided then that I wasn't going to be like that when I grew up. It wasn't until Dad had a breakdown that things changed and we moved down here. " She shrugged. "I work hard, but I love it and I also make time for the things I love to do."

"I've never stopped to ask, never considered anything else." He looked so conflicted, so concerned.

"Aside from surfing, what do you enjoy doing?"

"I honestly don't know." He shook his head. "Sorry, I'm not being a fun date. I had this epiphany this afternoon that I hated my work and I thought I could put it aside but it's hit me for six." He stared out the window at the vineyard. "I don't know anything else but Shadbolt. I wouldn't know what else to do."

She'd felt the same when he'd announced he was knocking down the bakery. "Is there anything you do like about working there?"

"Not really," he finally said, turning back to her, his eyes sad.

Mai squeezed his hand. She wanted to be able to help him. "What was your favourite subject at school?"

"Woodwork."

She sat back in surprise. She couldn't imagine this business man in a workshop, getting dusty and dirty. Though now the thought was in her head ...

"I spent three months working for a construction company while I was at university and I loved every hot, sweaty minute of it."

Mai suppressed the image of him hot and sweaty. "What were you building?"

"Mostly pre-fabricated granny flats."

Maybe she could help him. "Hannah's building a holiday retreat not far from town. Each cabin is pre-fabricated and she's doing the interiors herself. If it still interests you, I'm sure she could do with some help."

He hesitated and then straightened his shoulders. "Could I have her number? I'd love to take a look."

"Sure." She rattled it off for him and he put it in his phone. "So what do you do when you're not working?"

He laughed. "Go out to dinner with you."

"I meant back in Perth."

He sobered. "Nothing. It was all work, all the time. I've been more social here than I've ever been."

"You can always come jogging in the evenings with Fleur

and me."

"You surf, you jog, you bake and you volunteer in fire and emergency rescue. How do you find the time?"

"I make the time. In winter I also ride vintage motocross."

His eyebrows rose. "You're kidding me."

"No." She laughed. "We've got a motocross track not far out of town and the club has quite a few members. Fleur is president."

Their meals arrived and Mai inhaled the spicy scent of her chorizo and mushroom risotto. "Bon appetit."

"To good food and great company." He raised his wine glass and she gently clinked her glass against his.

"Cheers.

It was getting dark when they left the restaurant, the insects chirping noisily as Mai got into Nicholas's car. She wasn't ready for the evening to end. They'd talked for hours about favourite movies, world politics and business tactics. She discovered he shared her love of superhero movies and agreed with many of her own ideals. It was fantastic to have such stimulating conversation from a date.

Nicholas navigated the winding road, shadowy in the dusk, and Mai kept her eye out for kangaroos. As they approached her new cafe, there was a battered dark blue sedan parked in the car park, its headlights on. Mai sat up straight. "Pull in."

Nicholas did as she asked and she unbuckled her seatbelt, her heart pounding. It had to be Gordon, but what was he doing there? She reached for the door handle and Nicholas put a hand on her arm.

"Wait. Shouldn't we call Lincoln?"

"No. It's Gordon – the same guy who almost ran us off the road the other day. I know him. He's harmless." She stalked across the gravel as fast as she could in her heels. Gordon probably didn't know she'd leased the place, but he would soon. And she wouldn't put up with him dealing drugs in her backyard.

She turned the corner of the building. "Gordon, what on earth—" Her words caught in her throat as she took in the scene.

Gordon was on his knees, head bowed, while three guys stood over him. One was the creepy guy she'd seen with him at the park, another a tall blond, and the third was a great hulking man covered in tattoos. The hulking man had a gun pointed directly at Gordon's forehead.

Shit.

All eyes whipped to her as did the gun the man held.

Mai froze, her eyes locked on the hard metal weapon now pointing directly at her.

What the hell did she do now?

"Mai, is everything all right?" Nicholas's voice was over by the car, but his footsteps were coming closer.

"Get rid of him," Creepy Guy snarled.

Her palms were sweaty as she forced herself to turn and wave. "Yes. I won't be a second. Stay there." She stepped forward, out of Nicholas's view and prayed he wouldn't follow her.

Gordon's eyes were wide, his face full of fear.

"You have a nasty habit of turning up where you're not wanted," Creepy Guy said.

She didn't dare say a word.

"You're going to turn around and forget this ever happened," he continued. "You didn't see a thing. If you call the police, we'll kill Gordon and your bakery will burn."

Hot flushes of fear swept over her. They knew who she was.

"You've got some lovely sisters as well – very pretty."

She wanted to be sick. What would he do to her family? She couldn't risk it.

But how could she leave Gordon there by himself? What if they hurt him?

"Mai, go." Gordon's smile was forced. "I'll be fine. We're just having a minor disagreement."

Creepy Guy nodded. "Listen to your friend."

The crunch of footsteps behind her made her decision. She couldn't drag Nicholas into this, couldn't risk him getting hurt. She spun around and hurried away, meeting Nicholas halfway across the car park.

"What was it?"

"It was Gordon." In the dark he couldn't see her fear. "Let's go." She grasped his hand and pulled him towards the car.

Maybe she should call Lincoln. No, she couldn't. He'd threatened her sisters.

She had to protect them.

"What was he doing there?" Nicholas's voice was loud in the car and she jumped.

She needed an excuse. "He didn't realise I'd leased the place, and it's become a meeting place for drug deals."

"That's not good."

"No. He said he'll move elsewhere."

"Are you all right?"

She shook her head. Her skin tightened, but she couldn't tell him the truth. Clearing her throat, she said, "Sorry, it upsets me that Gordon is dealing. I went to school with him and he dated Kit for a while." She paused. "He was made redundant and now he's struggling to find any work."

"It's been tough with the economic downturn," Nicholas agreed. "Maybe I can find him work on the development."

Mai glanced at him. "Really?"

"Well it depends on his skills, but there might be something he can do."

"Thank you." She'd talk to Gordon tomorrow, ask about his qualifications. Her conscience pricked. Maybe she should call the Albany police.

But what if they didn't arrive in time? Would Creepy Guy actually hurt her sisters or burn down her bakery? He'd said he'd kill Gordon if she contacted the police – did that mean he wasn't planning on killing him now?

She had no idea.

They pulled up behind her apartment. Mai didn't want to be alone. "Do you want to come up for coffee?"

"Sure."

They walked upstairs and she turned on the light, its brightness chasing away some of her fear. Immediately there was a meow and Calypso ran over, rubbing himself against both of them.

Nicholas chuckled. "Looks like someone missed you."

She liked his laugh, liked the way he was kind to her cat, she liked him. She wanted to focus on him, wanted to forget everything she'd seen, wanted to delay making a decision. "He's always vocal when he's been alone for too long."

"I can understand that. My apartment seems empty if I'm the only one there."

Did he realise how lonely he sounded? She was surrounded by friends and family, and if she needed some time to herself, her apartment was her refuge.

She stepped closer to him and slid her arms around his neck. "You're here with me now."

His smile was slow and warm. "I am." He bent his head and she rose onto her toes and they kissed, slow and sweet. Heat swam through Mai's body, tracing the slow journey of his hands as they slid down her back. Here was a man who knew how to kiss.

This was what she needed. "Do you want to see my bedroom?"

"I'd love to."

Mai took his hand and showed him the way, shutting the door behind them. He pulled her into his arms, pressing her back against the closed door and kissed her again with more urgency.

Oh, sweet yes.

Mai fumbled with the buttons of his shirt, needing to feel him. His chest was firm with a smattering of hair, and his skin warm. She ran her hands up to his shoulders and pushed his shirt off. They needed to get naked – now.

Nicholas reached for her again, running his hand down her back to her zip and sliding it down. She liked where he was going.

Quickly she shrugged out of her dress and the fabric pooled at her feet, but before she moved, his hands were on her skin, warm but urgent, and he kissed her again.

Yes, please.

It had been a while, and every nerve ending in her body celebrated, zinging in pleasure. She needed more.

Pushing him back, she stepped out of her dress and heels. "Bed," she ordered. She took a condom out of the drawer.

When she turned back Nicholas was in his underwear. For a guy who had a desk job, he was in fine shape. She needed to touch every inch of him. Nicholas picked her up and she shrieked as he lowered them both on to the bed. Then his lips were on her breast and Mai's head fell back.

Sweet bliss. This man was good with his mouth.

And his hands. They roamed her body, found her centre, stripping off her underwear and she bucked at the pleasure coursing through her. She was ready for him.

She reached for the condom which was just out of her grasp. Nicholas looked up and grinned, the desire on his face sending a further shot of lust through her. In a second he was naked and sliding the condom on and then he was inside her.

Oh, yes.

Mai moved with him, loving the way he filled her. She bit his neck and he moaned.

"Mai, you're so damned incredible."

She liked him saying her name, the way it was almost reverential. She felt pretty damned reverential herself.

His thrusting hit a spot in the right place and she groaned. "More."

He complied, rubbing her perfectly and before she could prepare herself she came and he was right there with her.

Mai stretched in satisfaction as Nicholas cleaned himself up. Her whole body was relaxed and she was pretty mellow. Maybe he could stay a while and they could have another round.

Nicholas glanced at the clock she had on her bedside table. "I should go." He picked up his underwear and pants and slid them on.

She blinked in surprise and then frowned. "So soon?"

He nodded as he did up his shirt. "Yeah, I don't want to keep you up."

Well that wasn't an excuse she'd heard before. Mai sat up, crossing her arms as the hurt stung.

He brushed a kiss over her cheek. "I'll call you tomorrow." He grabbed his shoes and was out of the door before Mai could think of something to say. A moment later the apartment door closed.

Wow.

That had to be a world record for the wham, bam and thank

you ma'am exit.

She stared at her bedroom entrance. She'd just had fantastic sex and Nicholas hadn't even let her get her breath back before he'd left.

Did he really care that much about keeping her up? Or was it an excuse? Maybe this was only a quick dalliance to mark a successful deal.

She got up and confirmed the door was locked, that he'd actually left.

He had.

Shaking her head, she climbed into bed, curled into a ball. She'd thought it might be the start of something good. Though he had said he'd call.

Maybe he would.

Chapter 11

Mai groaned as the chime of her alarm stabbed through her consciousness. She'd only just fallen asleep after tossing and turning most of the night, unable to stop thinking about Gordon, the gun, the threat to her sisters and her business, plus Nicholas and his sudden departure.

She flung back her sheets and stood up.

Maybe she should drive by the cafe, make sure Gordon had gone. It was hours since she'd seen him, so he should have left, but it would stop her from imagining his dead body lying on the ground amongst the weeds.

She hesitated. It wouldn't be dangerous if there were no cars out front, and if there were, she'd keep driving and figure out what to do next.

It wouldn't take her more than ten minutes to check.

Decided, she showered, dressed and hurried downstairs, dashing into the kitchen to turn on the ovens to heat before going out to her car.

The streets were quiet and dark, everyone tucked up inside asleep, the only light from the street lamps lining the road. She slowed as she approached the bend the cafe was on and pulled into the empty car park.

He was gone.

Her breath puffed out in relief.

She drove in a circle around the car park to illuminate part of

127

the backyard and there was nothing there, no one there. Gordon was fine. She'd call him later today to make sure.

On the way back to the bakery, her pulse rate slowed and her restless night caught up with her. She would need a lot of caffeine to keep her going today.

Once safely inside, auto-pilot kicked in as she tipped the right quantities of ingredients into her two mixers to make the first batches of dough and then went out into the shop area and switched on the coffee machine. While she waited for it to heat up, she reviewed what pastries remained in the cabinet. A couple would have to be discarded because they were past their awesome date. She wouldn't sell anything that wasn't top quality, but there were a couple of community groups who would take them.

With her list created, she got out the ingredients for the quiches she needed to make and then made her coffee.

The first sip reminded her of Nicholas.

Would he call today?

She'd thought they'd clicked, but if they had, he wouldn't have been in such a rush to leave. Seriously, who finished having sex and then fled the scene? She hadn't expected cuddling or declarations of undying love, but a little bit of talk before he went home would have been nice.

She cracked an egg a little too hard and had to fish out all the little bits of shell. Crap.

The mixer switched off and she dumped the dough on to the table to knead before cleaning the bowl and putting in the next ingredients.

It didn't matter that Nicholas had left.

It showed her he wasn't interested in a relationship. And if sex was all he was after, well she had no complaints. He was excellent at it.

She could do friends with benefits while he was here. They could both be satisfied with that.

Penny walked into the kitchen. "Morning!" She headed straight for the coffee machine.

"Morning." Mai wouldn't dwell on last night any longer. The next time she saw Nicholas, she'd set some guidelines so they were both on the same page.

She might as well have some fun while he was here.

The birds squawking outside Nicholas's window woke him on Sunday morning. Sunlight streamed through the open blinds. He stretched, every muscle in his body feeling amazing.

Last night had been incredible. Mai had met him kiss for kiss and had given as much as she'd taken. But it wasn't just the sex. The conversation had been stimulating as well. He hadn't clicked with anyone in a long time, hadn't confided in anyone the way he had with her. It seemed natural – right.

If only he could have stayed longer, maybe even the night, but it had already been past her usual bedtime. He wouldn't be the kind of guy who put his own desires before hers. She needed her sleep.

He got up and made a coffee, taking it out the front to look at the ocean. It was calm this morning, only a gentle swell, with no waves in sight. Maybe he'd go for a swim later, or Mai had suggested he start jogging to improve his fitness. He could probably manage to jog to the rocks and back.

His phone beeped and he immediately tensed. Was it his father?

He didn't want to know but he would drive himself crazy wondering. Striding back inside, he snatched up his phone.

Traffic accident, calling volunteers to help.

The tension morphed into nerves. His first rescue call. It had to be a serious accident. Would he be able to handle whatever he saw?

He didn't know.

But if Mai answered the call and he wasn't there he'd appear like a complete wimp.

He typed a reply and collected his kit bag. The jog would have to wait.

At the fire station, he walked over to Lawrence. "What have we got?"

"Car ploughed into a karri tree off Smith Road. Ambulance is there but they need the jaws of life to get the driver out."

Nicholas's mouth went dry. "Who else is coming? Mai?"

Lawrence shook his head. "She doesn't do traffic accidents.

She has a thing about blood. Jeremy and Foley are on their way. Suit up."

Of course. He hadn't thought about that. He changed and then helped Lawrence put the trailer on the fast attack. When the others arrived Nicholas got into the vehicle with Jeremy, taking a long slow breath to calm his nerves.

"First accident?" Jeremy asked.

Nicholas nodded.

"Try to distance yourself. Don't look at the people in the vehicle, focus on the task, which will be cutting the car open to get to them out."

It sounded easy but he was sure it wouldn't be.

When they arrived, the police had already cordoned off the road and were redirecting traffic. Ryan let them through and they parked next to the ambulance already on site.

The old dark blue sedan was completely off the road, down an embankment, its bonnet crushed into a huge karri tree that had stopped it from falling down into the gully below. The car was a lot like the one that had been parked at Mai's cafe the night before.

A male paramedic stood at the driver's window talking to the driver.

Jeremy swore. "No skid marks."

He was right. It looked as if the driver hadn't noticed the curve in the road.

They both got out of the vehicle and met Lawrence and Foley on the road. "We need to stabilise the car before we do anything else," Lawrence said. "We don't want it slipping into the gully." He pulled some ropes and chains out of the trailer. "If we can, we'll winch it out. Let me talk to the paramedics."

Lawrence beckoned Nicholas to follow him and they picked their way down the steep embankment. One paramedic, a guy in his forties spoke to the driver in quiet, calming tones, the other, a female, stomped down the low bushes next to the car, clearing some space so they could access the driver more easily.

"They're trying to kill me!" The voice was high pitched and frantic.

"You're safe now," the paramedic said. "The fire department is here to help us get you out."

Nicholas glanced inside the car and winced. Big mistake. The driver's face was covered in blood, his nose at an odd angle and his eyes wide, the pupils dilated. The steering wheel was pressed hard against his chest and his legs must be crushed, but he didn't appear to be in any pain. Maybe the paramedic had given him medication. He was already wearing a neck collar.

The car was too old to have airbags and the whole front bonnet was concertinaed to half its original length. It was a miracle the guy was still alive.

Lawrence and the female paramedic discussed options and agreed to stabilise the car with cables before cutting it open. Back at the fast attack, Jeremy and Foley had already set up the jaws of life. Nicholas helped them loop the cables around the sturdiest parts of the car and tighten them.

"You need to work fast," the woman said. "He's been there for at least a couple of hours and I suspect the circulation's been cut off in his legs. Once the pressure has been released, we're going to need to get him to hospital as soon as possible."

"He must be on some great painkillers," Nicholas said.

The paramedic by the driver glanced at him. "He's high on something. He doesn't feel a thing, but he will when he's moved, and then he might get violent. He's already full of delusion and paranoia. He thinks someone ran him off the road." His disdain was clear.

Right. They were dealing with someone who might attack them for saving his life. Not something Nicholas was used to.

"Nicholas I want you to talk to the guy, tell him we're going to cut him out. You need to convince him we're his friends," Lawrence said. "Jeremy and I will cut the roof off."

Nicholas went with the paramedic to the driver. What the hell was he supposed to say?

"Gordon, this is Nicholas. He's one of the fire-fighters who are going to get you out of here," the paramedic said.

Nicholas gasped. Gordon. This had to be the guy Mai had spoken to last night. The one who had been dealing drugs – and obviously doing them. Recognition sparked as Nicholas looked at him again. He was also the guy who'd protested the development at the council meeting. Nicholas still didn't know why. "Hi, mate."

Gordon squinted at him. "You're one of them."

What? "I'm a fire-fighter, mate." He tried smiling.

Gordon shook his head. "No, they want to hurt you too, you have to be careful."

He was clearly tripping. Nicholas needed to keep him calm. "My colleagues are cutting the roof off. You might hear the crunch of metal, that's them cutting through the roof supports." The jaws of life made surprisingly fast work of the wreck. Lawrence prepped another tool, this one a spreader rather than a cutter. Some of Nicholas's training came back to him. "When the roof's off, we'll try opening the door again and if that doesn't work, they'll use a machine that will pry the door open, all right? We'll take care of you."

Gordon nodded, then gasped. "I can't breathe."

The paramedic shoved Nicholas aside and yelled to his partner near the ambulance.

Shit. Gordon was in real trouble. Nicholas stared, unable to do anything to help.

"Nic, we need this roof off," Lawrence called.

That was something he could do. He got into position at the mid-point of the car and lifted, the metal roof surprisingly light. Shuffling to the side until it cleared the car, they dumped it on the incline out of the way.

"His lung has collapsed." The man tried the door but it didn't budge. The woman seized a large syringe from her kit and inserted it into Gordon's chest. Nicholas grimaced and looked away.

Jeremy took the other tool and pried the door apart.

Gordon's lips were turning blue.

He was dying.

Nicholas's heart thudded hard in his chest as he watched them all work, helpless to do anything. Gordon needed a hospital and he needed it now.

In the distance a woman screamed. Nicholas looked up at the road. Ryan and another police officer were holding back a woman at the edge of the cordoned area.

"Gordon!" she yelled.

Shit. "Should I go and fetch her?" he asked Lawrence.

"No, she'll get in the way, make it harder for us to do our

work. Go tell her he's alive and she needs to be ready to drive to the hospital."

He didn't want to. He didn't want to tell the woman something that might change in an instant.

Bracing himself, he climbed up the embankment and strode towards her hoping he looked authoritative and calm. The woman sobbed and hit Ryan who was doing his best to restrain her.

"Is he alive?" the woman demanded when she noticed Nicholas.

"Yes, but he's been badly injured. He'll be rushed to hospital when we get him out. You need to be ready to follow the ambulance."

She nodded, calming down now she had some news. He exchanged a glance with Ryan who nodded his thanks and then he strode away. He was giving her hope when he wasn't sure there was any.

By the time he returned to the crash they had the door open and Gordon was lifted out and on to the stretcher. His legs were a crushed mess of blood and cuts.

Nicholas's stomach heaved as Gordon screamed once, a cry full of pain before he fell silent. Unconscious.

One of the paramedics took his pulse, then swore and started CPR.

Not unconscious. Dead.

And Nicholas had told the woman he was alive. His chest tightened and he tried to breathe, gasping for air.

He squeezed his hands into fists, praying as they carried the stretcher up the incline and into the ambulance, one paramedic continuing CPR while the other got into the driver's seat.

Lawrence shut the door and the ambulance took off. He let out a deep breath. "He's not going to make it."

Jeremy shook his head. "Those injuries were too severe. They're not going to be able to resuscitate him."

Both men were calm, far too calm for Nicholas whose whole body shook. He'd just witnessed a man dying in front of him, and those injuries … he retched again, his stomach spasming in pain.

Lawrence turned to him. "Sit down, put your head between

your legs." He put a hand on Nicholas's shoulder and helped him to the ground. Nicholas's legs buckled under him and he landed hard on his butt. He couldn't get enough air.

That poor woman.

And Gordon. Mai had said he was a good guy. He was younger than Nicholas. It was too young to die.

"I'd like to say it gets easier, but it doesn't." Jeremy handed him a bottle of water. "We had a two-car crash a couple of weeks ago with more people involved, and it's seriously the worst part of this job."

He appreciated they weren't trying to cheer him up, or making fun of him. This was fucking hard. No one deserved to die like that. It didn't matter if Gordon was high on drugs.

That could have easily been Shane behind the wheel of the car. It could have been him dead. Shane had admitted afterwards that he'd turned to drugs to tune out the stress of work. This guy had turned to them because he'd had no other work.

Life sucked.

"Lawrence, can we start the investigation?" It was Ryan's voice.

"Yeah. We're done here."

There was a hand on his shoulder and Nicholas glanced up.

Ryan gave him a smile. "Do you want to faint or vomit?"

"It's a tough call." Nicholas's stomach heaved again and he closed his eyes.

"There's a psychologist at the hospital who's available for all emergency responders," he said. "Maybe you should go and talk to her."

Nicholas nodded. He might, but right now he wanted to stop feeling so sick. Every time he closed his eyes he saw the mess of Gordon's legs and the blood on his face. He put a hand to his stomach as if he could hold everything inside.

Around him people were talking, but he couldn't get himself to move, to listen to what was going on. On the ground in front of him an ant carried a speck of something white over the leaves, its path defined by something Nicholas couldn't see. It was determined, barely pausing when an obstacle appeared in front of it.

Something warm and thick covered his shoulders. A blanket. "We're about finished here," Jeremy said. "Can you make it back to the truck?"

Nicholas nodded. He needed to get out of here, needed to stop thinking about what might have been.

They drove back to the fire shed and he moved on auto-pilot as he helped Jeremy, Foley and Lawrence stow the gear and replenish stock. Lawrence handed him a card. "This is the psychologist's number. Call any time."

"Thanks." He didn't want to talk to a stranger right now. What he wanted was … to see Mai. The thought of her soothed some of the frenetic thoughts in his head. It wasn't even midday yet, though it felt like he'd been at the crash for hours, and Mai might still be at work. If he stopped by the bakery, he'd at least get to say hello.

"Do you want to go for a drink?" Jeremy asked.

Nicholas shook his head. "No, I'm right, really. I need to go home."

Lawrence slapped him on the back. "You did well today."

Nicholas picked up his kit bag and drove to the bakery, where he parked at the back next to Mai's car. Then he walked around to the entrance. One of the customers gave him a second look and he realised he was still wearing his fire-fighting gear.

He waited until everyone had been served before he asked the woman behind the counter, "Is Mai here?"

"No, sorry. She's just finished work."

"Thanks."

He returned to his car and looked up at her window. It was empty. Would she be asleep already? He stood there for a long moment. He desperately needed to see her breathing, feel her heart beating, even though his rational brain knew she was. Perhaps if he was quick she would still be awake. He rang the doorbell and heard her coming down the stairs, her steps loud and fast.

The door opened and Mai was there, wearing satin boxer shorts and a fitted tank top. She had never looked more beautiful, more alive. "Mai." Relief swept through him, blowing away some of his fears.

She frowned at him for a second. "What are you doing here?"

He took a step back. "I'm sorry, I woke you." Now that he'd seen her the tightness gripping his heart relaxed. "I needed to see you were all right. I'll let you go back to bed." He turned to go and she reached out and gripped his arm.

"You went on the call-out." Her eyes were full of concern.

He nodded.

"It was bad?"

He nodded again. There was no way he could verbalise it yet.

"Come in then." She took his hand and led him inside.

Relief flooded him as he followed her upstairs.

He could be with her for a little longer.

Chapter 12

Nicholas stood next to the bench, his shoulders slumped, staring into space, unblinking. He was somewhere else. Mai couldn't turn him away, couldn't ignore his pain. She put the kettle on and then turned to him.

She couldn't be angry at him for last night, not when he looked so lost, so confused. She pulled off his thick jacket, dumping it on the kitchen table and he barely moved. "Take a seat." She gently led him over to the couch and pushed him down. He obeyed without a word. She'd never been to a traffic accident, but she'd heard some of the guys talking about it and knew they were often nightmarish.

Quickly she made the tea, handing him his cup before curling up next to him on the couch. "Want to talk about it?"

He blinked as if coming back to himself. He cleared his throat. "A car hit a tree. The driver was stuck and we had to use the jaws of life to get him out."

"How badly injured was he?"

Nicholas shook his head. "He didn't seem too bad at first. He was talking and he had blood all over his face, but ..."

She was quiet, letting him find the words he needed.

"Then his lung collapsed and he had trouble breathing. One of the paramedics drained his chest and we finally got the damned door open." He put the mug on the coffee table and pulled her into his arms, holding her tightly. Mai wrapped her arms around him, trying to take away some of his pain.

"His legs were crushed. The paramedic thought the drugs in his system were keeping the pain at bay. When we moved him though he screamed … then he stopped breathing." He took a breath himself. "The paramedic was giving him CPR as the ambulance drove away."

She prayed it wasn't someone she knew, but now wasn't the time to ask. "I'm sorry you had to witness that."

"Somebody had to help him."

"You're a braver person than I am," Mai said. He was cold to touch and staring straight ahead, probably reliving the event. She needed to help him, needed to get through to him, needed to get him out of the clothes that would remind him of what had happened. "Come with me." She tugged him to his feet and took him through to her ensuite bathroom, turned on the shower.

As the water heated, she unlaced his boots and helped him out of his clothes. Without needing prompting, he stepped into the shower. She waited to make sure he didn't collapse, then gathered up his clothes and took them into her bedroom so they wouldn't get wet when he got out. When she went back into the room, he sighed and opened his eyes. Then he frowned. "I'm sorry, Mai. I shouldn't be here, you need to sleep."

Maybe he really *had* been concerned about her getting enough sleep last night. She put a hand on his chest to stop him getting out. "It doesn't matter. You need me."

He looked at her for a long moment, his eyes intense before he nodded. "Yeah, I do."

His confession warmed her. When he was done, she handed him a towel and went into her bedroom so he had room to dry himself. Calypso wandered over, so she picked him up and gave him a cuddle, needing a little comfort of her own. Being here for Nicholas like this was more intimate than sex. Could she really do friends with benefits? She wasn't sure. Not anymore. Not when her heart ached to see him in so much pain.

Nicholas came out with the towel wrapped around his waist. His eyes were still sad, but more alert than they had been.

"You need some rest." Mai put Calypso on the ground and pulled the covers off her bed.

He glanced at the bed and then back at her. "I've disturbed you enough. First last night and now this."

She wouldn't put the sex into the category of a disturbance. "Do you hear me complaining?"

He shook his head. "It's not right, it's selfish of me. You don't get much sleep."

"You really are worried about my sleeping habits." She laughed, shaking her head. "And here I thought you'd got what you wanted and couldn't get away fast enough."

His eyes widened and he took a step forward. "No. Of course not. Last night was … incredible."

Pleasure flowed through her. Maybe she hadn't misread their connection. She climbed on to the bed and patted the spot next to her. "How about we both lie down and get some rest?"

He hesitated, glancing down at his towel. Was he shy?

She slipped her tank top off and slid out of her shorts and then held out her hand.

With a small smile, he dropped the towel and lay on the bed next to her, his body tense. She curled up against him, wrapping an arm around his waist and spooning him. "Close your eyes, Nic. I'm here."

His sigh was loud and deep, and his whole body relaxed.

He was warm, male and naked. It was arousing as well as comforting and she shut her eyes. They would both feel better when they woke.

The gentle charm of Mai's alarm brought her to consciousness, but it was the warm, male body spooning her that really woke her up. It took her a second to remember what had happened and she shut off the alarm before turning to him. He watched her and her belly tightened. "How are you feeling?"

"Better."

He looked better as well. The haunted look in his eyes had been replaced by a hunger and her body responded. "I'm glad."

"Thank you." He leaned forward to kiss her and then jerked back. "Is there such a thing as afternoon breath?" He put a hand over his mouth and breathed into it.

Mai chuckled. "How about we find out?" She kissed him and

he tasted like Nicholas.

He pulled her closer. "I'm sorry for the way I left last night. I was mindful you had to be up again in about five hours and I wanted you to get some sleep."

She pushed a stray lock of hair off his face. She believed him now.

He ran a hand down her side and her body woke all the way up. "Do you need more sleep?"

Hell no. "I've had enough."

"Then let me make last night up to you." As they kissed, his hands made a slow exploration of her body, running along her skin, brushing past her breasts and skimming over her groin.

She wanted more. "Touch me."

He smiled. "I am."

What was he playing at? "Touch me harder."

"In a minute. You're so beautiful."

It wasn't true, but she'd take the compliment all the same. His hands caressed her breasts and she moaned. It was torturous pleasure and she arched into his touch, needing to feel him. She wasn't normally this sensitive, but then again, her previous lovers hadn't taken their time.

"That's cheating," Nicholas said. He kissed her slowly and then dipped lower to suck her breast.

Need and want filled her as his tongue tasted her and her nipples puckered in response. "Yes."

"Do you like that?"

Did he really need to ask? She nodded.

He turned his attention to her other breast and Mai's eyes closed as pleasure filled her. He began a slow, steady descent as his kisses trailed over her stomach and down between her legs. That's where she wanted him.

Right there.

He licked her and she moaned. Thank goodness she hadn't sent him packing – he was definitely good at this.

His thumb rubbed her gently and she needed more. She lifted her butt and pushed off her underwear and then thank you God, his tongue was on her. She gripped the covers, trying not to move, wanting him exactly where he was, tasting her.

He slid a finger into her and she widened her legs to give

him better access and oh my, she would come if he didn't stop. "Nic, stop."

He glanced up at her. "How many times have you come in a day?"

What was he talking about? Orgasms? Now? He waited for an answer. "Um, a couple."

"Let's see if we can break that record today."

Before she registered his words, his mouth was back on her and she tumbled over the edge and was gone.

Mai's eyes were closed, her head thrown back and body trembling as she came. Her groan sent a surge of satisfaction through Nicholas. He'd made her feel this way. He'd pleasured her.

It was one way he could make last night up to her. Looking back on it, he saw how she'd got the wrong impression. He'd been so intent on letting her sleep that he'd come across as an arsehole. He was an idiot.

He cared about her and wanted to show her how much she meant to him.

Just what *did* she mean to him?

There'd been no one else he'd considered going to after the call-out. No one he wanted to call. Only Mai.

And that was strange. They barely knew each other. How had she become someone he could turn to?

He'd never had that before. Someone to really talk to, someone who would hold him when he needed comfort, take care of him when he couldn't think.

He'd never known he needed it.

But now that he did, he wanted more. He didn't care about the development or that he shouldn't mix business with pleasure. He cared about showing Mai he wasn't just after sex.

When she opened her eyes, he slid up the bed to kiss her. Her little moan of appreciation sent a shot of lust right down to his groin. He wanted her.

"Feeling all right?" he asked, brushing her hair out of her face, loving the way it spread out beneath her like a curtain.

"I'm feeling great." Her hands slid down and ran over his

hard erection. "And so are you." She grinned.

He jerked at her touch. He was ready for her, but he wanted to tease her some more, wanted her to come again when he did. He captured her hands and placed them above her head. "I bet I can make you feel even better."

She smirked. "I'll take that bet."

He lowered his head until his lips hovered just above hers. "Game on."

After Nicholas had won his bet, he pulled Mai into the bathroom and they showered together though it was a tight squeeze in her tiny cubicle. He'd have to have her over to his place where the shower was the size of her whole bathroom. He washed her hair, unable to stop himself from touching her. He felt so much lighter with her, as if the rest of the world didn't matter.

The crash almost seemed unreal, like a nightmare.

Except for one family it wouldn't be.

He didn't want to think about that now – couldn't face the reality yet. Instead he slid his hands over Mai's butt and drew her closer to him.

She chuckled. "You're insatiable."

"For you, maybe." He kissed her. His stomach rumbled. "Do you want to go out and get some lunch?"

She nodded. "That sounds nice."

He turned off the shower and took the towel Mai handed him, drying himself quickly. Mai had already slipped on her underwear and Nicholas stared at his fire gear on the floor of her bedroom. There was no way he was putting that on again. "Could you do me a favour?"

"Sure." She noticed his clothes and grinned. "Have you got a change in the car?"

"Yeah. I'm not sure where I left the keys." He wrapped the towel around his waist and followed her out into the living area where his keys were on the table.

"I'll be right back," she said. The keys jingled as she left.

Nicholas picked up Calypso and stroked him. Maybe they could get some take-away so they could come back and keep Calypso company. He didn't want the cat to get lonely.

Hearing Mai's voice on the way up the stairs, he turned towards the door as her words carried to him. "I won't be a second!"

Was she talking to him?

"I'll meet you in the bakery, Kim."

Mai had company.

And he stood in nothing but a towel. He backed away from the door towards Mai's bedroom but he was too late. Mai came into the apartment carrying his bag and a moment later an Asian man about Mai's age followed her in.

"What the ..." The man's eyebrows almost disappeared into his hairline.

Mai spun around and groaned. "Kim, I told you to wait downstairs."

Was he Mai's brother? This was awkward. Nicholas nodded a greeting as Mai gave him the bag and pushed him into the bedroom. "Get dressed. I'll deal with him."

Nicholas closed the door and quickly changed as Kim asked, "Who was that?"

"That's Nicholas. I'll introduce you when he comes out."

"This is the guy you've been seeing, right? Didn't you just meet?"

Nicholas wanted to hear Mai's response, but he also didn't want her to deal with the situation on her own. He checked his appearance and then opened the door, smiling a little sheepishly at the man, hoping to get him on his side. "Hi, I'm Nicholas." He held out a hand and after a moment's hesitation the man shook it.

"This is my brother, Kim," Mai said.

"Nice to meet you."

Kim frowned. "Yeah."

"Kim dropped by for a visit." She turned to her brother. "We were heading out to lunch."

"It's three o'clock."

"Late lunch," Nicholas amended. "Maybe afternoon tea."

Kim shook his head, but his lips turned up at the edges. "You should invite him to the family dinner tomorrow night, Mai. I'm sure Mum and Dad would love to meet him."

The idea of meeting more of Mai's family appealed to him,

though hopefully under better circumstances than this. "I've met Bian," he said. "She's leasing one of my units."

At that news Kim's eyes almost boggled out of his head. "You're the property developer."

Nicholas nodded.

Kim's eyes flicked between him and Mai. He shook his head. "All right then."

Mai took her brother by the arm and led him to the door. "I'll see you tomorrow." She pushed him through the door and shut it. Then she sighed and turned to Nicholas. "Sorry about that. I told him to stay downstairs."

"Hey if my sister got a bag out of a strange car, I'd follow her to check out the situation too."

Mai chuckled. "I hope it didn't make you uncomfortable."

"Nothing I can't handle." Was she going to invite him to the family dinner?

"Shall we go and get something to eat?"

The disappointment was swift, which was ridiculous. They'd only been on one date. "Sure." He followed her out of the apartment.

There wasn't a cloud in the sky and the sun caressed his skin. It was too nice to be indoors. He took Mai's hand and they walked down the street together. "Shall we get something to go and eat by the river?"

"Yeah. The cafe on the corner has some nice sandwiches."

Mai took him between a couple of buildings, avoiding the crowds on the footpath. She waved to people they passed, but didn't stop to chat. Quite a few looked at them with speculation. He wasn't used to that level of scrutiny, but he liked staking his claim. Mai was with him now.

"Is there a reason we're avoiding people?" he asked.

"Everyone will be talking about the crash, and you don't need that yet."

No, he didn't.

"Mai!" The shout had them both turning around.

Fleur jogged towards them.

Mai dropped his hand and gave her a hug. "How are you?"

"Great," she said. "What are you two up to?" She didn't appear surprised to see them together.

"We're getting lunch," Nicholas answered.

Fleur grinned. "Had a longer siesta than normal, did we?" She winked.

"Sure did."

Mai took his hand again and he felt warm all over

"All right, I'll leave you be, but I wanted to ask if Friday night is a good time for a girls' night."

Mai frowned. "I'm not sure. The next couple of weeks are going to be full on setting up the new bakery so I'm not sure if I can handle the lack of sleep."

"What's this?"

Mai ran a hand over her hair. "I'm leasing the Mortimer Road place. We've got to paint and that kind of thing."

"Why don't we do a busy bee then?" Fleur said. "I'll check if the girls can get Saturday free. You know you suck at painting."

Mai didn't seem offended by the comment.

"That would be great."

"All right then. I'll rope Jamie and the guys in too. See you later." She walked away.

"You have nice friends." Blackbridge was a real community.

Mai nodded. "They're the best." She let out a breath. "If everyone turns up, we could have the cafe finished on the weekend."

"I'll help too."

She beamed at him and kissed his cheek. "Thanks. Now let's get some food, I'm starving."

They bought a couple of gourmet sandwiches from the cafe and wandered down to the river. The foreshore was relatively empty with only a single family making use of the barbecue facilities.

"So what do you need to do on the weekend?" Nicholas asked.

"The big thing is prepping the walls and painting." She grimaced. "Not my favourite thing to do. I also need to put up shelving in the store room and cafe, and I need to buy some more tables and chairs." She sipped her drink. "Outside the grounds need tidying and I want to put a ramp up to the front door, but I might need to get a builder to do that."

"I can do it."

Her eyebrows raised in surprise.

"It's one of the things I can do," he reminded her.

She grinned. "That would be great. You can come to the cafe during the week and tell me what tools and supplies you need."

"Sure." Excitement built in him. The idea of building something again appealed. It had been so long since he'd worked with his hands.

When they finished eating, Mai asked, "Do you want to go kayaking?"

"Yeah, why not?" They threw their rubbish in the bin and went to chat to the guy hiring kayaks, who Mai knew of course.

"Half an hour or an hour?" the guy asked.

"An hour," Mai answered, shooting a look over her shoulder at Nicholas. "Are you up for that?"

He nodded though he wasn't convinced. He hoped Mai knew what she was doing.

Mai got in the back of the kayak, so he took the front and they started up river. "It's really nice this way," Mai said. "You get to see some of the town and then paddle into the countryside."

Nicholas paddled slowly, getting used to the rhythm. The trees lining the bank were a mixture of paper barks, with their white, flaky bark, and gums. The scent was fresh and rich, and as they paddled, a family of black swans kept pace with them for a short while before losing interest.

They crossed under the main traffic bridge and the further away they went, the quieter it became. In the distance a lawn mower hummed, the cicadas whirred and a child shrieked in play, but here there was only the quiet splash of their oars.

They had nowhere to be, nothing to do, for the next hour it was just him, Mai, the kayak and the river. Exactly what he needed. "This was a good idea."

"I'm glad you think so."

He twisted to look at her and the kayak rocked alarmingly. He clutched the sides and waited for the rocking to subside.

Mai laughed. "Careful. I don't want to go for a swim."

He grinned, loving the sound of her laugh. "It might be a little fresh," he agreed. The river was shaded and the gentle breeze cooled the day a little more.

"There's a place a kilometre or so upriver that's nice," she said. "We can stop and rest." She winked at him.

He grinned and paddled harder.

Chapter 13

Mai followed the river up its twists and turns. It was such a beautiful day and Nicholas relaxed further as they paddled out of town. She was pleased she could help him, pleased his eyes had lost some of the haunted look he'd had when he'd arrived. It would take him some time to come to terms with what he'd seen at the accident, to decide whether he wanted to continue to respond to those kinds of emergencies.

"Does the river go through Kit's property?" Nicholas asked.

"Yeah, it's one of the borders." He had a good sense of direction. "On the weekends, when we were teenagers, we'd occasionally take Fleur's dad's dinghy and motor all the way up the river to visit her."

"That sounds fun."

She smiled. "It was. We'd pretend we were adventurers off to discover new lands. Fleur was always the captain."

"Didn't your parents worry?"

"Kit would bring a two-way radio down and let her parents know we'd arrived safely and they'd call our parents."

"How did she get down to the river?"

"Motorbike. We all learnt to ride at Kit's farm." Those were some of her favourite memories, the days when it was just the four of them or five if Jamie came over. They would swim or ride or talk about life and what they wanted out of it. It was there that she'd first confided to her friends that she wanted to leave school and become a baker. Hannah would talk about the retreat she wanted to build, Fleur would worry about telling her father she wanted to become a nurse, and Kit was adamant that all she wanted to do was inherit the dairy farm and be a farmer.

"We did the first official musketeers ceremony by the river at Kit's place," Mai said. The memory was sweet.

"What's with that nickname?"

"Kit, Hannah and Fleur were inseparable from the time Hannah moved here when she was eight," she said. "At school it was always the three of them, and whenever they were in town, they were together. They started getting called the three musketeers."

"Then you moved to town."

She nodded though he couldn't see her. "And we became the musketeers."

"It must have been rough coming in when they were already so tight."

"It actually wasn't." She smiled. "Kit and I clicked straight away. We bonded over having younger siblings to look after and that was that – I was part of the gang."

"What about Jamie?"

"He's an honorary member," she said. "He didn't hang around us at school and had his own friends, but whenever we visited Kit he was there. They lived next door to each other, the only kids in miles."

"There's Lincoln too, isn't there – he's Jamie's brother?"

"Yeah, but he's six years older – way too old in those days to pay any attention to us." Mai chuckled. "We did give him the title of being our knight protector though. We had a ceremony and everything, and good sport that he is, he went along with it, vowing to protect us for as long as he lived."

"That's nice."

"It was. Occasionally he still uses the title to boss us around, but he really is born to protect." She glanced at the shore to get her bearings. "The clearing is around this bend." Her back muscles were protesting slightly at the unfamiliar motion.

The bank sloped into a sandy beach only a few metres wide and she directed the kayak on to it. The grass that came down to the beach was longer than she'd anticipated, though it had been flattened in places. "Keep an eye out for snakes," she told Nicholas as she followed him out of the kayak.

Nicholas paused mid-stretch and examined the grass behind him. "What do you get here?"

"Just tiger snakes and dugites." She stamped her feet and there was no rustling in response. They were probably fine. She walked around the area, treading down the grass and when she'd made a space big enough for the two of them she lay down, propping herself up on her elbows.

Nicholas frowned.

She patted the ground next to her. "It's fine. All my stomping would have scared away anything nearby."

As he sat Mai heard the thud of hooves. She sat up and spotted the rider cantering along the trail that ran parallel to the river on the other side. Recognising Trent's girlfriend, she waved. The girl waved back and continued on.

"How far does the trail go?"

"A fair way. It's shared by horse riders, motorbikes and cyclists, so there are often disputes about going too fast." She lay down again and this time Nicholas joined her, turning on his side to look at her.

The intensity in his eyes stirred her. She had never felt this level of passion or intimacy with a man. "You know we're all alone out here."

His lips quirked upwards. "You mean aside from the occasional trail user across the river?"

"We'd hear them coming." She raised herself up on to her elbow and brought his head close to hers. Their lips met in a soft, sweet kiss. She felt it all the way through her body. This was right, so very right.

He deepened the kiss, pressing her back so she was lying down and he was on top of her, his body warm.

She hummed in approval when his hand slid up her top to her breast. He had such clever hands. She cupped his butt and brought him closer to her, his hardness pressing into her. She caressed him and he broke the kiss breathing heavily.

"Mai, we should head back to your place."

She grinned and took the condom out of her pocket.

His glanced at the opposite side of the river.

She didn't want him to be uncomfortable. "Come on." She got to her feet. "We've got a record to beat." She winked and pulled him up and then walked further along the shore up river where the paper barks met the water. There was another spot where they could have a bit more privacy. She pushed a bush aside and a sharp ammonia smell hit her, making her eyes water. "Wait." Her arm shot out to stop him.

The ground in front of them was covered in a blue liquid coming from a whole lot of white plastic containers of kitchen cleaner scattered on the ground. How could anyone use that much all at once? The grass around it was already dying. Someone didn't care about contaminating the ground or river. Selfish bastards.

"This reminds me of the containers in the shed at Foley's place," Nicholas said.

He was right. Worry replaced the anger and she took her phone out of her pocket and dialled. "Lincoln, I hate to bother you on your day off, but I thought you'd want to know."

"What's wrong, Mayday?"

"You know those barrels at Foley's?" she asked.

"Yes." His voice was suddenly more alert.

"Nicholas and I have found a pile of similar chemicals by the river. They're mostly empty but a couple are leaking on the ground so we need to notify Parks and Wildlife too."

"Where exactly are you?"

"We took the kayaks upstream to Lovers' Landing."

Nicholas's eyebrows raised and Lincoln chuckled. "I'm not going to ask what you were doing."

"Best not to," she agreed.

He sighed. "All right. It's going to take me some time to get out there. I'll have to call Albany and wait for the detectives. Can you see any car tracks?"

"No." Maybe they came via the river.

"Send me some photos so I can forward them to Albany. Can you wait out there until I arrive?"

"Sure, as long as you let Ted know we're going to be late back with the kayak."

"Deal."

She hung up and took a few photos, careful not to disturb

anything further.

"What did he say?"

Mai repeated the conversation as she sent the photos and she gestured him back towards the landing. "We'll wait on the shore."

Nicholas smiled. "Lovers' Landing? Were you planning to seduce me this whole time, Miss On?"

Her cheeks flushed. "Well I do believe you said you wanted to break a record today."

He grinned at her. "I do indeed."

But there would be none of that while they waited for Lincoln.

"Do you think this is drug related?" Nicholas asked, nodding towards the barrels.

"Maybe, but whoever dumped them can't be local. Everyone knows this spot is popular. Those drums were bound to be spotted sooner rather than later."

"Yeah, or someone was desperate to hide them quickly."

He had a point. Could it have been Gordon? She still hadn't called him. "Shoot."

"What's wrong?"

She couldn't tell him the whole truth. "I just remembered I need to call Gordon about last night."

Nicholas's face went white. "Shit. I didn't tell you."

She grabbed his arm. "Tell me what?"

"The accident this morning." His voice hitched. "Same blue sedan as outside your cafe, driver was called Gordon."

Mai's legs buckled and Nicholas hauled her against his chest.

The drug dealers, the guns.

What had she done?

What had she allowed to happen? She shook her head. Get the facts first. "My age, bald, kind of shifty looking?"

He nodded.

She closed her eyes. It had to be him. She should have called Lincoln last night. If she'd called him, he would have arrested Gordon, and Gordon would still be alive. "What caused the accident?"

"Jeremy thought he'd missed the curve in the road. He was high as a kite, delusional as well, saying someone was trying to kill him."

She'd left him in that situation, left him at the mercy of men with guns. But it didn't quite make sense. Creepy Guy could have shot Gordon, but he'd let him go, let him drive home high.

He hadn't been high when she'd seen him. And he'd said he wasn't a user – but he could have been lying. She needed to ask Lincoln for more details, had to know if the crash was an accident.

"Mai, are you all right?"

She nodded, stepping away from him, straightening up. "I'll call the hospital when we get home."

What if Creepy Guy had given Gordon the drugs, or run him off the road? Gordon must have done something to irritate him. And if Creepy Guy was behind it, was she putting herself in danger by calling Lincoln?

She didn't know what to do.

Nicholas's arms came around her in a hug. "They might have been able to save him."

Mai could tell he didn't think so, but she could pretend as well. "I hope so." She tilted her head so she could see him. His eyes had the haunted look again. "How are you feeling about the crash?"

"I won't forget it in a hurry," he said. "But I'm all right."

"I'm glad." She looked at him, really paid attention to his face. He was a lot kinder than she'd given him credit for, a lot more fragile than she'd expected him to be. She enjoyed being with him, being someone he turned to. In a short space of time she'd come to care for him. "Do you want to come to my parents' for dinner tomorrow night?"

His eyes widened and she hurriedly added, "No pressure or anything. You might enjoy a home-cooked meal."

"I'd love to. What time?"

"Six. I'll pick you up just before."

"I'll be ready."

They settled into a comfortable silence. Another family of swans, or perhaps the same ones, swam past and there was the occasional splash as a fish jumped. Little wrens flitted amongst the trees, calling to each other and some kind of insect chirped. She lay back using one hand as a pillow as she stared up at the tree branches above her. It didn't seem right to enjoy this peace, when Gordon could be dead, when her decision had directly affected whether someone lived or died.

Nicholas lay next to her and took her hand. "Thank you for suggesting this. It's what I needed."

She forced a smile. "Me too."

They lay like that until the hum of a motor downstream reached them. They both sat up and a few minutes later a large dinghy came into view with Lincoln at the helm. It was quite crowded with three others in the boat: a darker skinned man who looked like he had Middle Eastern heritage and a blonde female, both in plain clothes and whom she assumed were detectives, and Will, the Aboriginal park ranger who worked for the Parks and Wildlife Service and came into her bakery daily.

She got to her feet, brushing the dirt off her shorts. Lincoln threw her a rope and she steadied the boat as they all disembarked.

"Can you show us what you found?" Lincoln asked. "Use the same path as you did last time."

Mai wanted to ask him about Gordon's condition, but instead she nodded and took them through the grass to the containers.

"Thanks, Mai. We'll take it from here."

"We'll need a statement from them both," the female detective said.

"Do you want it now, or shall we come into the station tomorrow?" Mai asked.

"Sergeant Zanetti can take it now."

Lincoln stood behind the woman and rolled his eyes.

She hid her grin. "All right."

Together they walked back to where Nicholas waited and Lincoln got out his notebook. "Tell me all your dirty secrets."

Nicholas chuckled. "The only dirt is on the back of Mai's shorts."

"And yours," Mai pointed out.

She couldn't mention Gordon now, not with Nicholas here. She didn't want him involved. She focused instead on what Lincoln asked, giving as much detail as she could, though there wasn't a lot to say.

"Thanks, guys. You can go now, but don't leave town." Lincoln winked.

"I hope it doesn't take too long."

Lincoln sighed. "Me too."

"Any news on the crash victim this morning?" Nicholas asked, shuffling his feet. "Did he make it?"

Lincoln's face fell. "No. They couldn't revive him."

Mai gasped and stumbled back. It was her fault he was dead.

Lincoln caught her. "Shit, Mai, I didn't think. Did you know him?"

She nodded. "He dated Kit in high school."

"I'm sorry."

She had to tell him everything. Had to explain why she hadn't called him last night. How would she ever face Gordon's wife again? "Slinky, I saw Gordon last night. He wasn't high."

"It doesn't take long to get high, Mai."

Frustration skirted her skin. "I know that—"

"Sergeant!" The call came from the male detective standing under the trees. "We could do with another set of hands."

Lincoln glanced over his shoulder and waved, swearing under his breath. "I've got to help." He turned to Nicholas. "Can you take care of Mai?"

Nicholas nodded.

She bristled. "I don't need to be taken care of. I need you to listen to me."

"Sergeant!"

Lincoln sighed. "I'm sorry, I have to go. Call me later." Before she could protest, he was gone.

Damn it.

"What's wrong?" Nicholas asked.

She couldn't tell him, couldn't risk him getting involved. She sighed. "Nothing. Let's go home."

Mai didn't get the chance to call Lincoln until Monday afternoon. She'd convinced herself she needed to be alert, needed to write down what she'd seen to make sure she'd got the details right, so she'd waited until after her siesta.

Her call went straight to voice mail, and she left a message, asking him to call her.

Maybe she should call the station, but she wasn't comfortable talking to the others. It had to be Lincoln.

Not wanting to be left with her guilt, she collected the keys to the Mortimer Road cafe from the real estate agent. She needed to write a list of the work to be done, had to make sure she had all the supplies for the busy bee on Saturday.

As she drove into the car park, her skin tightened. This was the scene of the crime, the place where she'd put her own welfare above someone else's, the place where she could have made a difference, and hadn't.

She walked around the back to where Gordon had been on the ground. There was nothing there to show for it. No drop of blood, no scrap of clothing, not even the weeds were crushed.

Only her guilt

Not wanting to be out in the open, she hurried back to the front door. The faster she wrote her list, the sooner she could leave.

By the time she finished she had filled two pages. She could drive into Albany to get the supplies now. She didn't want to go on her own though. Nicholas would be working, but maybe Jamie was free. She dialled his number as she locked up.

"Please tell me you want me to do something," Jamie said as he answered.

His plaintive tone made her smile. "Don't tell me you're getting tired of sitting around doing nothing."

Jamie laughed. "As if Mum would let me," he said. "I've been working at the cheese factory and I'm sick of the smell of milk."

"I'm doing a supplies run to Albany. Want to come?"

"Yes, a hundred times yes," he said. "Do you need me to pinch the ute?"

"That would be great. I'll be out in twenty." She hung up and then headed out to the Zanetti farm.

Jamie was lounging on the old sofa out on the wrap-around verandah when she pulled up. He was on his feet and at the gate before she got out of her car. "In a hurry much?"

"Yeah. Let's go." He seemed agitated, his palms rubbing

against his jeans and shuffling from foot to foot so she quickly got into the old Zanetti ute.

When they were on their way, she asked, "What's wrong?"

"I'm feeling a little stir-crazy."

It was more than that. Her own concerns forgotten, she took a good look at him. His fingers tapped the steering wheel and he bit his bottom lip, his eyes glistening. "What happened, Jamie?"

He shook his head, not looking at her.

Something was definitely wrong. Concern fluttered over her skin. "Pull over." When he kept driving, she put a hand on his arm and said more sternly, "Pull over."

He pulled off the road and lowered his head to the steering wheel. He started shaking.

Mai's heart leapt into her throat and she undid her seatbelt, sliding across the bench seat to put her arm around him. "Tell Mayday what's wrong."

The noise that came out of him was half laugh, half sob.

She'd never seen him so upset. She held on to him until the shaking subsided and he took a deep shuddery breath. He lifted his head and wiped the tears away. "Sorry about that."

Mai shook her head. "Are you going to tell me what it was about?"

"Everything kind of hit me at once."

She waited, knowing he would explain in his own time.

"My teaching contract wasn't renewed at the end of the year," he began. "I've been applying for jobs, but so far no luck. I might be unemployed when school goes back in a couple of weeks."

That was ridiculous! Jamie loved teaching, and was so damned good at it. "I'm sorry."

"That was the first hit," he said. "Then Sandra wasn't happy about me coming back to Blackbridge for the holidays."

Mai had never met Jamie's girlfriend, but she didn't like what she'd heard about her. She was demanding and high maintenance, and anytime Mai had called Jamie while she'd been over, the conversations had been cut short. Sandra didn't like Jamie having female friends.

"Surely she knows how much you love coming home, and how you help your parents out while you're here."

He shook his head. "She doesn't understand. She called me just after you did today and announced she was coming down to visit for the weekend." He sighed. "She hasn't accepted any of my invitations and now she decides to come on the one weekend when we're working on your cafe."

She didn't want to cause him any trouble. "That doesn't matter, Jamie. You don't have to come. I'm sure there will be plenty of people there."

"No, Mai, I want to help." He turned to her. "I told her I had plans, that I was helping you and she got angry, accused me of cheating on her and dumped me."

Mai gaped at him. "Who are you supposed to be cheating with?"

He raised his eyebrows at her.

"Me?" Mai laughed and held out her hand. "Give me your phone and I'll call her back. Tell her she's mistaken."

"The thing is, Mai, I'm not upset. I'm relieved."

"Huh?" She frowned, examining him to make sure he wasn't losing it.

"I stayed in Perth because of her. I liked being in a relationship and she was really good in bed, but I've missed you and the other musketeers."

"We're not quite the same as your girlfriend."

"No, you're better." He sighed. "I miss my family and I'm always jealous when you tell me what you've been up to."

"So what are you saying?"

"I've got no job, I've got no girl, and there's nothing stopping me from coming home."

Mai squealed and hugged him hard. "That's fantastic! Wait until the others find out. Kit's probably got a contact at the School of Agriculture. You might be able to get a job there. And there's not a lot of cheap accommodation around town, but you could probably bunk in with me at Fleur's."

Jamie chuckled and held up a hand. "Slow down, Mayday. I'll sort out my own accommodation thanks very much, but I hadn't thought about the ag school. I'll give them a call when I get home." He started the car. "Thanks, Mai. I feel better. Now, let's get your supplies."

"Absolutely." She smiled. She'd needed some good news.

And Jamie moving back to Blackbridge was the best news she'd heard all day.

159

Chapter 14

Nicholas paced the living room while he waited for Mai to arrive. He should have picked her up, then he wouldn't have to wait here considering all the things that could possibly go wrong.

When was the last time he'd met a girlfriend's parents?

When was the last time he'd had a girlfriend?

Maybe at university, which was far too many years ago to count.

At least he'd already met Bian and Leanne. They'd both been friendly, but he'd made a crappy first impression on Mai's brother. Would he have told the others? Nicholas cringed. He hoped not.

Surely they wouldn't say anything about him being naked in Mai's apartment. It was none of their business.

But there was no denying he wanted to make a good impression. Mai's family were important to her. He wanted them to like him.

He let out a sigh of relief when Mai pulled up, picking up his keys and leaving the house before she knocked. She greeted him on the front path with a kiss.

"Hi."

"How was your day?" he asked.

Her smile was big and bright. "Really great."

Something had happened to make her so happy. She

positively radiated it, and his nerves evaporated. "What did you do?" He got into the car, moving Calypso on to his lap.

"Jamie and I went into Albany to get the things we need for Saturday."

She hadn't asked him to go with her – not that he expected her to invite him everywhere – but it would have been nice.

"And Jamie mentioned he's moving back to Blackbridge." She smiled. "Isn't that great?"

He pushed back the jealousy. Jamie had said he wasn't interested in Mai. Still, they had a bond he envied. "Yeah. How long has he been in Perth?"

"Basically since he went to uni – about eight years."

"Has he got a job down here?"

"Not yet, but if necessary I can give him a few hours in the bakery. I'll need more staff with the bigger seating area."

He could understand why Jamie wanted to move back. It was such a great community and Nicholas didn't want to think about leaving it either.

Mai pulled up at a huge modern, two-storey house on the hill above the town. It had stylish lines and wouldn't look out of place in one of the wealthier suburbs in Perth – not quite the small family home he'd been expecting. It was even more modern than his parents' house on the beachfront.

"Ready to meet the horde?"

He winced inwardly, before nodding. Were all her siblings going to be there?

"Don't worry, you'll have fun."

He could do this. He took the bottle of wine and Calypso, and followed Mai into the house. Inside, the hallway was large, with light-coloured walls adorned with bright artwork. On the dark wooden hall table stood a carved wooden statue of a dragon which could have been Vietnamese in origin. Mai walked straight through to the back of the house in the direction of the voices.

The kitchen was epic. One wall was covered in glossy white cupboards and the other contained a huge oven and stove top, almost commercial size. It was stainless steel and white, bright and airy but welcoming with its touch of colour in the fruit basket and the green kettle and toaster next to the stove. Mai's family was gathered around a large island bench covered in food – four siblings and her parents.

An older man looked up and grinned. "Hi, Mai."

Everyone turned and Nicholas found himself the centre of attention.

"Everyone, this is Nicholas." Mai pointed to each person in turn. "Eden, Sarah, Leanne, Kim, my mother, Bian and father, Anh."

Nicholas stood there holding a cat and a bottle of wine. He must look a fool. "Nice to meet you."

Eden moved forward and claimed Calypso. "Let me take the Cal-man from you." She left the room.

Leanne sighed. "She always gets out of the work."

Nicholas relaxed at the normal sibling complaints. He could relate.

Anh asked, "Have you ever made dumplings?"

He moved closer. That's what they were doing around the bench. Making dumplings and some kind of spring roll. "No, I can't say I have."

Mai took the bottle of wine from him. "It's tradition and you can't really mess it up. Wash your hands and Dad will show you how."

He did as requested and found himself standing between Kim and Mai with a small ball of dough in his hand. It was soft like plasticine and easy to flatten out into a disk. He followed Anh's instructions, adding some filling and pinching it together, and ended up with something that looked like it would collapse if anyone touched it. "I think I failed."

"It's still edible," Anh said. "It takes practice."

Next to him Mai made dumplings at three times his speed, making it appear easy. He'd need a *lot* of practice.

"Nicholas, I have those contracts here for you," Bian said. "Remind me to give them to you before you leave."

"I will." Another contract signed. The development was almost at full capacity. His father would be pleased.

"Bian showed me the revised development plans," Anh said. "It's a nicer looking building with the few changes you made."

"Thanks, I agree."

"What other stores are going in?" Kim asked.

There was no hostility in his question. Kim didn't seem upset about catching him in Mai's apartment. That was a relief. "A restaurant, Mai's bakery and a homewares store so far. I've still got two more units to lease."

"What kind of restaurant?"

"Tapas."

"That will be nice," Bian said.

Kim and Anh shared a glance. "Shouldn't be any competition."

Nicholas frowned and Mai explained. "Dad and Kim run the Vietnamese restaurant in town."

He hadn't realised. His development affected the whole family. It was a wonder they didn't ask him to leave right now, but neither man appeared particularly concerned.

He focused on the dumpling he was making and this one turned out slightly better than the last one. He added it to the plate of finished ones and his were clearly more mangled looking like overstuffed pillows.

"What's next when this development is finished?" Anh asked.

"I don't know," Nicholas admitted. "I'm enjoying it down here."

"We know all about that." Anh exchanged a fond look with his wife. "There's something about Blackbridge that is soothing to the soul."

It was poetic, but he was right. Nicholas had been able to de-stress and re-evaluate his life down here.

"The city has a way of making you forget that there's more to life than work," Bian said. "We've been so much happier since we made the move."

He hadn't considered moving down here permanently, but the idea was enticing.

"So how long have you and Mai been a thing?" Leanne asked.

Sarah smacked her sister on the arm and Mai shook her head. "That's none of your business."

Nicholas's cheeks warmed. He guessed they were a *thing*.

"All right, we're done here," Anh said. "Leanne, set the table outside, Sarah can organise drinks and I'll get steaming."

Relieved by the reprieve, Nicholas followed Mai outside into the lush and shady garden. A couple of big eucalypts towered above them and parrots sat in the branches, nibbling on the nuts. Underneath were a collection of Australian natives and shade-loving plants and the small patch of lawn was in immaculate condition. "It's a lovely garden."

"Thank you," Bian said as she followed them out. "It's my relaxation. Do you garden?"

"No. I live in an apartment in the city."

"You're missing out. There's something tranquil about pulling up weeds and tending to plants."

Mai snorted. "Except when the weeds grow back and the plants wither and die."

Her mother chuckled. "Mai didn't inherit my green thumb."

"Speaking of which, could you and Dad drop by the cafe on Mortimer Road sometime this week and tell me what I can do with the yard?"

"I'll get your father to stop by tomorrow."

Mai stiffened. "Thanks."

Why was Mai upset? It was nice for her father to help her. The relocation was really going to mess with her business and he regretted that most of all. But with her family and friends' help, she would be a success.

Dinner was a fun, boisterous affair with everyone talking about their upcoming plans. Leanne had finished university and was searching for work and Mai's other two sisters were on summer break for another six weeks. They talked half-heartedly about getting jobs, but neither was too interested. Nicholas couldn't remember a time when he hadn't worked. All through university he'd had part-time jobs at Shadbolt or working in construction. He envied their free time, their freedom to do absolutely nothing if they wanted to.

What would that be like?

He had no idea.

After Nicholas helped clean up, they all sat in the lounge room.

"Mai, we're going on a family picnic this weekend," Anh said. "Can you come?"

Mai screwed up her face. "I'd love to, but we're having a busy bee at the cafe. I'm hoping to get most of the work done over the weekend."

"You do nothing but work," Eden grumbled.

"It's what happens when you own your own business," Mai snapped back.

"Dad doesn't work as much as you do."

"Dad has a different business to mine."

"They're both food."

Anh interrupted Mai's retort. "Mai's move is going to take a bit of effort."

Eden pouted.

Nicholas shifted. It had been a long time since he'd squabbled with his siblings like that. He wouldn't have dared argue in front of guests – that wasn't acceptable in his family.

Mai checked the time. "We'd better be going."

"Yeah, you'd better get your beauty sleep," Kim teased.

Mai rolled her eyes as she got to her feet.

"Thanks for having me." Nicholas stood up and shook hands with Anh and Bian.

"It was a pleasure," Bian replied.

It had been. He'd enjoyed getting to know Mai's family, enjoyed their family dynamic. On the drive to his place, he said, "Your family is nice."

"Thanks." She pulled up outside his house. "I like them."

He wasn't ready for their evening to end. "Do you want to come in?" he asked. "You could stay the night."

Mai hesitated. "I really do need to get a decent night's sleep tonight," she said. "I should go straight to bed, and you won't want to."

He didn't care. He wanted her to stay, liked the idea of her being asleep in his bed. "I can tuck you in and I'll be sure to be quiet when I come to bed."

She studied him for a moment and then turned off the car. "All right."

He grinned, elation coursing through him. Mai was staying. "Can I get you a drink?" he asked as he opened the front door.

"No." Mai wrapped her arms around his waist. "I'm going to bed. You mentioned you'd tuck me in?" She squeezed his butt.

He hardened. "I thought you needed sleep."

"I'm sure you can help me relax."

He liked the way she thought. "I'm sure I can." He led her into the bedroom.

Mai woke in a strange bed with a warm man curled up beside her, his arm cuddling her. She vaguely remembered Nicholas coming to bed sometime after she'd gone to sleep. After she'd been thoroughly relaxed. She smiled and reached for her phone to confirm the time. Two minutes until her alarm went off.

She sighed, turned it off and then carefully tried to slide out of bed without waking Nicholas.

His arm around her tightened. "Awfoserwkdlksjd," he mumbled.

"I have to go."

"I thought you were staying the night," he said.

She smiled. "I did. It's time for me to go to work."

"But it's dark outside."

He was still half asleep. "That's when I go to work, remember?" She kissed his cheek and slipped out of bed, before gathering her clothes and leaving the room. She ducked into a spare bedroom, switched on the light and dressed quickly. She'd have a shower when she got home.

In the kitchen she grabbed her car keys and looked around for Calypso. He hadn't been in the bedroom and he wasn't on the sofas either. She didn't have time to search for him now. Instead she wrote a note asking Nicholas to bring Calypso home when he had a chance and left it on the kitchen bench. Then she drove through the dark, quiet town to work. There wasn't a single other car on the road and the lamp posts seemed far apart. The whole town was sleeping.

She yawned, forcing her eyes wide to focus on the road. She would have to get used to this. No more going down the stairs and into work. It would completely suck.

It had been inevitable that one day she'd move out of her apartment, but she'd hoped it would be further in the future.

Mai pulled into the car park at the back of the bakery, her lights illuminating the dark corner. A black van was parked outside the empty unit and a man stumbled into view, his clothes dark, his hair blond. She slammed on the brakes, her headlights illuminating the whole area.

Her heart raced.

He was the same guy who'd been with Gordon and the creepy guy at her cafe.

She leapt out of the car. "What the hell do you think you're doing?" She strode over to him.

"Miss On, you do consistently turn up at the wrong time." Creepy Guy stepped out from behind the van, his tone mild.

Fear slammed into her and she took a step back.

The blond guy turned towards her, his face bruised and bleeding.

Shit.

What on earth had she just walked into?

It didn't matter. She couldn't show her fear, even though every urge screamed at her to run. She wouldn't get very far. Puffing herself up so she stood tall, she said, "You're at my workplace, I start early."

"You should go inside," Creepy Guy said. "I'm teaching Shane a lesson. He didn't listen to me." The threat was there.

Had he killed Gordon? Had Gordon done something he didn't agree with? She couldn't ask, couldn't even hint that she suspected. "You're not burning down my building?" What a stupid thing to say.

"Have you gone to the police?"

"No." Not yet. She itched to get her phone out and take his photo but she wasn't that stupid. The car number plate however … she glanced over. It was covered in thick red dust and she could only make out the first two letters.

"Then I'm not burning your bakery."

"Well that's good." She took a step back, glancing at the blond who was silently watching them both but making no move to run or ask for help. "My staff starts in half an hour." She didn't want Penny getting involved.

A hint of a smile crept on Creepy Guy's face, making him look even scarier. "I'll be done by then. As long as I'm not interrupted further."

Mai backed away, not wanting to turn her back on them. She

was in way over her head. This time she had to call Lincoln, had to get help.

Creepy Guy reached into his pocket and pulled out a cigarette lighter. He flicked it on and then glanced casually at the building.

Her heart jumped. His message was clear.

She got back into her car, the urge to drive out of there and straight over to Lincoln's place strong. But what if Creepy Guy didn't stop with the bakery? What if he hurt her family?

No. She parked and hurried up the steps, her hands shaking as she tried to unlock the door. Finally it opened and she raced in, slamming and locking the door behind her before sinking to the floor.

How had she got into this mess?

How could she get out of it?

She had to talk to Lincoln. People were getting hurt. She had to tell him about Gordon, Creepy Guy and the blond. He'd be able to protect her family.

Her apartment, her bakery didn't matter.

That was a lie. Her bakery was everything to her, but she couldn't put it before people's lives. That wasn't right.

She slid her phone out of her pocket and stared at the screen for a long moment. Maybe she could get some footage, some proof of what was happening. She slipped off her shoes and quickly padded up the stairs to her apartment, unlocking it and tiptoeing to the kitchen window. She couldn't see anything through her lace curtains and she didn't dare move them in case Creepy Guy was watching.

She strained to hear voices and there was a murmur but she couldn't make out any words.

She had to act now. Had to call Lincoln.

A car engine roared to life and seconds later the black van peeled out of the car park.

They were gone.

A figure wandered into the light by her back door. Creepy Guy.

He looked straight up at her window, straight *at* her, and flicked the cigarette lighter on and off. Then he walked down the street as if he had all the time in the world.

Mai didn't start breathing until he was out of view.

This was not a guy to mess around with.

She had to be careful what she did. Had to make sure nothing could be traced back to her.

But how on earth did she do that?

All morning Mai debated how she could speak with Lincoln without risking her family. She kneaded the bread dough, hoping inspiration would strike, but it didn't. Creepy Guy would know it was her if the police started searching for him.

"Has someone annoyed you?" Penny asked.

Mai blinked and looked up, her hands buried in the dough. "What?"

She nodded towards the table. "You're really giving that dough a good workout."

Mai relaxed her hands and shook her head. "Just thinking." She set the dough aside to prove and went to the storeroom for more flour.

She needed to talk to her family, let them know to be careful, make sure her sisters didn't go anywhere alone.

Surely there would be no reason for Creepy Guy to hurt them.

With all of the bread prepared and proving she started on her list of pastries. Top of the list was bee stings – Lincoln's favourite. He bought one every day when he came in for his morning coffee.

She grinned. That's when she could catch him, take him into her office so she didn't need to go to the station.

It was the perfect solution.

When Lincoln strode into the bakery he greeted Sylvia and asked for his usual. Mai hurried into the front room. "I've got this, Sylvia. Lincoln, can I talk to you for a moment?" He was dressed in his full blue uniform, looking as handsome as ever. The bell above the door rang as a new customer came in and she automatically checked who it was. Her heart stopped.

Creepy Guy.

He wore the same clothes as he had last night, and he shifted his black jacket to show the hand gun beneath it. Her blood froze. Somehow she'd ended up in an American cop drama — except this was real.

He was real.

"Sure, Mayday. Sorry I didn't return your call yesterday. What's up?"

Mai blinked. This wasn't good. She couldn't ask Lincoln out the back and she couldn't talk to him in front of Creepy Guy. She got a bee sting out of the cabinet and boxed it.

"Mai?"

"I, uh, wanted to ask you about Jamie." Jamie was a safe topic of conversation, a reasonable thing to talk about.

"What's he done now?"

"Nothing. I wanted to ask if he's really all right after breaking up with Sandra."

Lincoln frowned. "I didn't know he had."

Great, now she was betraying Jamie's confidences. Crap. "Don't worry about it." It took all of her willpower not to look at Creepy Guy who was ordering from Sylvia. "I'll call him this afternoon." She made his coffee and handed it to him. "I'd better get back to work. I'll see you later."

"Thanks, Mai."

She didn't wait for him to leave. She hurried back into the kitchen and shut herself into her office, her pulse racing.

What the hell should she do now?

Mai spent the day trying to convince herself that she didn't need to say anything to Lincoln. Blond guy and Gordon were involved in drugs in some way which meant they were doing illegal things.

But any way she spun it, it didn't feel right. No one deserved to be beaten up, no one deserved to be killed. Gordon deserved justice like anyone else.

She had to talk to Lincoln, but Creepy Guy was obviously watching her. Was he able to tap her phone, trace her calls?

She had no idea what he was capable of.

So she needed to be covert. The station or Lincoln's place were out. Perhaps she could get Fleur to invite everyone over for dinner – no, she didn't want to get her friends involved.

Maybe she should invite Lincoln surfing – but that would look suspicious as well. It could only work if she happened to bump into him at the beach.

And she didn't know what his roster was, or even if he'd been surfing lately.

She hugged herself as she searched her apartment for Calypso. He usually met her at the door. So where was he?

She'd left him at Nicholas's place. She sent him a text.

Do you still have my cat?

The response came a moment later.

Cat? I don't remember a cat …

Mai frowned.

Big, fluffy beige animal with blue eyes.

Ah, that cat. I'm keeping him.

Surprise had her chuckling.

You can't, he's mine.

Possession is nine-tenths of the law.

That's a myth.

Then I'm holding him ransom.

She grinned, the tension of the morning melting away.

What are your demands?

A kiss and one Mai's Delight.

Done. When do you want to do the switch?

How about now?

Interesting. It was the middle of the morning and he wanted to see her.

Where?

The bridge at dawn.
Just kidding.
My place?

Be right there.

She should be sleeping, but her apartment didn't feel safe. She felt too exposed. Besides it wouldn't take long to drop off the pastry and pick up Calypso, and she wanted to see Nicholas.

During the drive over, Mai kept an eye on her rear-view mirror to make sure she wasn't being followed. Traffic was light and she couldn't see Creepy Guy anywhere. Maybe he was convinced she was suitably frightened.

She hoped he was.

Nicholas met her at his front door, Calypso around his neck. "The pastry?" he asked, waggling his eyebrows and twirling a make-believe moustache.

It was absurd, and a little of the stress faded as she swallowed her smile and showed him the box. He reached for it and she snatched it back. "The cat first."

"We'll do a switch on the count of three – one, two, three."

Mai handed him the box and before she could reach for Calypso, Nicholas had taken off down the hallway. "Oi!" She laughed and followed him inside, glancing down the street before she shut the door behind her.

He was in the kitchen, the box already open and the pastry on a plate. "Want to go halves?"

"No, thanks. I should take my cat and have my siesta."

"Why don't you nap here?" he suggested. "Calypso's not ready to leave yet."

Her cat did appear to be rather comfortable slung around Nicholas's neck and the idea that Nicholas wanted her to stay appealed. Plus his bed was far more comfortable than her own.

And she had zero desire to be by herself now that Creepy Guy knew where she lived.

No, she wasn't going to think about that now. She had a very sexy man in a playful mood in front of her. She wanted to make the most of it.

How far would Nicholas's playful side go? "All right. Mind if I take a shower?" She stripped off her T-shirt without waiting for an answer and dropped it on the floor, heading towards his bedroom. Her bra soon joined it and Nicholas said, "Sorry, Calypso, you're staying out here."

She laughed.

This was exactly what she needed.

Chapter 15

Nicholas leaned back in his chair, his gaze going to the time at the bottom of his laptop screen. Mai had been asleep for two hours. Was it too soon to wake her? He wanted to spend more time with her.

His phone rang as he got to his feet. "Hi, Mum."

"Honey, how are you? Are you getting enough rest? I haven't heard from you in over a week."

Nicholas smiled at the worry in her voice. It was nice to know someone still cared. "I'm fine, Mum."

"Your dad isn't working you too hard is he? The doctor said you're only allowed to work on the one project."

"Don't worry, after my stuff up Dad doesn't want me working on anything else." It didn't hurt anymore, not now he was debating changing his career.

"It wasn't your fault, Honey. None of it was."

That wasn't true, but he appreciated her support. "How are you?"

"Good, I'm good." She paused and he heard her hesitation.

"What is it?"

"Have you heard from Shane recently?"

His best friend's name jolted him. "No. He's not allowed to make phone calls in rehab."

"Ah, well that's the thing … he checked himself out."

Nicholas sank into the chair. "When?"

"Right after Christmas. Vicki only just called to tell me. They haven't been able to contact him."

Shane's parents had stopped talking to his parents after the fire. The police had treated the Jamesons as suspects as well and they'd all blamed him for the insurance failure. "Do you want me to ring him?"

"You can try, he hasn't been answering his mobile."

And wasn't likely to answer Nicholas's call. But what if Shane was in trouble? Neither of their parents knew the truth about Shane's debts, or about him ripping off the company. Could his drug dealer have killed him? Worry skittered over Nicholas's skin. "I'll let you know if I hear from him."

"None of this is your fault, Nicholas. You can't control what he does."

He had nothing to say to that. He should have tried harder to get through to his friend. He hadn't wanted to believe the figures, had wanted to trust Shane was telling the truth when he said he wasn't involved. He should have known better. His friend had a tendency to take the easy option if it was offered.

"Your father and I thought we'd come down to visit for a couple of weeks. Do you mind?"

In other words his mother wanted to check up on him. It was kind of sweet but he didn't want to see his father. Gerald would go through all his work, would visit the building and the contractors he'd lined up, would micro-manage.

Did it matter anymore?

Did he care if his father took over?

It would be a relief if he was sure his father wouldn't change things on Mai, make things harder on her. No, this was one development he needed to follow through to the end. He would see Mai set up her new bakery and then he'd walk away from Shadbolt. Find his own direction.

A movement caught his eye. Mai walked down the stairs, her long hair a little mussed from sleeping, and she was wearing one of his shirts.

She was gorgeous. Everything he needed. He didn't want to think about work, or his family or Shane. He wanted to be with her.

"Nicholas?" His mother's voice in his ear.

"Sure, come down. Let me know what day."

"We'll be down this weekend. I love you, Nicholas." She hung up.

Nicholas put down the phone and moved over to Mai, taking her into his arms.

"Work again?"

"No, my mum."

"Is everything all right?"

He hesitated. Should he tell her about everything that had happened before the fire? "Sort of." He wanted to. He wanted to confide in her. Wanted to know if she thought he'd done the wrong thing.

He took her hand and led her to the couch.

"What's wrong?" Mai squeezed his hand.

"I told you about the last development, the one that burned down."

She nodded.

"There was a little more to it." He took a deep breath. "The development was a joint venture between Shadbolt and Jameson. The Jamesons have been friends of the family for years and own a construction company. I worked for them when I was at university."

"Where you discovered a love for building things?"

"Yeah." He tugged on his earlobe. "My best friend Shane took over the company about a year ago when his father retired. It was the first project we'd worked on together and Dad put me completely in charge."

"What was that like?"

"They say never do business with family." And Shane was like a brother to him.

"What happened?"

"A couple of months in, I noticed changes – cheaper materials were being used, but the budget stayed the same. I questioned Shane and he told me I was mistaken." He ran a hand through his hair. He hadn't been able to ignore his gut feeling that something wasn't right. "I kept looking into it, thinking maybe a supervisor was involved, was skimming the extra money and Shane didn't know."

She ran a hand over his arm. "What did you do?"

"I examined everything, work schedules, deliveries, turning up on site unannounced – I spent more time on site than Shane did. Finally I realised it could only be Shane who was responsible."

"Did you confront him?"

"I was going to. For about a week he avoided me, saying he had to work on other projects, so I took up the slack on our development. Then we had the fire." Everyone was in shock. "When I discovered the insurance hadn't been paid, I told Shane first and he went mental." He closed his eyes. Shane's face had contorted into a mask of fear. He'd said they were going to kill him, that Nicholas had ruined his life. "He had some debts, big debts." Nicholas hated thinking about it even now. He hadn't known anything had been wrong. "He'd become addicted to meth, said the stress of running the business was too much to handle, and he owed his dealer over fifty grand."

"Wow." Mai sat back. "That's a lot of meth."

How had Shane been taking so many drugs without Nicholas having a clue? Some friend he was. "They were coming after him hard, and skimming off the project was his way of paying back the dealers." It had been one of the worst days in his life. His best friend was in trouble and he couldn't help. Nicholas glanced at Mai. "How could I tell our fathers that Shane was in such a mess?"

"So you said nothing?"

He nodded. "He agreed to go into rehab and we were going to work out a way to settle his debts."

"Do you think the fire was related?"

His gut clenched. "I asked Shane, and he said it was the dealer." The heaviness in his gut dissolved. "It was part punishment for not paying off the debt fast enough and part expectation that Shane would pay him back with the insurance money."

"But you hadn't paid the insurance."

"Right."

Mai shifted closer to him. "What happened next?"

"The police started saying it was arson. They knew I suspected something, but it wasn't my story to tell. I couldn't turn Shane in, not when he was dealing with so many other things at the same time." He'd failed his friend once, he wasn't going to do it again.

"You took the brunt of the accusations?"

"Yeah."

"That was incredibly loyal of you."

He couldn't read her expression. "Do you think that's a bad thing?"

"No, it's a selfless thing to do. Courageous. And I need to stop thinking of myself."

He frowned. "What do you mean?"

She stood up, biting her bottom lip. "Can I use your phone?"

He handed it to her. "Is something wrong?"

"Yeah. I need to speak to Lincoln."

Why did she need to talk to the police?

Whatever it was, he would be there for her.

Like he hadn't been for Shane.

Mai's heart pounded as Nicholas went to let Lincoln in. She'd asked Lincoln to make sure he wasn't followed, and to park in the garage. Nicholas had left the door up for them and it was now closing.

"This way." Nicholas led Lincoln and Ryan through to the living area to where Mai waited. They were both dressed in their police uniforms, their shirts crisp, the crease in their pants perfectly straight.

Lincoln frowned. "What the hell is going on, Mai? What's with all this clandestine shit?"

She stood up, paced around the kitchen table, unable to look him in the eye, unable to sit still.

"Mai, what's wrong?" Lincoln stepped in front of her, his tone more gentle now.

She looked up at him. Shadows darkened the skin under his eyes. She didn't want to add to his stress, but there was no helping it.

Nicholas switched on the kettle. "Drink anyone?"

"Tea, please." She wasn't sure where to start.

"Spill it, Mayday," Lincoln demanded, taking her by the shoulders and steering her towards the kitchen table.

She sat, assessing their expressions. Lincoln and Nicholas were both frowning, but Ryan waited patiently for her to explain.

"It started New Year's Eve with Gordon," she said.

Ryan got out his notepad as the water in the kettle bubbled and Nicholas made the drinks, the teaspoon clinking against the china mug.

This was it. She had to give them as much detail as possible. She told them about seeing Gordon and the blond at the party, witnessing Gordon's meeting with Creepy Guy at the park, and then seeing them at the bakery and the cafe as well.

Each man's expression got darker and darker as she spoke until Lincoln burst out, "Why didn't you call me immediately?"

"He threatened my *family*, Lincoln," Mai said.

Lincoln swore. "What did he say?"

"That my sisters were pretty." It didn't sound like much but the threat had been clear to her. "I'm sorry."

"We can protect them," Lincoln told her.

"I was scared. For my sisters and for you. The tattooed guy had a gun. Then Gordon died and I knew Creepy Guy would burn the bakery if I said anything."

"Risks like this are part of the job." Lincoln sighed. "I need you to go through it again in detail."

It was the right thing to do, she'd already left it too long. She nodded and began to talk.

"Jesus," Lincoln said when she finished. "I'm going to need you to work with a sketch artist to get a description of the creepy guy."

Tension coiled in her stomach. Lincoln was right but the fear bubbled in her. "All right. He was in the bakery with you this morning."

Lincoln shook his head. "That's why you were acting strangely." He swore. "I didn't notice him. You didn't recognise the other guys you saw."

"The blond was kind of familiar, but not a local." Her eyes widened as she made the connection. "He was the guy Gordon was with on New Year's Eve," she said. "I thought he was buying drugs, but maybe he gave them to Gordon."

Lincoln nodded.

Nicholas put his arm around her and his warmth seeped into her skin, thawing the stiffness that had taken residence. "Should Mai be alone?"

"We don't know what this guy could do." Lincoln looked at Mai. "Keep someone with you as much as possible."

Annoyance and fear battled with each other. "I've got a cafe to clean up," she said. "I can't have someone with me all the time."

"I'll help," Nicholas said.

She glanced at him. "You've got better things to do than babysit me."

"Not really, and I can work from the cafe as easily as I can work from here."

It was sweet, but she didn't want him involved in this. It was bad enough she'd involved Lincoln and Ryan. She didn't want another man she loved involved.

Oh.

Wow.

She squeezed her eyes shut for a second hoping to calm her suddenly racing heart. She'd gone and fallen in love with Nicholas.

"That's sorted then." Lincoln got to his feet. "I'll call you when I've arranged the sketch artist appointment."

She nodded, managed to wave as Nicholas walked them out the door.

Nicholas was going back to Perth when the project was over.

What was she going to do?

On Saturday morning Nicholas headed downstairs to the bakery early to see Mai. He'd barely left her side since she'd told him about the creepy guy. He'd slept at her apartment and gone to the Mortimer Road cafe with her while she cleaned and patched. He'd taken her to the Albany airport so she could fly to Perth to meet with the sketch artist, and then picked her up again afterwards. He'd stood next to her while she'd cried at Gordon's funeral, had comforted her after she'd given her condolences to Gail and the children who weren't old enough to really understand what had happened. He hated to see her so upset, refused to leave her to wallow in her guilt.

He loved being the one she turned to, loved holding her in his arms, loved just being by her side.

Mai was wrist deep in dough and she grinned at him when he walked in. "Morning, sleepy head."

He chuckled. Seven o'clock was hardly a sleep in. He kissed her and greeted Penny, then walked through to the serving area to make a coffee. "What time will you be finished here?"

"I'll be another half an hour," Mai said. "Then Penny should be able to cope with the rest."

"You betcha," Penny said.

"Can I help with anything?"

Mai pursed her lips. "No. It will be faster if I do it."

Burn. He raised an eyebrow. "Don't think I can cut it?"

"I haven't seen much of your baking skills," Mai said. "Besides, by the time I explain what you need to do, and I've made sure you're doing it right, I could have it finished."

She had a point. In the past few days he'd watched Mai work and she was a machine when it came to kneading and all things baking. The speed with which she and Penny turned out bread, rolls and pastries was incredible. He leaned up against one of the stainless steel benches to wait and his mind drifted.

There had been no sign of Creepy Guy. Nicholas spoke to Lincoln every day and it appeared the thug hadn't discovered Mai had talked to the police. He shuddered. It killed him that Mai had had a gun pointed at her while he'd waited oblivious by the car. He wouldn't make that mistake again. He wouldn't fail her.

She'd have to get used to him being her shadow.

She glanced at him as if sensing his thoughts and smiled. "I won't be long."

"There's no rush." He sipped his coffee. "Who's going to be there today?"

"I'm not sure who Fleur invited. Dad is doing some gardening and all of the musketeers will be there."

He wanted to get to know Mai's friends a little more. She'd

told him tales of their adventures during their evenings together and if he wanted Mai in his life, he needed to win over her friends.

And he did want her in his life.

He wasn't quite sure what he would do when the development was over, but he'd make it work. His savings were enough that they would carry him through until he found something permanent. He enjoyed living in Blackbridge, liked the slower pace. And working on a single development was a luxury – there was no longer the stress and aggravation of juggling a million things.

In a couple of weeks, Mai would move out and the demolition crew would take down the building. The concrete fabricators were manufacturing the slabs needed for the new structure and he had someone else interested in one of the last units. Once the build began, there wouldn't be much to keep him busy.

What would he do next?

Mai put the tray of pastries in the oven and wiped her hands on her apron. "I'm done. I'll just get a few things to take with us." She hurried into the bakery.

The day was already sunny, with blue skies stretching endlessly as he drove them over to the cafe. When he pulled up, he followed Mai inside. "Where do you want to start?"

"The walls behind the display cabinets. If they dry in time we can put up the shelves by the end of the day." She walked through to the kitchen. "You're going to do the ramp, aren't you?"

"Yeah. I'll get one of the guys to help me with it."

"Kit's your best bet," Mai said. "She's a genius at building anything."

He winced at his unintentional sexism. "I guess as a farmer she's got to know how to do a lot."

"That's right." She disappeared into the storeroom. "I'll get a couple of people painting in here as well. It only needs one coat to freshen it up, and then I'll put together the shelving."

"The cavalry have arrived!" a voice called from the cafe.

Mai grinned. "That would be Kit."

He walked out the front where Kit and Fleur were both

dressed in singlets, shorts and boots, their brown hair tied back in ponytails.

"Good to see you again, Nic," Kit said. She pinched a doughnut from the box Mai had left on the display cabinet and took a bite. "Where do you want us to start?"

"You can help Nicholas build the ramp," Mai said. "Fleur can start painting."

"What are you going to do?" Fleur asked.

"I've still got the fridges to clean."

Fleur shuddered. "Better you than me."

Nicholas showed Kit the ramp he'd designed and she nodded. "That shouldn't be too hard. How good are you with a hammer, City Boy?"

He smiled at the nickname. "I can hold my own."

She grinned at him. "Good."

He dug the holes while she measured and cut the lengths of wood for the posts.

"I should apologise for the thing at the council meeting," Kit said as she mixed the rapid set concrete in the hole while he held the new railing posts steady.

He glanced at her. He'd forgotten about it. "Should you?"

"Yeah. I stuck my nose in where it wasn't needed. I should have checked with Mai first, but sometimes she doesn't ask for help."

"Sometimes she doesn't need it."

Kit smiled at him. "That's right. She's pretty self-reliant." She inspected the level and nodded in satisfaction. "I was ready to dislike you for her sake," she said. "But I'm glad I don't have to. You seem like a nice guy."

"I think I am."

"I hope so, because if you hurt Mai, you'll wish you'd never been born." Kit laughed.

Nicholas wasn't certain she was kidding. He needed to change the subject. "How many dairy cows have you got?"

"About two hundred."

He let go of the post, satisfied it wasn't going anywhere.

"How much longer are you going to be down here for?" Kit asked.

Not subtle, but at least Mai's friends were looking out for

her. "At least until the development is completed."

"And after that?"

"I'm not sure." And when he was, he'd tell Mai first, not Kit.

They worked well together, changing topics as it suited them until Mai came out. Nicholas hammered the last nail in place and stood back. The ramp was finished.

"You've done a fantastic job." Mai kissed him.

"Hey, it wasn't just City Boy," Kit complained.

"Yeah, but we both know you don't need a bigger head."

Kit chuckled.

A car drove around from the back of the cafe, its trailer piled high with branches and cuttings from the yard. Anh wound down the window. "I'm doing a tip run. Do you need me to pick up anything?"

Nicholas leaned against one of the posts as Mai trotted down the steps to talk to her father. It was great that so many people had come to help her, even if her mother and sisters had gone on a picnic instead. A black van slowed down as it rounded the bend in the road. Nicholas straightened. It matched the description of the van Mai had seen, and its windows were tinted too dark to make out who was inside.

He didn't like it and waited until the van continued down the road and Mai headed back inside before he went to find Lincoln. "Got a second?" Nicholas asked, glancing around to make sure no one was close enough to hear.

"Sure." Lincoln put his paint roller down. "What's up?"

He told Lincoln about the car.

Lincoln scowled. "Did the driver see Mai?"

"Yeah. She was out the front with her father." A perfect target.

"You'd better tell Mai. Are you still staying with her?"

He nodded.

"That's good. It's better to be safe."

Nicholas's shoulders were tense and he looked over to where Mai chatted with Hannah. He didn't want her out of his sight. "Have you found anything about the guys?"

Lincoln hesitated. "Not yet."

He wasn't telling Nicholas everything. That wasn't good. But he couldn't pry him for more details here, not with Fleur making her way closer to them as she painted the wall.

It was up to him to keep Mai by his side at all times.
He needed to protect her.

Chapter 16

It was late afternoon when Mai waved goodbye to the last car and then stretched, groaning as she did so. She was exhausted but exuberant. They had done so much work today and the new cafe was almost finished.

"Happy?" Nicholas asked.

"Ecstatic. All that's left is the shelving behind the display cabinets and moving in." She would book the removalists for the week school went back, and get the shire out to approve the premise. She let out a sigh. "It's all coming together." She walked up the ramp Nicholas and Kit had built. "You've done a great job on this. You could become a carpenter."

"Thanks."

He hadn't said anything else about hating his job since their date, and when he'd been working next to her during the week, he hadn't seemed stressed. Maybe he'd just been having a bad day. "Have you thought any more about quitting Shadbolt?"

"Not a lot." He ran a hand through his hair. "I want to finish this development before I do anything."

"I'm glad. I trust you." She wanted him to stay.

She wandered through the cafe confirming that everything had been tidied up and all the doors were locked. The seating area was so much bigger than she'd had before and she could picture how it would look with the tables inside, a couple of large pieces of artwork on the walls to add a little colour. She trailed her hand over the metal shelving in the storeroom which was ready for her ingredients. This was hers for the next six months and she would use it to build her brand further, to attract more people. It would be harder with the smaller kitchen and she'd miss Penny's company in the mornings, but she would make it a success.

She moved back into the kitchen where Nicholas waited. She hadn't pictured him as a handyman, but he'd worked as hard as everyone else and had helped whenever anyone needed it.

"Is there anything else that needs to be done?" Nicholas asked.

"No. Let's go home."

Home. She wasn't sure whether she meant her apartment or Nicholas's house – home was wherever he was. She got into her car and squeezed her eyes shut for a second. It would break her heart when he left.

"Are you all right?"

She opened her eyes and forced a smile. "Just tired." She started the car. She wanted Nicholas to stay in Blackbridge, she wanted him to find a job he loved and to heal from the incident with his friend.

She wanted him to love her.

Did she want too much?

It was dark when Nicholas opened his eyes and he lay there, not sure what had woken him. He should be dead to the world after working on Mai's cafe all day. His muscles screamed at him not to move as he shifted.

Thunk.

He lifted his head. Mai was asleep beside him and Calypso was curled at his feet.

Thunk.

It was outside. Had Creepy Guy discovered Mai had spoken to the police? He took his phone from the table and slid out of bed, careful not to wake Mai. He slipped on a T-shirt and shorts and tiptoed to the kitchen window.

The car park was dark.

Slowly he unlocked the apartment door, tucking Mai's keys

into his pocket as he crept down the stairs. At the base of them he stopped. Should he turn on the outside light and hope it would scare off whoever it was? Or would it make him more of a target?

From what Mai had said, a little light wouldn't frighten Creepy Guy.

Thunk.

The noise was definitely coming from the empty unit next door.

He opened the back door and slipped outside. The air was cool and the streetlamp down the road gave a measure of comfort. But he wasn't heading that way.

Nicholas crept down the steps and clung close to the building's wall as he moved closer to the unit, his eyes adjusting to the dim light.

Thunk.

It sounded as if someone was chopping wood, one strike at a time. He scrolled through his phone to find Lincoln's number as a figure moved out of the unit. The glare from the phone was bright and the figure swore.

Heart thumping Nicholas swiped his torch on and held it up.

He froze.

Shane.

His friend was dressed all in black, jeans, T-shirt, jacket. His blond hair stuck out all over the place, not his usual styled hairdo, his face was bruised like he'd been in a bar fight and his hands were empty.

Nicholas lowered his phone. "Shit. You gave me a heart attack, Shane."

"Nicholas." Shane took a couple of steps back towards the unit so he was in front of the open door. "There you are."

He frowned. "What are you doing here?"

"I, ah, needed to get away for a few days, you know?"

"Why didn't you come by the house?" He had stayed there enough times to know the way.

"You weren't there. Then I drove through town, searching for a place to stay and saw your car here. I figured this was your development." He glanced towards the unit. "Thought I'd stay the night here and catch you in the morning."

There was something off with what he said. Nicholas held his phone higher to see Shane's eyes, to see if he was high. Shane squinted and looked away.

"Why didn't you call?"

"I wasn't sure you'd answer after the things I said." He cleared his throat.

"Of course I would have." He wouldn't let his friend down again. Hadn't Shane listened to the message he'd left on his mobile? "Why did you check yourself out of rehab?"

"The place was for pussies, talking all sorts of bullshit. I didn't fit there."

Shane still couldn't see he had a problem. After everything that had gone on, the fire, the debts, he still thought he was fine. "What about the men you owe money to?"

"I've worked out a payment plan." Shane glanced at the unit.

Nicholas didn't trust him; every nerve in his body told him there was more to the story, but he needed to help his friend. "Why don't you get your things and go to my parents' place? There's a spare key under the pot plant on the back patio." Hopefully being there would remind Shane of the good times they'd had together. Of everything he had to lose. "Stay there tonight and we'll talk in the morning. Where's your car?"

"I parked it down the street." He shrugged. "Figured people would disturb me if they saw it here."

Or he was hiding something. Nicholas would inspect the unit after he left. "Do you need a lift?"

"Nah, I've got it." He stayed where he was for a second and then said, "Thanks, Nicholas." Slowly he walked away.

As Shane rounded the corner of the building, Nicholas's phone buzzed.

Fire call out.

Then he read the location, and sprinted for the stairs.

A loud high-pitched ring split the air, and Mai sat straight up in bed, her pulse racing. What the? It wasn't her alarm … it was her phone. No good news came at midnight. She reached for it and her other hand dropped to the empty place beside her. Where was Nicholas?

She leapt out of bed as she recognised the number. "Where's the fire, Lawrence?"

"Mai, it's the cafe out on Mortimer Road. You leased it didn't you?"

Her heart stopped momentarily as she flicked on the light and grabbed her fire gear. "Yeah. How bad?" She wouldn't panic. Maybe it was a fire in the backyard.

Nicholas raced into the room already dressed. Where had he been?

Lawrence's words brought her attention back to what mattered. "It's well alight."

She squeezed her eyes closed as she fought down the nausea. "Many responders?"

"We've got a full crew. Maybe you should sit this one out."

"Nicholas and I will meet you at the cafe." She hung up.

"How bad?" Nicholas asked.

"Bad." There was a lump in her throat but she refused to let her emotions get the better of her. "We didn't leave anything on, did we?"

He shook his head as he threw on his gear. "No, you inspected everything before we left."

She checked Calypso's water bowl and then Nicholas held the back door open for her and she raced out to her car.

The fire glowed bright orange in the dark sky, a beacon to where they were heading. Even as she drove fast, her focus on the turns ahead of her, she knew there was no hope. A glow that bright meant the building had been consumed. She parked out of the way and ran to the fire tanker, the fire-fighters already suited up wearing breathing apparatus, dousing the flames with water.

There was no saving it. The cafe was fully engulfed, with smoke pouring out of the roof and flames shooting from the broken windows. The smoke stung her eyes and the heat made her sweat as she stared into the inferno, her heart in her throat.

All of the work they had done that day burned in front of her.

Her future was going up in flames.

She'd been warned.

And Creepy Guy had delivered on his threat.

Anger settled over her shoulders as Nicholas joined her, pulling her into his arms.

"We'll sort it out, Mai. Don't worry."

She pushed him away. He was spouting platitudes. There was no way to sort this out. The cafe would be a skeleton by the time the fire was out. She wouldn't be moving into it by the end of the month. She would have to start again – again.

Lawrence strode over to them. "Either help or get out of the way."

His tone snapped her out of it. She would worry about the consequences later. First they had to put out the fire, stop it from spreading to the trees or the neighbouring houses.

She picked up a hose and worked with Nicholas. The heat was a shimmering wall and the smoke was dark and acrid. The water was having little effect.

"Mai!" The yell and a hand on her shoulder had her turning to Jeremy. "The bakery is on fire."

Mai blinked. "I can see that," she shouted, gesturing to the burning building.

He shook his head, his eyes full of concern. "The one in town."

She froze. No, not that too. She couldn't handle them both burning. That was her life. Then her heart stopped. "Calypso ..." She shoved her hose at Jeremy and turning, she ploughed straight into Lawrence, bouncing off him with a thud. He was *not* stopping her.

"Take the fast attack," he shouted at her. "There's another brigade on its way, but we can't leave here."

Gratitude swept through her. She ran towards the vehicle. By the time she had it going, Nicholas was in the passenger seat beside her.

"What the hell is going on?" he asked.

"The bakery is on fire. I have to get Calypso out."

He swore. "What do we need to do?"

"It depends on what we find." Had the fire started in the front or the back of the building?

It had to be the back, the front was too exposed. And if that was the case, she wouldn't be able to use the stairs. She'd need the ladder to get to the kitchen window.

Her heart thudded as she sped into the back car park. Smoke billowed from the door. There was so much of it – too much of it. Was Calypso already dead?

She jerked the vehicle to a stop and ran to the fast attack trailer, snatching up a BA set while Nicholas set up the hose. "I'm going in." She hefted the set on to her back and put the mask over her face, then grabbed a torch from the toolbox. "Turn the hose on." Sirens sounded in the distance. Help was on its way, but she didn't have time to wait.

He didn't argue with her.

The door jamb was already splintered, the lock broken. This was where they'd entered.

"On the count of three." She counted down and then kicked the door open. Heat and smoke rushed out and Nicholas directed the hose into the bakery. The water cleared some of the smoke momentarily. Her kitchen was ablaze. There would be no saving it.

But she had to save Calypso.

She raced up the stairs, and into her apartment, slamming the door behind her. The smoke wasn't as thick in here but the room was hot, the heat coming in waves from the floor. "Calypso!" The mask and the crackle from the fire muffled her voice.

No response.

She had to be careful. There was no telling how stable the floor was, but she wasn't leaving without her cat. She moved quickly, as lightly as she could, to Calypso's favourite sleeping corner, but he wasn't there.

Shit.

Where else would he be?

The smoke was thicker at the front of her apartment and it was warm, too warm. She scanned the room with the torch, moving towards her bedroom.

She didn't have long.

"Calypso." The light beam shone over her bed and hit her cat curled up against her pillow. She ran forward and seized him, tucking him under her arm as she ran for the stairs.

"Mai, you've got to get out of there." She jumped at Nicholas's voice coming through the radio of her BA.

"On my way." She opened the door and a thick cloud of smoke and flame rushed at her. She slammed it shut.

"I'm coming out the window. Get me a ladder," she ordered, racing for the kitchen.

As she reached the sink there was an almighty crash behind her. She didn't stop. She vaulted on to the bench and kicked out the glass in the window frame. Someone had leaned a ladder up against the building and a fire tanker was below, with fire-fighters yelling at her. She couldn't hear what they were saying, but she had to get out of there. She didn't have much time.

She placed Calypso on her shoulders as she backed out on to the ladder. Her heart lodged in her throat at the gaping hole where her living room had once been. She could see down into the kitchen full of flames. Her bakery was gone.

Her lungs hurt and her eyes watered as she shimmied down the ladder. When she reached the ground, hands gripped her, pulling her away from the building.

Nicholas.

"Over there," he yelled and pointed.

Lincoln stood there with Oscar, the town vet. Thank God someone had called him. She raced over and gave Calypso to the vet.

"Let me check him." Oscar laid him on the ground and examined his vitals. "He's breathing, but I need to take him to the surgery."

Mai ripped off her BA. "Do you need my help?"

He shook his head. "You're needed here. I'll call you."

In moments he was gone. Mai looked back at the bakery. Flames and smoke condensed where once her dreams had been. Two brigades were attacking the fire from different angles and while it wasn't spreading, there was no saving the building. Her bakery was gone.

She seized control of her emotions. She couldn't afford to grieve yet. She had to see this through. "You need to call Albany," she said to Lincoln. "This was deliberately lit. The back door was kicked open."

Lincoln's nod was short, his face grim. "Already done."

Nicholas wrapped his arm around her waist.

As her pulse rate came down and the pressure in her chest

cleared, the enormity of what was in front of her hit her. Her home and business were burning to the ground in front of her.

Her eyes filled with tears that had nothing to do with the smoke. She had lost everything. Her ovens, her mixers, all of her supplies. Everything she had worked so hard for, all the time she'd sacrificed to make it a success, gone with the strike of a match.

Gone because she'd spoken to Lincoln. Gone because some bastard thought he could threaten her, thought that he could control her.

She'd show him she couldn't be bullied. She'd do everything in her power to see him behind bars.

If he knew what was good for him, he wouldn't show his face near her again.

As the roof caved in, in a roar of defeat, so did her resolve. Everything was gone. She sank to the ground and hugged her knees. Nicholas pulled her into his arms and she buried her face in his chest and sobbed.

The sun had appeared on the horizon by the time the fire was out, its glow so reminiscent of the burning building that it would be some time before Mai would be able to enjoy a sunrise again. She'd taken her turn on the hose and had spoken with Lawrence who had dropped by after the cafe fire had been extinguished. There was only a shell left of both buildings.

Penny had arrived for work and watched in horror as the building burned before Mai sent her home. She had to ring the rest of her staff today, she had to tell them they no longer had jobs. They were going to be devastated.

She squeezed her eyes shut. Her throat hurt from the smoke she'd inhaled and from trying to keep the tears at bay. She kept hoping this was a nightmare and she would soon wake up.

But it wasn't.

The only positive of the night was that Calypso was all right. Oscar had called to tell her he was fine but on oxygen and he would monitor him for the day. Mai wanted to cuddle her cat, to reassure herself he was really OK, but that would have to wait.

First she had to answer questions from the Albany detectives who had arrived to investigate. They were the same two who'd come to investigate the containers she and Nicholas had found.

"Do you want me to call your parents, or Fleur?" Nicholas asked her. "They can bring you something else to wear."

She had nothing left but the clothes she wore. She swallowed past the lump in her throat and shook her head. "Let's not wake them yet." The bad news could wait.

"Are you ready to come to the station?" Lincoln asked.

"Yes." There was nothing left to do here.

She and Nicholas sat in the back of the police car and Lincoln drove. Once inside the station, Lincoln put a hand on Nicholas's chest to stop him from going into the office with Mai. "We need to interview you separately."

Mai frowned. Why? She wanted him with her.

The male detective glanced down at his notepad. "Nicholas Shadbolt, you're the owner of the building?"

Mai jolted. That's right, he was. And it had burned to the ground like his last development. She hadn't even thought to ask how he felt.

Nicholas nodded, his expression grim as he followed Lincoln into another room. He didn't even look at Mai.

Something was wrong.

"Take a seat, Miss On," the detective said.

Mai sat in one of the hard plastic chairs in front of Lincoln's desk. The whole office was so impersonal, grey and functional with a crappy desk, an ancient four-drawer filing cabinet and a couple of chairs. The man sat in Lincoln's chair and the woman sat next to Mai.

"I'm Detective Khan and this is my colleague, Detective Bosch," the man said. "Can you tell us what happened last night?"

Last night her whole world had burned to the ground, but that wasn't what he wanted to hear. She swallowed hard and started from when the phone call had woken her up.

"Nicholas was with you the whole night?" Bosch asked.

"Yes." She hesitated. That wasn't right. He'd been awake and dressed when the phone call had come. Her skin prickled, not liking where her thoughts were headed. "Actually, I'm not sure."

Both detectives' gazes sharpened on her.

"What do you mean?" Khan asked.

"When the phone woke me, Nicholas wasn't in the bedroom. He walked in as I was talking to Lawrence and he was already dressed."

"You don't know where he was?"

"No, I didn't hear him get out of bed." But he couldn't have driven to the cafe and back to light the fire. She would have heard the car start and woken up.

Bosch looked up from where she wrote a note. "Was the back door locked when you left?"

Her mind ran through what had happened. "I don't know. Nicholas held it open for me." They were thinking what she was thinking, but she wouldn't vocalise it, wouldn't believe it.

"Did you notice the back door at all?"

"No, I was more worried about getting to the cafe." She hated the suspicion, hated that she could even consider Nicholas had done this. "It had to be Creepy Guy."

Khan raised an eyebrow.

"Did Lincoln tell you about Creepy Guy? There was a police sketch."

Bosch reached for a file on the desk. "This man?" She held up the sketch.

"Yes. He threatened to burn down my bakery if I told the police what I saw."

"Were you aware Nicholas has been suspected of arson before?" Khan asked.

Didn't they believe her? "Yes. He told me all about it. It wasn't him." He couldn't have been lying to her – could he? He'd been so cut up, so distressed about Shane, about the whole situation.

"Did he say who it was?"

She swallowed. "He doesn't know for sure."

Khan sat straighter. "But he suspects someone?"

It wasn't her secret to tell, but she didn't have the loyalty to Shane that Nicholas did. She nodded.

"Who?"

"Ask him," Mai said. "Can we forget about Nicholas and get

back to Creepy Guy? He's the one who threatened me. Nicholas knew I was moving out at the end of the month, he even helped me in the cafe yesterday – there's no reason for him to burn the building down." She had to believe it.

"There's always insurance," Bosch said.

"No." She couldn't believe Nicholas would do that. He knew how much her bakery meant to her.

"How long have you known Mr Shadbolt?" Khan asked.

"About two weeks."

"That's not much time to get to know someone." Bosch smiled at her sympathetically. "But it's flattering when an attractive man pays us attention."

Mai glared at her. But there was a tiny niggle of doubt in her mind. She gritted her teeth and answered their questions until her phone rang. Scanning the display she saw it was already seven o'clock. "It's my father, I need to get this." She didn't wait for their answer. "Dad."

"Oh, thank God you're all right," he breathed.

She winced. "I'm sorry, I didn't want to call you too early."

"That's nonsense! You should have called us straight away. What happened?"

That was the question of the day. "I'm not sure. I was at a call-out when the blaze started. I'm at the police station answering some questions."

"Do you need us to come and pick you up?"

"I don't know how long I'll be. I'll call you later."

"All right. We're here for you."

She hung up. The detectives were watching her, waiting for her. They could wait a little longer. She sent a text to the musketeers so they'd know she was all right. The response was immediate with a flurry of texts and then her phone rang with Kit on the line. She sent it to voice mail. "Are we finished?" she asked. "I need to call my staff and reassure my friends and family."

"We're done for now." Khan got to his feet. "We may need to ask you some more questions later."

"Lincoln has my contact details." She walked out of the room. Lincoln sat at one of the desks. "Where's Nicholas?"

"We still need to question him," Bosch told her.

She didn't want to leave him here, but she needed to call people, needed to get out of her smoky gear.

The realisation crashed down around her. She had no clothes to change into, no home to go to, she had nothing.

Mai squeezed her eyes shut and took a deep breath.

"Do you want me to call someone to pick you up – Fleur, your parents?" Lincoln put his arm around her shoulders.

She wasn't ready to face anyone yet, she needed time to process what had happened and to call her staff. But she had little choice. She had to go somewhere. "I'll call my parents." She dutifully made the call as Lincoln turned to the detectives. "Nicholas is in the interview room."

Khan nodded and he and Bosch went into the room.

She didn't have the energy to worry about Nicholas now. If he was innocent, he'd be fine. She had to deal with her staff.

Mai walked outside to wait for her father and Lincoln accompanied her. She yearned to lean up against the building wall and rest, but if she did, she might fall asleep. She couldn't succumb to the fatigue yet.

"Mai, this doesn't look good for Nicholas," Lincoln said.

She glanced at him. "He didn't do it." Maybe if she said it enough times she could get rid of the tiny sliver of doubt.

"You don't know that. We barely know the guy. He was suspected of arson at his last development."

"I know." She wanted to clamp her hand over his mouth to stop him from speaking. Fatigue was messing with her logical thought process.

"I know you like him, but you need to be careful. You shouldn't spend any more time alone with him."

Anger coursed through her and she placed her hands on her hips. "*You're* the one who said I shouldn't be alone, who told him to stay close to me. I don't understand why he's suddenly the suspect and not Creepy Guy."

"Because Creepy Guy is a man for hire." Lincoln's voice was soft.

"What?"

"We got a lead on him on Friday. He's a guy who will do anything if you pay the right price ... and Nicholas has a lot of money." He placed a hand on her arm, his expression concerned.

"No." She shook him off. He was making her doubt Nicholas and she didn't want to. She *loved* him.

"I'm sorry, Mayday. We have to explore the possibility." It was his gentle tone that got to her.

"It can't be him, Lincoln," she whispered.

He pulled her into his arms and hugged her. "I really hope it's not, but you need to be prepared in case it is."

She dashed the tears from her eyes as her father pulled into the car park. "I've got to go."

He nodded. "Take care of yourself, and call me if you need anything."

"I will." She walked over to where her father waited for her. He pulled her into his arms and squeezed her tightly. "I'm so glad you're all right," he whispered in Vietnamese.

Mai hugged him back, trying her hardest not to cry. She couldn't break down now. She had too much to do. There were staff to call, insurance to sort out, a life to rebuild. She swallowed hard. "I'm fine, Dad." Or she would be eventually. Getting into the car, she closed her eyes and rested her head against the side window.

"What did the police say?" her father asked. "What happened?"

"Can we wait until we get home? Mum will want to know too." She didn't have enough energy to explain it repeatedly.

He nodded.

At the front door to the house she was swamped, her mother, sisters and Kim all crowding her, hugging her and demanding to know what happened. She wanted to disappear, wanted to sink into the floor and pretend it was all a bad dream.

"Give her some space!" her father called, shooing them away. "First she needs a shower and clean clothes, then she needs food."

Her mother put an arm around Mai. "Come with me, Honey."

Mai let herself be led into the bathroom. Leanne handed her a pair of shorts and T-shirt to change into and then they left her alone.

Bliss.

She stripped off her clothes and ran the water, stepping under the warm, soothing spray. If only she could wash off her fatigue and worries as easily as she could wash off the sweat.

She had staff who would be turning up to work soon, and she needed to tell them not to bother. Jodie and Sylvia were both single parents and would be equally devastated and there was nothing she could do to fix it.

When she was dressed, she found her family in the kitchen. Her father had made banh mi and as she sat at the table, he pushed a roll over to her. "Have you eaten anything this morning?"

She shook her head, and though she wasn't hungry, she took a bite. The flavours were plentiful and tasty as always.

"Can you tell us what happened?" Kim put a mug of coffee in front of her.

"Where's Calypso?" Eden asked.

There was silence as her family looked at each other as if fearing the answer.

"At the vet's. Oscar says he'll be all right." She would need to pick him up this afternoon.

"How did he get out?" Leanne asked.

"I went in and got him."

Her mother gasped. "You went into a burning building to save a *cat?*"

She didn't have the energy to defend herself. "Calypso's family, Mum. I'd do the same for any of you."

Her mother opened her mouth to say something else, but her father put a hand on her shoulder and shook his head. "Tell us what happened."

So she did. She went through the whole nightmare of a night again, sticking to the facts, not letting her emotion rise to the surface. If she thought about everything she'd lost she wouldn't be able to continue talking. When she'd finished she stood up. "I need to call my staff."

"Use my office," her father said.

"Thanks." She closed the door on the room and sat behind his desk. This would be hard. She braced herself and called Jodie.

It took her twenty minutes to calm Jodie down. When Mai

finally got her off the phone she dumped it on the desk and closed her eyes. She desperately wanted to handball the task to someone else, but there was no one else. It was her business, her staff, her responsibility.

Her life.

She continued down her list.

Mai hung up from the last person and sighed. She was done. Her body was so heavy, her mind so tired that she was tempted to go to sleep right here. But she needed to call the insurance company, and find out whether her safe had survived the fire. Her phone rang. She groaned. She couldn't handle any more conversations.

But the caller ID caught her attention.

It was Nicholas.

She reached for it, needing answers, needing to convince herself Lincoln and the detectives were wrong.

"How are you?" His voice soothed her.

"Exhausted."

"Where are you?"

"My parents'."

He was quiet a moment before he said, "Can I come and see you?"

She did want to see him, did want to talk about where he was last night. "Yeah."

"I'll be right over."

Mai left the office and returned to the kitchen. Only her mother was there.

"How did it go?" she asked.

"As well as you could expect. They're all now unemployed until I can figure out what to do."

Her mother frowned. "What do you mean? Won't you just wait until the new development is built?"

Mai gaped at her mother. "That's six months away."

"Yes, but what else can you do?"

She had no clue, but giving up wasn't an option. "I don't know yet."

"Mai, be sensible. There weren't any other suitable premises available to you. You should take a break from work."

Fatigue and anger surged together in a wave that rolled through Mai. She'd had enough of her mother's negative attitude towards her work. "You never wanted me to be a baker, but I won't go to university to make you happy. It's my decision, my life. I will continue to bake and nothing you say will stop me." Her lungs hurt and her skin was so tight. She wanted to cry, but she wouldn't – not here, not now. She wouldn't show her mother how much it hurt.

"Mai, no." Her mother shook her head. "I wasn't against you becoming a baker because I wanted you to go to university. It was because I knew the hours you would need to work. I understand how hard it is to run a small business, how stressful it can be. Your father and I had been consumed by our jobs in Perth and I didn't want that for you." She placed a hand over Mai's. "I'm so incredibly proud of what you've done, of all of your hard work. I hope the rest of my children are as successful and as happy as you are. It grieves me that you've lost everything."

Mai stared at her mother, the lump in her throat growing larger. She blinked rapidly. If she started crying now, she wasn't going to stop. She swallowed hard. "I never realised."

"I should have told you."

Mai sniffed, and the doorbell rang. "That will be Nicholas." She got to her feet. She needed to move, needed to focus on something else. Her eyes burned but she couldn't give in.

"I love you, Honey," her mother said.

Mai nodded, unable to speak, and hurried down the hallway, stopping for a moment before she opened the door to get her emotions under control. Her mother was proud of her, believed she was successful. It soothed some of the pain inside. Taking a deep breath, she opened the door.

Nicholas still wore his fire-fighting gear, his eyes shadowed. She stood back to let him in.

"Some night, huh?"

"Yeah." She led him into her father's office. Now she needed to deal with where Nicholas was when the call came in. She wasn't sure she'd be able to handle any more bad news today. "Were you with the police all this time?"

He sighed. "I was. They had a lot of questions."

So did she.

Nicholas pulled her into his arms. "You scared the shit out of me when you went in after Calypso."

His arms were strong, warm and comforting. He smelled like smoke, sweat and Nicholas. She wanted to forget about what had happened, about her suspicions and be with him, but she couldn't. She gently pushed him away. "I couldn't have left him there."

"Just don't scare me like that anytime soon."

"I'll try not to." She closed the door. She had questions.

She just hoped he had the right answers.

"We need to talk."

Chapter 17

Nicholas's heart thumped hard in his chest. He'd known this was coming. It was only a matter of time. But he didn't want to do this now, with Mai looking as if she could barely keep her eyes open. "We should both get some rest first. It's been a long night."

She straightened, lost some of the fatigue in her eyes. "No. I need to know. Where were you when Lawrence called?"

For the first time since he'd met her, she appeared uncertain. He had put that look on her face. And her expression when she found out the truth would be far worse.

"You were dressed."

He nodded. "I heard something downstairs and went to check."

She frowned at him. "Was there anything?"

He hesitated. How could he tell her that he might have interrupted Shane in the middle of setting the fire and then had left him to it?

"Nicholas?"

If he didn't tell her, Lincoln would. He'd told the police everything when he'd been questioned, including his suspicions about the Baldivis fire. Bracing himself, he said, "It was Shane."

"Shane?"

"My friend – the one who checked himself out of rehab." That sounded better than 'the one who was responsible for my last development burning'. "He recognised my car and was searching for a place to stay."

"Why didn't he call you?"

"He wasn't sure I'd answer. I told him where the spare key was to my parents' place. He left just as I got the message about the fire. I didn't get a chance to check what he was doing in the empty unit."

She shook her head. "The empty unit?"

"He was in there when I came downstairs. He said he was going to camp overnight until he could get in touch with me." He'd known something was off. But he never would have believed his best friend would burn down a building knowing he was inside.

What had his friend become?

"Wait, this is the friend you think was involved in arson?" Her voice rose with incredulity.

He winced. "Yes."

"And you left him behind while we went to fight the fire?"

"I reacted to the call out, just like you did. There was no reason for Shane to burn down the bakery. He has no financial interest in it at all."

"How about revenge?"

"For what?"

"For not having insurance, for ruining his plans, for sending him to rehab."

Every word was a dart right on target. Shane had blamed him, but to want revenge ... it had never occurred to him. And it should have. Looking back, it was clear Shane had broken into the unit, and may have been the one responsible the first time. He'd been so blind.

"Did you tell Lincoln?"

"Yeah."

She stood up. "You should go."

The abrupt change had him blinking. "Mai, I'm so sorry."

She nodded. "I know, but I need to sleep. I can't deal with this right now." Her eyes were shadowed and there was such conflict in them. She walked out of the office and down the hallway.

He followed her, his heart aching. "I'll make this up to you,

Mai."

She opened the front door, her smile sad. "I don't think you can."

Before Nicholas could say anything, she'd shut the door on him.

And ripped his heart right out.

A thud downstairs woke Nicholas and he was immediately alert, on edge. He got up and slid on some shorts. Had Shane come back? When Nicholas had arrived home he'd brought the spare key back inside. There was no way he would give Shane access to the house now. He threw on a T-shirt and crept into the hallway.

"Nicholas, are you home?"

Relief swept through him. It was his mother. Hurrying down the stairs he found both of his parents in the kitchen unloading bags of groceries.

"There you are." His mother raised her eyebrows. "It's midday. Don't tell me we woke you?"

He kissed her cheek as his brain worked to catch up. "I was up all night putting out a fire. What are you doing here?"

"I told you earlier this week we were coming."

Nicholas smothered a groan. "Sorry, I forgot all about it."

"It's not inconvenient is it?" she asked.

"It's our house, we can do what we like," his father growled.

Nicholas held up a hand. "Just give me a second." He went over to the kitchen sink and splashed water on his face. He needed to be more awake for this conversation.

His mother placed a hand on his arm. "Is something the matter?"

"Yeah," he said. His father would go ape-shit. "The fire last night was the building we bought. It's completely destroyed."

"What the fuck!" his father roared, as his mother sunk into a nearby chair. "How the hell has another one of your projects burned to the ground? Have the police questioned you yet?"

Nicholas wasn't going to cower, he wasn't going to be intimidated. He simply nodded. "I was there this morning."

"And?"

"Gerald, go easy on him. It's not his fault," his mother said.

"We don't know that," Gerald snapped.

Nicholas couldn't breathe. The air disappeared from his lungs as the accusation hit him.

"Gerald!"

"I didn't burn down my girlfriend's bakery," he said when he was able to breathe again. "But I think I know who did."

"Girlfriend?" his mother asked.

"Who?" his father demanded.

Nicholas answered his mother first. "I'm dating Mai who was one of our tenants." At least he hoped he still was. She hadn't dumped him straight out.

"Who cares? Who burned the building?"

His father wasn't going to like this. "Shane."

"What?" his parents asked in sync.

"He was there last night. I caught him coming out of the empty unit and he said he was looking for me. I told him to come here and then I got the call out for the other fire."

"Other fire?" his father asked.

"Mai had leased a cafe to work out of while the development was being built. That burned last night too." She really had lost everything.

"Why would he do that?" his mother asked.

"Because he blamed me for not having paid the insurance," Nicholas said. "I can't prove it, but I think he lit the Baldivis fire, or it was burned as punishment. He needed the money to pay for his drugs – he owed about fifty thousand."

His mother put a hand over her mouth and his father sank into a chair, his face white. "Why didn't you say anything sooner?" he asked.

"I thought he'd get better by going to rehab." He'd believed the bullshit his friend had told him.

"Do you know where he is now?"

"No." If he did find him, he'd take him straight to the police station, no hesitation this time. Shane had gone way too far. He'd destroyed Mai's livelihood and could have killed them. He needed help.

"I can't believe it," his mother said. "Vicki is going to be devastated."

"Not as devastated as Mai – she's lost everything."

His father banged his fist on the table. "You should have turned him in months ago."

Wasn't that typical? It was back to being his fault again. Well he wouldn't take it this time, even if he did regret his actions. He was tired of being the martyr. "These are Shane's actions; they are his fault, and he's going to have to answer to them." He couldn't stay here. He wouldn't shoulder the blame.

"I'm going for a walk."

He strode out.

After Nicholas had left, Mai went upstairs to her old room and slept for a few hours. She hadn't thought she'd be able to, not after Nicholas's confession, but the second she'd hit her bed exhaustion had claimed her. Now though, it was time to think, to plan, to figure out what on earth she was going to do.

She found some paper in a desk drawer and sat on the bed to write a list. She needed to call the insurance company, put in a claim, access her fire-resistant safe, confirm it had survived the inferno, and she needed to get some clothes of her own.

She looked up the number of her insurer and dialled. After an intense conversation, she received assurances that they would be out on Tuesday to assess the damage. There wasn't a lot she could do in the meantime.

Next she called Lincoln.

"Everything OK, Mayday?"

"Yeah. Have the investigators found my safe yet?"

"I don't know. They've only just arrived."

She knew the guys and they were thorough and methodical. She wouldn't get anything out of them until tomorrow. "Thanks." She hung up and her phone rang.

She'd been avoiding her friends, knowing she hadn't been ready to handle their kindness, but now she was. "Hey, Fleur."

"What do you feel like doing more: crying, screaming or getting stupidly drunk?"

Mai laughed, surprised that she could.

"'Cos I've got two other women here who are willing to help you out."

"What I really need is to buy some clothes," she said.

"Are you at Nicholas's?"

Her throat ached. "No, my parents'."

"I'm sensing there's a reason for that."

"It's a long story, but I'm ready to tell it if you're interested."

"Of course."

"Can one of you pick me up?" Her car was still parked outside the cafe, and she didn't have the energy to face the remains of the building just yet.

"We'll be right there."

Mai hung up and then made the bed and headed downstairs. Her sisters were in the lounge room and her mother was outside gardening.

Mai needed to say something to her, needed to apologise for the outburst. Her mother stood and brushed her hands against her shorts. "How are you?"

"A little less tired."

"Good. What are you going to do now?"

"The musketeers are taking me shopping."

Her mother smiled and walked with her back inside. "That's a great idea. Take my card." She took her purse off the kitchen bench and handed the card to Mai.

Of course. The loss hit her again. Her own purse had burned in the fire. She had nothing. "I'll pay you back when the bank opens."

Her mother hugged her. "Don't worry about it now."

Mai hesitated and then said, "I'm sorry for yelling at you earlier."

"I'm sorry you didn't realise how proud I am of you. Now, go, have fun." Her mother squeezed her hand and then nodded towards the front door.

Mai went out the front to wait for her friends and Fleur pulled up in her white Hyundai, the rest of the musketeers in the passenger seats. Before she could get in, they were out of the car surrounding her in a hug, their voices blending together.

Mai squeezed back the tears. She wouldn't break down now, not out here in public.

"Let's get you to my house and I'll make you a cup of tea," Fleur said.

She nodded and got into the car.

"So what happened?" Kit asked.

There was so much she had to tell her friends she wasn't sure where to start.

"Let's get to Fleur's before she starts." Hannah squeezed her hand.

It was a short reprieve and she was silent on the drive over. They didn't know anything about Creepy Guy, or Gordon, or Shane. At Fleur's house she followed them through to the kitchen. This was when she usually put a box of pastries on the table for them to share. She swallowed hard. "Sorry I didn't bring anything to eat today."

"We did," Hannah said and Kit waved at the packets of Tim Tams on the table.

"They won't be as good as yours, but they'll do," Kit said.

Mai took a deep breath as her gratitude and the understanding of her friends threatened to overwhelm her. "Thanks."

Fleur put mugs in front of her and the other girls. "Do you want to tell us about it?"

She nodded. They deserved to hear the whole story from her, but she'd start with last night. When she was finished, Hannah said, "Oscar will take good care of Calypso."

"I know." He'd saved Hannah's dog's life about a month ago.

"What did Lincoln say about it?" Kit asked.

"He called the arson squad in. Both fires were deliberately lit."

"Why would anyone want to do that to you?" Fleur asked.

"That's a long story." And they weren't going to like that she'd kept it from them.

She went through all that had happened since Kit's New Year's Eve party, keeping to the facts, reporting it as if it had happened to someone else, not her.

"Someone pointed a gun at you, *threatened* you, and you didn't tell us?" Kit was outraged.

"There wasn't anything you could do." There was no way she would have messed her friends up in this. She didn't want them in danger too.

"So what happens now?" Fleur asked.

That was the million dollar question. Mai hadn't allowed herself to think that far ahead. "The insurance company is coming on Tuesday." She sighed. "Even if I can get new equipment, I've got nowhere to bake or sell from." Images of the charred remains of the building flashed through her head and all at once her defences crumbled. Her whole body shook and the tears she'd been holding back for so long breached the flood banks. She sobbed, letting her friends crowd around her, hug her and tell her everything would be all right.

She didn't believe them, even though she wanted to.

She couldn't see a way out of this mess, a way to rebuild. And until Shane or Creepy Guy were caught, there was no point.

After she'd cried herself out, Fleur pulled her up and led her into the lounge room to sit on the couch. "We'll work something out, Mayday."

Mai shook her head. "I can't think of anything. The warehouse was the only other available space and it's too big."

"What about a mobile option?" Kit asked. "Lease one of those food vans and sell from there, offer delivery to customers."

"She'd need somewhere to bake from," Hannah said.

She would, but the idea had some merit. She wiped her tears, playing the idea around in her mind.

"You could bake here," Fleur said.

Fleur's kitchen wasn't the biggest, but it might do. She would have to think about it. It was the first glimmer of hope she'd had all day, and it gave her the strength to sit up and wipe the tears from her cheeks. She *would* work it out.

Fleur put her hand over Mai's. "We'll think of something. You're going to stay here with me while we sort it out, right?"

We. The plural reminded her she wasn't alone. "If you're happy with that."

"Of course." Fleur smiled. "Now, you're going to need some new clothes and such. Are you up to going out, or do you want to borrow mine?"

She'd had enough of feeling sorry for herself. She needed to do something, to take action. She let out a deep breath. "Let's

go shopping."
Perhaps some retail therapy would help.

Chapter 18

Just over twenty-four hours since Mai's bakery had burned to the ground and she was going insane. She'd spent the morning making phone calls, trying to think of everything she needed to replace and everyone she needed to contact. The bank had promised to send out a new card, she'd cancelled all of her utilities and when she'd finally been given access to her fire-proof safe, she'd picked up her car and headed into Albany to buy herself a new laptop.

She didn't have the energy to sift through the blackened remains of either of the buildings yet. It hurt too much.

Everything took her twice as long because she didn't have anything she needed – no identification, no cash, nothing.

Her emotions were a see-saw, going from optimistic to doomsday, from perfectly fine to devastated in a matter of minutes. She hated it.

For that reason she hadn't answered any of Nicholas's calls. She didn't know how she felt about what he'd done, didn't want to risk saying the wrong thing.

Calypso meowed and rubbed her leg.

She picked him up, cuddling him, his fur soft and comforting against her skin despite the lingering smell of smoke. He'd been discharged the night before and she'd bought him a new bed and bowl and he seemed settled at Fleur's place. It had taken her no time to move in – she had nothing except for her fire-fighting gear, and she'd picked that up from her parents yesterday when she'd dropped by to tell them she was staying with Fleur.

She strode over to the window. Maybe she should go for a jog, clear out the cobwebs in her head.

No, she couldn't. She hadn't replaced her sneakers yet.

The now familiar feeling of loss threatened to drown her.

Her phone beeped in her pocket and she fished it out. One glance had her heart racing.

Bush fire in national park. All units to respond.

It had to be a big one if the message was going out to all the brigades in the area. She leaped to her feet as Fleur walked through the front door. "I've got to go."

"What is it?" Fleur followed her into her bedroom.

"Bush fire – it's a big one." She threw on her gear, which still smelled of smoke and headed for the front door.

"Be careful."

"I will." As she strode outside, the siren at the station wailed. Fleur's car was parked behind Mai's, and since Fleur only lived a block away from the station, Mai jogged down the road, scanning the activity. Lawrence was there and Jeremy. The roller doors were open and more cars were pulling into the car park. Everyone was responding. That was good.

She waved to a couple of kids playing in the front yard as a dark van screeched to a halt in front of her, almost running her down. She stumbled and crashed into the back of it. What on earth? Her heart pounding from the shock, she turned to give the driver a piece of her mind. It wasn't like she was invisible in her high-vis fire-fighting gear.

She registered his blond hair and the bruised, scowling face.

The man Creepy Guy had been teaching a lesson.

Fear spiked, but it was too late. His fist ploughed into her face.

And everything went black.

Someone had filled Mai's head with the whir of ten mixers on high. Her head buzzed as her body rolled and bumped. Carefully she opened her eyes. Where was she? What had happened? She braced one hand beside her, felt the thin carpet she was lying on, and lifted the other hand to her head hoping to dull the pain.

The fabric-lined roof above her was almost close enough for her to reach up and touch it and she shared the space with a white surfboard, still a little sandy and smelling of the ocean. Why was she in the back of a van? And why was she wearing her fire-fighting gear?

Memories came back to her. The fire call-out, jogging down to the station, the van, the blond punching her.

She'd been kidnapped.

She closed her eyes to push away the incessant buzzing and tried to focus. Where was he taking her? What did he want? Had Creepy Guy sent him because she hadn't died in the fire?

She needed to talk to him, needed to convince him she wasn't his enemy. Creepy Guy had said his name when he was beating him up. She closed her eyes, trying to remember.

Her eyes flashed open.

Shane.

Was he Nicholas's friend? Was this how he was repaying his debts?

Shifting slowly, she twisted her head to see the man. There was a metal grid safety screen between them, but he would see her if she sat up. He was about Nicholas's age, could very well be his friend. Which meant this might not be about drugs, but his vendetta against Nicholas.

Anger flooded her. This bastard had burned down her bakery. She was certain of it. She wouldn't let him get away with it, she wouldn't try to reason with him.

She also wouldn't lie here and let him take her wherever he was headed. The surfboard was too bulky to make an effective weapon and there wasn't even a toolkit in the back of the van.

She wasn't restrained though, so she could jump out if the van slowed down enough.

Taking a deep breath, she calmed herself.

The van jolted some more and her head cracked against the floor. Stars flooded her mind. She needed to be careful, had to stay conscious. The way the van shuddered indicated they were on an unsealed road – they could be anywhere. Depending on the direction Shane had taken, outside could be thick forest or low beach scrub.

She'd either have a chance to lose him, or be a sitting duck.

But she couldn't just lie here and wait for the van to stop. She had to do something.

A particularly nasty bump in the road jolted her and she shut her eyes, using the momentum to fling herself closer to the door. She waited for Shane to say something or to slow down.

Nothing.

Opening her eyes a sliver, she looked at him. His grip was tight on the steering wheel and he stared straight ahead. From where she lay she saw the top of eucalyptus trees and blue sky. Bush. She might be able to escape. She watched him for a minute, waiting to see if he would check his rear-view mirror and then realised he wasn't going to. The back of the van had no windows.

She rolled towards the door and reached up to pull the handle.

Locked.

But there had to be a way of unlocking it from the inside.

The bumps were less frequent and the noise of the tyres on gravel lessened. They were slowing down.

She wiped her sweaty palms on her pants. Fight time. She had to use the element of surprise. At her size, she needed all the help she could get. The surfboard would have to do.

The van stopped and the engine switched off, the ensuing silence all-encompassing until a kookaburra laughed.

The front door slammed and footsteps crunched closer as Shane came around the back of the van. She crouched, picked up the surfboard and waited, straining to hear, to sense what he was doing.

Eyes and throat – the most vulnerable areas.

She would aim for them.

The door swung open and the second it was wide enough she yelled, thrusting the point of the surfboard directly in his face.

"Fuck!" He staggered back.

Mai leaped out of the van and ran, fighting through a wave of dizziness. The red gravel road was potholed, with slippery ball-bearing like pebbles. Eucalypts towered on either side of her, the undergrowth scrubby and not very thick. She wouldn't be able to lose him in there. Far better if she kept to the road, she could go faster. Heart pounding, she glanced behind. Shane was right there, no more than a couple of metres away.

She couldn't let him catch her.

Pushing herself harder, she pumped her arms, keeping an eye on the road and her surroundings. She was a jogger, there was no way he would outrun her.

She checked behind again. He was falling back, his face red and angry.

Suddenly her foot hit a pothole and her ankle twisted, pain shooting straight up her leg. Her arms flailed as she stumbled and her ankle gave way. She yelled, sprawling palms first into the gravel. The tiny pebbles tore into her skin and tears pricked her eyes.

She had to keep going.

She pushed herself up, clenching her teeth as her ankle screamed at her not to move.

Shane came to a stop in front of her, panting, hands on his hips. His pupils were so dilated they almost blocked out his irises. "You're not getting away from me, bitch," he spat out.

Mai tried again to stand, but it was no use. She couldn't run any further. All she had left were words. "What do you want with me?"

"Get up." He grasped her ponytail and yanked her to her feet.

Mai wanted to vomit at the pain. She swayed, trying not to put any weight on to her twisted ankle. "Shane, please. I've done nothing to you."

"You're a means to an end." He clutched her arm and dragged her towards the van and the rickety corrugated iron shack behind it. There were gaping, rusted holes in its side, a rotten wooden verandah and part of the roof had fallen off. It looked like something that would fall down in a strong gust of wind.

She needed to keep him talking. Needed to get his keys and get into the van. She'd only have one chance. "What do you mean?"

"You saw too much, you're a loose thread that needs to be

tied off." He grunted as she slipped and fell against him. "And if that means Nicholas suffers too, then it's all the better."

He *was* Nicholas's friend.

Mai gritted her teeth and struggled to keep pace with Shane. Every step was pure torture. Her foot was swollen more than over-proved dough. "Why?"

The van was getting closer.

"He didn't pay the damned insurance," Shane yelled. "That was my ticket to freedom and he stole it from me. I was forced into rehab, my parents cut me off, and now I've got to do horrific shit for the Tiger to pay off my debts."

"It was a mistake," Mai said.

"Nicholas doesn't make mistakes – he's the goddamn golden child. He knew what I was doing. He wanted me caught." Shane's face screwed up in anger. "His parents didn't even punish him. Instead they gave him a cushy job in his favourite town, while I've been living in this shit hole." Shane pointed to the shack.

Only ten metres to the van now. Where were the keys? He was a city guy so they wouldn't still be in the ignition.

As they drew next to van, she stumbled and fell to her knees to force Shane closer to her, the thick fire-fighting pants cushioning some of the pain. Her pulse beat loudly in her ears as he swore.

"Get to your feet." He jerked her up and she fell against him. This was her chance.

She reached into his jeans.

They were too tight. Her fingers brushed metal and he slapped her hand, pushing her away. She sprawled on the ground.

"Sneaky bitch." He slapped her hard and her head snapped back. The pain made her eyes water and her ears ring. Before she recovered, he hauled her over his shoulder, pinning her legs tight against his chest. "Lucky you're a tiny thing."

She wasn't going down without a fight.

She elbowed the back of his head, forcing it forward. Shane swore, then squeezed her twisted ankle hard. The searing pain left her breathless and weak, as he clomped up the front steps of the shack and then dumped her onto the dusty, dirty floor.

Around her were bags of rubbish from various fast food outlets and some meth pipes. The only chair in the room, a fold-up camp chair, was too far away.

There was nothing she could use as a weapon. He dug a packet out of his jacket pocket.

Cable ties.

Shit.

She wouldn't get away if he used those on her. She sat up, ignoring the pain and punched him square in the balls. He bent over with a bellow and his fist connected with her face again.

She fought the darkness this time, but lost.

As Nicholas strode into the fire station he scanned the faces of those prepping the vehicles for Mai. She wasn't there.

She'd refused to answer his calls since he'd told her about Shane, texting him to say she needed a little more time.

He didn't want to give it to her, wanted to show her how sorry he was, but he wouldn't force it. He had to respect her wishes.

As much as he hated it.

Lincoln strode into the building and went straight to Lawrence, his face grim.

Something was wrong.

Was it just the bush fire?

He kept one eye on the two men as he performed the necessary checks.

When Lawrence called everyone around the table, Mai still wasn't there.

Where was she?

"It's a big mother," Lawrence said. "Lincoln's the incident coordinator for Blackbridge, but the Department of Fire and Emergency Services is in charge. They're getting the water bombers in the air as soon as possible. We don't want this to become like Esperance."

A fire that had burned for more than ten days.

"At the moment no properties are threatened, but that will change if the wind alters direction in line with the forecast. We're waiting for further instructions." He looked up from the map. "I want half of you to go home and sleep. This is going to be a long one and we'll need a fresh team to do the night shift."

As they discussed who was going on the first shift, Nicholas rang Mai. It went straight to voice mail. He frowned, worry prickling his gut.

"Nicholas, do you know where Mai is?" Lawrence called.

"No. I just phoned her – no answer."

Lincoln glanced up. "I'll call Fleur."

Nicholas strode over to him and caught the end of the conversation.

"No, she's not here yet. I'll call you when she turns up." Lincoln hung up. "Fleur said she left ten minutes ago. She was on foot."

Nicholas's mouth was dry as he headed to the entrance and scanned up and down the road. A couple of kids kicked a football in the front yard of a house, but there was no one else on the street. "Which way is Fleur's house?"

"That way." Lincoln pointed up the hill. "Where is she?"

There was no ditch she could have fallen into, no bushes to hide behind. And she wouldn't have stopped at anyone's place on the way. "I'm going to take a look," he said and walked up the road. It was a pointless exercise, but he couldn't ignore his instinct. Something was wrong.

He met Fleur halfway to her house. They didn't need to say anything. Fleur strode over to the kids playing on the lawn. "Jacob, did you see Mai walk past in the last few minutes? She was wearing fire-fighting clothes like Nicholas."

Jacob shook his head.

"I did," the little girl next to him piped up. "She fell down when the van almost hit her and the driver took her away."

Nicholas's heart stopped. "She was hit by a van?"

The girl shook her head. "No. She almost ran into the back of it. Then the driver got out and she fell down and he put her in the back."

Fleur and Nicholas exchanged glances. "I'll call the hospital," Fleur said.

Nicholas squatted down so he was closer to the girl's height. "What colour was the van?"

"Black."

Every hair in his body stood on end. Hell. Had Creepy Guy taken her? Had he not been satisfied by burning her buildings? His throat tightened and he swallowed. "What did the driver look like?"

She shrugged. "Just a regular old man."

"As old as me?" Nicholas asked. "Or as old as your granddad?"

"You."

"What colour hair did he have?"

"Yellow, like mine."

Blond man, Nicholas's age. Could it have been Shane? He reached into his pocket and pulled out his phone, scrolling until he found a photo of his friend. "Did he look like this?"

The girl squinted at it and nodded. "That's him."

Why the hell had he taken Mai?

Fleur hung up. "No one's been admitted to the emergency room."

"We need to get Lincoln." He thanked the kids and together they ran down the road to the station.

His phone beeped as he entered the building and he pulled it out of his pocket. The photo in the message stopped his heart and his feet. Mai sat in a camp chair, her arms tied behind her, her head down, eyes closed, face bruised. There was a map location and the words *Come alone.*

Fleur bumped into him. "Nicholas?" She peered over his shoulder and snatched the phone out of his hand. "Lincoln, Mai's been kidnapped!"

No. The message said come alone.

He lunged for the phone, but Fleur evaded him, reaching Lincoln and Lawrence. Silence. The rest of the fire-fighters were all staring at them.

Shit.

Now what?

Lincoln glanced at the photo and swore. "Who has her?"

"Shane."

Lincoln glared at him. "What does he want with her?"

"I don't know." He didn't want to contemplate it. It was his fault Mai was in this mess. "I need to go."

"That's in the middle of the national park," Lawrence said.

"It's north of the fire, but if you don't get her out before the wind changes direction you'll be right in its path." He scanned the map on the table and pointed out the location.

Nicholas didn't care. He had to save Mai.

"Call the number," Lincoln told him.

He dialled and headed for the street away from eavesdroppers.

"You got my message." The voice was painfully familiar.

He squeezed his eyes shut. "Shane, what are you doing? Why have you taken Mai?"

"Because you took away my options," he growled. "I've got no choice, and now you don't either. Let's see how you like it."

His pulse raced. Shane sounded a little crazy. He had to reason with him. "There's a bush fire in the national park. You need to get out of there."

He chuckled. "Who do you think lit it? Don't worry, we're nowhere near it, but the fire-fighters and police will have their hands full for a while. You've got fifteen minutes before I start poking holes in her."

"Wait!"

Shane had already hung up.

Would he really hurt her? After the fires he wasn't sure. He pushed past Lincoln, heading for his car.

"Nicholas!" It was Lawrence not Lincoln who called out. "Take the fast attack vehicle." Lawrence tossed him the keys. "It's more protected if you get caught."

He'd be driving directly towards the fire. Something he was getting used to. "Thanks."

"Nic, I need to call this in." Lincoln strode next to him as he headed for the vehicle. "We need to put a plan in place."

Nicholas climbed behind the wheel. "Here's my plan. I'm going to go in, save Mai and get out before the fire arrives. You do what you need to do." He hit the accelerator and the sirens.

He had fourteen minutes to go.

The distance to destination on his phone decreased far too slowly for Nicholas's liking. Once he hit the gravel road, he was forced slow. The road could have won a record for the most potholes in a single stretch.

He checked the time. Eight minutes.

He slammed his hand on the steering wheel and pushed the car faster.

As he drove, Lawrence fed him fire updates via the radio. "The wind change came early, Nic. The fire's heading your way."

He swore. There was nothing he could do about it. He had to push on, had to get to Mai.

His phone rang and he hit the answer button.

"I've been in touch with Parks and Wildlife Service, there's an old, disused shack in that location," Lincoln said. "We think that's where Shane is. There's only one road in, so he can't leave without passing you."

That was only partially good news. There would be no other way to escape the fire but this rough road.

"Albany police are backing us up and Ryan and I are on the way."

They'd be in the fire's path as well. Mai wouldn't forgive him if Lincoln got hurt because of this. "The wind has changed. It's heading this way."

"I know."

Lincoln was crazy. He had to keep him safe. He could handle his best friend. "Shane said to come alone."

"He didn't say anything about us turning up after you." Lincoln hung up.

Damn it. He reached for the radio as it crackled to life. "This is Blackbridge Station to Blackbridge Fast Attack One."

"Go ahead," Nicholas said.

"The wind is picking up speed. It looks bad. Be fast."

He smiled. Lawrence knew he wasn't turning back. "You need to stop Lincoln from heading in. He doesn't have the gear."

"I'll try."

Three minutes.

Nicholas wound down his window and sniffed the air. No smoke. The sky was clear and the forest looked like any other day. There was no clue a fire raged towards him.

Finally, up ahead was a black van, its back doors open, a

white surfboard on the ground and behind it the shack.

At last.

He slowed, scanning for Mai, for Shane.

They must be inside.

He pulled in and parked so the vehicle pointed back towards the road. He might need a fast exit.

Pocketing the keys, he got out, holding in his desire to race straight in there. He didn't know what his friend was capable of anymore.

The front door of the corrugated iron shack was open, and through one of the rusted gaps he saw movement.

"Shane, are you there?"

"Nicholas?" Mai's voice was low, a little weak.

She was alive. Relief filled him and he moved closer, scanning the nearby bush. "Are you all right, Mai?"

"Nicholas, you've got to run. Shane's got a—" A sharp crack cut off Mai's words.

Fury rushed over him and he stormed into the shack, pulling up short.

Fuck.

He blinked, not believing what was in front of him.

Mai sat on the camp chair, her hands behind her back and her feet cable-tied together. Her face was bruised, her head lolling to one side.

But that wasn't the worst part.

The worst by far was what Shane held in his hand.

He barely recognised his best friend who stood behind Mai. His eyes had a crazy glint to them, his normally styled hair was dishevelled and his nose was swollen and bloody.

He held a syringe full of something against Mai's neck.

Nicholas froze, then slowly raised his hands to show he was unarmed. "Let her go, Shane."

"No can do." His expression was grim. "This is what you've forced me into, Nicholas. If you'd paid the insurance, I'd be in Perth right now, not in this shit hole. Instead I've had to do things I never would have done, just to pay off my debts." He shook his head as if he didn't believe it. "And while I was trying not to get killed, you were going to New Year's Eve parties as if you didn't have a care in the world."

He needed to keep Shane talking. "I cared. I wanted to help."

"Bullshit. You got me thrown into rehab while you had a holiday down here."

"Dad wanted to hide me away. He was furious with me." Nicholas took a step forward and Shane gripped Mai's hair, tilting her head so her neck was exposed.

"Wait!" His heart pounded in his chest. He couldn't let Shane inject her.

Shane laughed, the sound frighteningly lacking in joy. "You really do like her, don't you? I mean, I know you were sleeping with her, but you should see the panic in your eyes." His smile was vicious. "The Golden Boy is in looove."

The words hit him like a bullet.

Shane was right.

He loved Mai.

And there was no way in hell he would let anyone take her away from him.

Shane lifted the syringe. "This contains one hell of a high. The same concentrated dose Gordon received before he drove away."

"Gordon." Terror clutched his chest.

"Yeah, that sad sap you pulled from the wreckage. He was attracting too much attention."

"You did that?" What had happened to his best friend?

Shane's eyes were haunted. "The Tiger said it was him or me. I chose him."

Shane was seriously unstable. Nicholas's eyes locked on the syringe. He had to get it. "You've got a problem with me not her."

"She put her nose where it didn't belong, just like you." He shrugged. "And like you, she has to pay." He lowered the syringe towards Mai's neck.

Nicholas lunged at him as Mai flung her body to the right. The force of her momentum caused the chair to tip and she crashed to the ground, out of Nicholas's way. He grasped Shane's hand and the needle flew out of it.

Shane swore, but recovered quickly. He roared and swung his fist at Nicholas's face.

Nicholas dodged, but not fast enough. The blow hit his cheek hard enough to make his teeth rattle. He channelled the pain, using it to fuel his anger. He wasn't as tall as his friend but he was stronger. He punched Shane back, throwing his whole weight forward and trapping Shane against one of the walls. The shack shuddered at the impact and the syringe rolled towards them.

Nicholas stamped on it, and there was a sharp crack as it broke.

Pressing his arm against Shane's throat, he growled, "It's over." This was his friend. He was sick and he needed help, but Nicholas wasn't giving him any more second chances. He needed to restrain him, tie him up.

He glanced around for more cable ties.

"Not until that bitch is dead," Shane spat and his knee connected with Nicholas's groin.

Pain shot through him, and Nicholas stumbled back, gasping for breath. He had no time to recover. Shane pounced on him, pushed him to the ground and pounded his fists into Nicholas's face.

Nicholas blocked the punches as best as he could, but each blow was like a jack-hammer.

Shane was beating him to death.

A metallic taste filled his mouth and he could barely see through the red haze in his eyes. He bucked, but it was no use. Shane had him pinned. The drugs had given him super strength.

He couldn't give up. Mai needed him.

He couldn't see her near him, didn't know where she'd gone, couldn't lift his head to look.

They were both going to die.

Chapter 19

Mai fought to stay conscious as she hit the ground. Her shoulders screamed at her and her ankle pulsed but she gritted her teeth. She had to get free. Had to help Nicholas.

She wriggled, glad Shane had only tied her wrists together and hadn't actually tied her to the chair. She glanced up. Nicholas had Shane against the wall of the shack, but Shane had crazy on his side.

Shuffling into a seated position, she tried to rise. Her ankle buckled, pain swamping her.

That wasn't going to work.

Changing tactics, she rolled towards the door. She had to find something sharp to cut the plastic ties.

As she reached the opening, the scent of smoke hit her. The bush fire.

She'd forgotten all about it.

Black smoke filled the sky, rolling towards her like clouds.

It was close.

She crept like a worm out of the doorway as Nicholas yelled. Her heart raced. She had to be quick, had to cut her restraints, but maybe she could distract Shane. "Fire!" she screamed.

Nicholas had brought the fast attack. There were tools inside, but she couldn't stand to get to them. The rusted holes in the corrugated walls weren't in a position she could reach either.

Scanning the surrounding bush, her eyes fell on a rusty sheet of iron to the left of the shack. It must be from the roof. She squirmed towards the step as Shane filled the doorway.

"Where do you think you're going?"

Nausea churned in her at his bloodied hands. Had he killed Nicholas?

Her heart spasmed. No, he couldn't have.

She wouldn't believe it.

"The bush fire's heading this way. We have to go."

As if emphasising her point, five grey kangaroos bounded out of the bush, almost crashing into the vehicles before continuing on – their panic clear.

Shane hesitated.

"There's only one road out of here. If we don't leave now, we'll be trapped." There was a sharp bang in the bush. "That's a tree exploding," Mai told him. "It's close." Too close. If he didn't help them, she and Nicholas were going to burn alive.

Shane was already moving towards his van.

"Wait! Nicholas is your best friend."

He hesitated, glancing back at her.

"At least untie me!"

He shook his head as he got behind the steering wheel. "You both have to die." With a spray of gravel, he was gone.

Mai coughed as the dust floated towards her. "Nicholas!"

The faint groan gave her hope.

Restraints first. If Nicholas wasn't fully conscious she wouldn't be able to help him as she was.

She bumped down the steps and rolled over to the rusted roof, relieved her fire-fighting gear offered some protection.

The light dimmed as the smoke clouded the sun. Soon she would be unable to see what she was doing. The bush started to spit and hiss as the fire crept closer.

Hands first. She shifted, twisting her neck to see what she was doing as she found a sharp edge. She sucked in a breath as it bit into her skin. Adjusting her position she tried again.

This time she found it.

In two swipes the plastic snapped and she yanked her hands in front of her, rubbing them quickly. "Nicholas, we need to get out of here. Are you all right?"

No response.

Using her freed hands, she swung her legs around and made short work of the ties on her ankles. She staggered to her feet, closing her eyes for a second against the wave of dizziness and then hopping the short distance to the shack. Around her spot fires were igniting.

They were running out of time.

She staggered up the steps. Nicholas lay in a heap on the floor, his face smeared with blood.

Oh, God.

She closed her eyes as the nausea hit her. She clenched her fists. No. She was not going to faint.

She could handle the blood.

She had to.

Nicholas needed her.

Focusing on the wall in front of her, she limped over, then crouched down by him. His blood was warm and wet as she shook his shoulder. "Nicholas!"

She risked a glance.

His eyes were open.

Thank God. "You need to move." She tugged at his arm. "There's a bush fire on our doorstep and if we don't move we're both going to die." She coughed as smoke flowed into the hut.

Suddenly it was dark. Very dark.

"Mai?"

"Yeah, it's me. Stand up for me."

He moved slowly, far too slowly, getting to his hands and knees. He groaned.

The shack was getting warmer.

There wasn't much time.

Mai got to her feet, all her weight on her good foot, and gripped him under the arms. "On your feet." He weighed a ton.

He lifted first one foot and then the other until he stood.

"Good. Let's go."

Every step was absolute agony as she put weight on her injured ankle in order to support Nicholas. The short distance between the shack and the fast attack seemed endless.

Smoke stung her eyes. The fire raged, engulfing one side of the road almost completely. The radiant heat burned. She threw open the passenger side door. "In you go." She shoved Nicholas inside and slammed the door behind him.

Using the tray of the vehicle for balance, she hopped around to the driver's side, snatching the two petrol-filled jerry cans off the back as she did so and leaving them on the ground. She didn't need them exploding if they got caught.

Ash swirled all around her and she coughed as she climbed into the driver's side.

No keys.

"Nic, where are the keys?"

His head was back against the head rest, his eyes closed.

Shit.

"Nic!" She reached over the centre console and shook him. He groaned. The keys had to be in his pocket. There was nowhere else they could be. She dug into his pocket and dragged them out.

Hallelujah.

She turned the engine and it spluttered, coughed and then roared to life. Gritting her teeth when her sprained ankle pressed the clutch, she stuck the vehicle into gear and drove.

It was dark as night now, the smoke completely blocking out the sun. She flicked on her headlights and reached for the radio. "This is Blackbridge Fast Attack One calling Blackbridge Station."

"Mai, where the hell are you?" Lawrence demanded.

"I don't know. I've just left a shack in the national park. The fire is to my left and it's bad."

"I can direct you out. Is Nicholas with you?"

"Roger that. He's injured. We're going to need medical assistance as soon as we get out of here."

"I'll have an ambulance on standby. When you get to a T-junction turn right."

The heat radiating through the windows was unbelievable, hot enough to make her skin burn, but the potholed road made it impossible to go any faster. She fumbled with the velcro of the heat shield curtain on the side window, rolling it down and sticking it in place. It blocked her view of the fire, but also some of the heat.

Nicholas moaned.

"Nicholas, stay with me." She glanced at him as the vehicle crawled forward as fast as the visibility and road would let her. Sparks of flame flew at the windscreen along with a whole heap of ash. She flicked on her windscreen wipers.

"Mai?" Nicholas's voice was soft, weak.

Relief flooded her. "I'm taking you to hospital." Mai put all the confidence she could in her voice.

How much further was it to the T-junction?

The engine warning light flashed on only seconds before the engine died and the vehicle slowed.

No, no, no.

Not now.

She turned the key off and on again. Silence.

The car was dead in the middle of a bush fire.

And they had no burnover sprinklers.

The fire had jumped the road and both sides of the bush were alight with flame, the heat burning her skin. She had to do something. "Emergency, emergency, emergency. Blackbridge Fast Attack One in burnover. Our engine has died." She checked the time.

There was a short pause before the response. "Don't leave the vehicle, Mai." Lawrence's voice was strained.

She wasn't stupid. "Roger that. We'll need someone to fetch us when it's safe to do so." Quickly she lowered the heat shield curtains on the windshield and behind her, then climbed over Nicholas to do the same on his side. She grabbed the burnover blankets and tucked one around Nicholas. His eyes flickered open.

"I need you to lie still for me," she said. "I'm going to get you some oxygen."

"It's hot."

"Yeah and it's going to get hotter," she said. The smoke seeped into the cab, eucalyptus and wood combined with melted plastic. She choked and lifted a breathing apparatus to her face, turning it on before doing the same for Nicholas.

Burnovers were counted in minutes. This wasn't going to last long.

She spread the other burnover blanket over herself and hunched down in her seat.

All at once she felt like the bread she baked. They were in an oven and it was horrific. It was so dark and she didn't dare lift the reflective curtains to peer outside. Seeing death coming towards her wouldn't change the outcome.

The fire roared and snapped, trees exploded, branches fell. There was a war going on outside. And all she could do was pray.

The radio crackled but she couldn't make out the words.

"What's happening?" Nicholas's voice was weak and he shifted. She placed a hand over his chest to stop him from displacing the blanket.

"Nothing much." She flashed him a smile. "We're stuck in a broken down car while a bush fire rages around us."

"Huh?" He tried to lift his head and she stopped him.

"Lie still. It will be over in a minute and then we can get out." Assuming they survived the baking heat, and assuming the doors didn't melt.

The noise outside was like a jumbo jet and Mai took another gulp of oxygen. Her whole body was heavy, lethargic, her ankle pulsing a steady, painful beat. She needed water but she was worried about removing her mask, worried about the chemicals that might be in the air. And only a few minutes had passed.

How much heat did it take to bake a human?

She didn't know, didn't want to know.

But this could be it for them. They might not make it out of the vehicle.

Her heart squeezed and her lungs burned. After all of the trauma of the past few days, this was the worst. But the scariest thought wasn't that she might die, but that Nicholas might.

He wasn't to blame for Shane's actions. Shane was crazy, irrational, blinded by the perceived wrongs against him.

Had he made it out?

She didn't care. She only cared about Nicholas.

Tears pricked her eyes and she squeezed his arm. "We've got to hold on," she said, more to herself than him. "When we get picked up, we'll get you to the hospital and have a nice cold shower."

He didn't respond.

His eyes were closed. Frantically she felt for a pulse in his wrist.

And found it, faint and thready. She choked out a sob. "I love you, Nicholas. Don't you dare die on me."

Nicholas's hand clutched hers. "I love you too, Mai." His eyes opened, met hers.

Her pulse pounded.

"We'll be all right," he whispered, his voice slurred, as his eyes slid shut again.

She prayed he was right.

It felt like an hour, but was only five minutes more when the temperature shifted. Either that or Mai was getting used to the industrial oven style heat. She peeled back the curtain next to her, peeked outside. There was less smoke in the air, the sky was lighter, and the flames in the bush weren't as intense.

The fire front had passed over.

And they were alive.

She reached for the radio and encountered a melted mess on the dash. Shit. She needed to call for help. To let people know they were OK.

"Mai?" Nicholas croaked.

"The worst is over." She opened the door, shoving her shoulder against it when it stuck, and then slid out of the car, taking off her BA. The bush still burned but there was none of the intensity. Smoke and ash danced around her and she sighed at the breeze. It was cooler out here. She needed to get Nicholas out of the car. She tossed her BA into the cab and grabbed a bottle of water from behind the seat and drank it in a couple of gulps. Then she slipped on her gloves, took another bottle and hopped around to Nicholas's side.

She tugged at the handle. It took a couple of attempts to pry the door open. Nicholas was still.

Her heart thudded as she slid off his mask, ignoring the congealed blood, and held the bottle to his lips. "Drink for me."

His eyes fluttered open.

"That's it. You need to drink something."

He lifted his head and she tipped the water onto his lips. He coughed and winced.

He needed to get to a hospital. She dug her mobile out of

her pocket. It had one bar of signal. She dialled Lincoln's number. He would be somewhere near control and could relay a message.

"Mai, tell me you're all right." His voice was frantic.

"We're both alive, but need to be rescued. The vehicle is toast, the radio has melted and Nicholas needs urgent medical attention."

He relayed the news to someone in the room.

"The fire's burned over where we are. You might be able to get a four wheel drive down the road when it's safe."

"What about Shane?"

She'd forgotten about him. "He left about five minutes before we did. I don't know where he is."

"Roger that. I'll call you back. I'm so glad you're all right, Mayday."

She smiled. "Me too."

Nicholas had his eyes closed and as she turned to him, he slid towards her.

"Nicholas?" She caught his shoulders, but the motion made her put weight on her bad ankle and she fell, taking him with her. Her heart kicked back into double time. "Nic, wake up." Reaching for his pulse, she found it.

The ground was hard and warm. Only the front half of the car gave some semblance of shade as the sun fought through the remaining smoke.

Gritting her teeth, she got to her knees and dragged him into the shade, putting him into the recovery position. She needed to clean him up, make sure his nose was clear of blood before getting the oxygen again.

She wouldn't lose him now. Not now they'd survived the inferno.

There was a first aid kit behind the seats.

She was almost numb to the pain as she used the roo bar to get to her feet and around the car to fetch the kit, the BA and the small esky of water.

She wiped his face, gritting her teeth against the waves of nausea and then fitted him with the oxygen, monitoring his breathing as she waited for a call back.

Her phone finally rang. "What have you got?"

"The fire's between you and the town," Lincoln said. "We've got an ambulance coming from Mount Barker and we're sending a PAWS vehicle to get you out."

"What's their ETA?"

"Twenty minutes."

A lifetime. "Nicholas is unconscious again," she said. "I can't wake him up." Her voice trembled.

"We'll be there as soon as we can," Lincoln said. "He might have heat exhaustion, Mai. You know what to do."

"Shane nearly beat him to death."

Lincoln swore. "Keep safe. We'll have you out of there soon."

She hung up and examined Nicholas. "Nic, wake up."

Not so much as a groan.

Tears blurred her vision, but she blinked them back. She couldn't fall apart, couldn't think the worst. She had to get them to safety. She had to cool him down.

She undid his jacket and opened it wide. He was pale and his T-shirt was wet with sweat. She checked the temperature of the remaining water bottles and poured one over his chest. He stirred but didn't wake.

Mai found the instant cold pack, activated it and shoved it under one of his armpits.

His jacket next.

She struggled to pull his arms out of his jacket, but eventually she managed it.

Her head pounded a steady, powerful thudding beat, and her stomach twisted uncomfortably. She clenched her teeth. She was fine. Nicholas was in worse condition than she was.

Grabbing another bottle of water, she took a few precious sips before tipping the rest over his chest. "Come on, Nicholas. Wake up."

Nothing.

The breeze came in flurries, kicking up ash and whirling it around them.

Nicholas groaned.

"Nic. Talk to me."

"Wet."

Her shoulders slumped in relief. "Yeah, sweetie. You got a

little warm and I needed to cool you down." She squeezed his hand. "You need to stay with me this time. You've got to stop slacking off and sleeping. I'm doing all the work here."

"Sorry." His words were still slurred.

"Can you drink some water for me?" She removed the BA and helped raise his head enough so he could drink from the water bottle she held for him. "Just little sips," she told him. "You don't want to choke."

He screwed up his nose. "Hot."

His words were precious. "Yeah, but it's the best I can do right now. We'll get you something cooler when we get out of here."

She prattled on, talking about anything and everything that came to her mind to keep him focused, asking him question after question so he had to answer.

Finally the beautiful sound of a car coming towards them reached her. "They're here, Nicholas. We're going to get you something cold."

"'K."

She waved as the white four wheel drive came into view. It pulled up and Will jumped out. He wore the khaki and bottle green uniform of Parks and Wildlife Service.

"Are you all right?" Will asked.

"I'm fine, but Nicholas isn't so great. He was attacked and beaten, and I think he's suffering heat exhaustion."

Will knelt down and examined him. "There's an ambulance waiting for us on the main road." He helped Nicholas to his feet and mostly carried him to the car.

Nicholas was safe. They were going to the hospital.

She pulled herself up, and her head spun. She staggered forward into Will's arms.

"Woah. I've got you." He carried her to the car, put her in the front passenger seat and handed her a cold bottle of water. "Drink this slowly."

Nicholas was in the back, his eyes open.

Mai closed her eyes as nausea swirled in her stomach. She had to get some fluids into herself, but the lid of the bottle was too tight. She didn't have the strength left in her arms to untwist it.

She was tired, so tired.

"Hold on," Will said. "I'll get you out of here as fast as I can."

Secure in the knowledge that someone else was looking after Nicholas, Mai let the darkness claim her.

Chapter 20

Nicholas woke slowly, his head cloudy, an overwhelming scent of smoke around him.

Smoke?

His eyes flew open, but his vision was restricted to a couple of small slits of light. He sat up, heart pounding, head spinning.

No fire.

But he couldn't see properly. He reached up to touch his face and found a tube connected to his arm. He was in hospital.

"Nicholas!" The relief in his mother's voice was clear.

He turned and found his parents sitting next to the bed, their expressions concerned.

What were they doing here? "Mum?" His voice was croaky and it hurt to speak.

His mother burst into tears and his father stroked her back. "It's all right, Bronwyn, he's going to be fine."

Nausea rose up and he clapped a hand over his mouth. His father shoved a sick bag at him and he used it, his body heaving, his ribs screaming.

"The nurses said you might feel a little sick when you woke," his father said.

A little? More like he'd been beaten with a sledge hammer. He closed his eyes. What had happened?

If he smelled like smoke, he must have been at a fire. He remembered the call out, remembered getting to the fire station, and then what?

It had something to do with Mai.

"Mai?"

"She's in the bed next to you." His father gestured towards the curtain.

His pulse raced. If Mai was in a bed, then she must be injured. "Is she all right?" Why couldn't he remember?

A nurse entered the room and smiled at him. "Glad to see you awake, Nicholas."

"How's Mai?"

As she took his obs, she said, "She's doing well. A little dehydrated, and her family is with her. I can open the curtain for you if you'd like. She's been asking about you."

"Please." His throat ached to talk, but he couldn't remember fighting a fire.

But he did remember driving in the fast attack vehicle, a bumpy road, a shack.

The memories flooded back.

Mai kidnapped. Shane threatening her. Fighting Shane. Losing.

Then what?

Heat. The most incredible heat he'd ever experienced.

And all the time Mai was there, talking to him, telling him things, asking him questions, telling him she loved him.

Had he imagined that?

The nurse spoke to someone behind the curtain and then opened it. Mai lay in bed, her family around her. The bruises on her face made him grit his teeth. Shane had done that.

He continued his scan. She was attached to an IV of fluids and one of her legs was raised with a bandage wrapped around it, but she was conscious and her smile lightened his heart, slowed his pulse rate.

"Nicholas, how are you?" She slowly swung her legs out of the bed and sat on the edge.

"Don't get up." His brain was working at half pace, but he was sure she shouldn't be moving.

"I'm fine, just a sprained ankle and a bit of dehydration, but they're pumping me full now." She gently lowered herself to the ground, taking the fluid bag off its hook, and Anh helped her move to his side.

"I'm more worried about you. How are your ribs?"

He frowned. Ribs? His whole body felt like it had been tossed into a cement mixer.

His mother said, "You broke your ribs, nose, have a concussion and heat exhaustion."

He shifted to the side, making room next to him so Mai could sit on the bed, wincing as he did so. "Sore. What happened?"

"What do you remember?"

He took her hand, caressing it, needing to touch her. If even half of what he remembered was true, they were both lucky to be alive.

He wasn't sure what to say though. He wanted to talk to Mai alone, make sure his memory was correct, find out what his parents had been told.

Detectives Bosch and Khan walked into the room.

"We heard you were awake," Khan said. "How are you feeling?"

"Not great."

Bosch nodded. "I'm sorry. Can you answer some questions for us?"

"He's just woken up," his mother snapped. "Give him time to recover."

Nicholas winced as he smiled. "Mum, it's fine. The quicker we get this resolved, the better. Why don't you get a coffee?"

"I could do with a drink," Bian said. She moved into his cubicle and smiled at his mother. "I'm Bian, Mai's mother. Why don't we go around the corner to the pub and get a drink? We could all use one after today's excitement. We can come back in an hour or so?"

The last was directed at the detectives who nodded.

"All right," his mother agreed.

The cubicle emptied and he was left with Mai and the detectives. "Did you catch Shane?"

"He was picked up on the highway heading back to Perth. He's being taken to Albany station now," Bosch said.

Nicholas relaxed a little. If Shane was in custody he couldn't hurt Mai.

"Take us through today's events," Khan said.

Mai started the story, filling Nicholas in on how Shane had snatched her from the street and what had happened up until he had arrived. "Shane admitted he'd lit the fire on the Baldivis development," Mai told them. "He needed money to pay off his drug dealers. He called one of them the Tiger."

"We've got an alert out for him," Khan said.

Nicholas then took over the story, letting the detectives know Shane had admitted to drugging Gordon. His throat was sore and he coughed, taking a sip from the glass of water Mai handed him. "I don't remember much after being hit in the head a dozen times."

Mai squeezed his hand and continued the tale. "While Nicholas was fighting Shane, I rolled out of the shack to find something to cut my ties. Shane came out, noticed the fire was close and took off." She swallowed. "I managed to untie myself, get Nicholas into the fast attack vehicle and drive off, but the engine overheated and cut out. We were stuck in the burnover and then Will from PAWS got us out."

Nicholas's jaw dropped open and he winced. That explained the intense heat. They'd been in the middle of a bush fire. They'd been trapped, but Mai had saved his life. He kissed her cheek. "Thank you."

"You're welcome."

He didn't want to answer any more questions, he wanted time to be alone with Mai. He wanted to ask her about their conversation in the fast attack, wanted to find out if she really loved him. He ran his thumb over the back of her hand and she leaned into him.

"What's the status with the fire?" Mai asked.

"Blackbridge is on a watch and act alert," Khan said. "But it's forecast to rain. If it does, they should be able to control it."

In other words it was still a threat.

There was commotion outside the cubicle and Fleur, Jamie, Kit and Hannah burst in.

"You're all right!" Kit yelled.

Nicholas winced at the shout.

Mai smiled. "We're both fine."

A nurse came into the room carrying another bag of fluid

and shook her head at the sight of Mai on the bed with him. "You're both supposed to be resting." She exchanged the nearly empty fluid bag attached to Mai.

"We are," she said. "We're just being economical, letting someone else use the other bed."

The nurse laughed and checked her obs. "I'll get the doctor in to examine you after you've finished this bag. You should be right to go home this evening."

"What about Nicholas?"

"We'll need to keep him in at least overnight."

As much as he ached, he wanted out of the hospital. He wanted to be alone with Mai.

"We brought you both some spare clothes." Fleur held up a bag. She glanced at Nicholas. "You're about the same size as Jamie."

He squeezed Mai's hand. They had thought of him as well.

Jamie grinned. "They're not as stylish as your usual garb, but they'll do until you get home."

"Thanks, mate."

Fleur and Kit perched on the end of his bed. "You're done here, right?" Kit said to the detectives.

Nicholas swallowed his grin at their sucked lemon expressions.

Finally Khan nodded. "We'll talk to you both again in the morning."

As soon as they left, Hannah asked, "What happened?"

"Mai saved my life," he said.

"Go, Mai." Kit gave her a high five.

"Only after Nicholas saved mine." Mai told the story again, calm and to the point.

"Weren't you terrified?" Hannah asked.

Mai nodded. "I thought we were both going to die."

His hands clenched. She'd made it sound like no big deal to the detectives. And he hadn't been cognitive enough to truly understand what was going on.

The thought of Mai dying was physically painful. He nuzzled her cheek, not caring they had an audience. "I'm so glad you didn't."

Jamie cleared his throat. "I think these two need some time

to themselves," he said. "Let's go get a coffee." He smiled at them. "We'll be in the cafeteria."

A wave of gratitude and affection washed over him. "Thanks."

Finally they were alone.

And Nicholas didn't know what to say.

Mai reached for the bed adjuster and moved the back rest so they reclined a little more. Then she cautiously lay next to him, careful not to put any pressure on his chest. "You look like hell."

He winced. "I feel like it too." He shifted and a stabbing pain went through his chest. Ever so slowly he moved so he could put his arm over Mai.

He'd survived a beating and a bush fire, and yet admitting his feelings was far scarier. Maybe he'd hallucinated what he thought Mai had said. He took as deep a breath as he was able. "You talked a lot when we were waiting to be picked up."

"I did," she agreed. "I was trying to keep you conscious. I was so scared that your head injury was really bad." There was still worry in her eyes.

He cleared his throat. "I'm not sure if some of what I remember is real or a dream."

"What part?"

This was it. He would be brave. He would put his heart out there. Slipping his hand into hers, he entwined their fingers. "I thought you said you loved me."

"I did." Mai's gaze was intense, her eyes on his.

The relief was instant, flooding him with joy and hope. She loved him. "Thank God."

She raised her eyebrows. "You're happy about that?"

"Of course." Why would she even question it? "I love you too. Didn't I say that?" It was part of the same memory.

She laughed. "It was more of a garbled murmur before you fell unconscious again."

He hugged her tightly, and then gasped at the pain. He would have to be careful how he moved for the next few weeks. "Mai, you're the most important person in the world to me. I don't want a life without you."

She sighed. "That's a relief." She kissed him long and sweetly and all the pain disappeared for a moment.

When she moved back he said, "I want to move here permanently. I'll sort out a job, and we can get a place together."

She put a finger on his lips. "Slow down, Nicholas. We can work it all out later. Right now I want to hold you and reassure myself that you're perfectly fine."

He grinned. "Well then, let me see if I can prove it for you."

He kissed the woman who had saved his life.

The woman who had shown him how to live.

The woman he couldn't live without.

His Mai.

Epilogue

"Are those scones ready yet?" Kit called.

Mai glanced across Fleur's kitchen table to her friend. "Should be." Before she could stand, Nicholas gingerly got up and took the scones out of the oven, pricking them with a skewer to check they were done.

"Here, let me." Fleur took the skewer from him and shooed him back to the table where the rest of their friends were gathered. "The pair of you are the walking wounded."

It was only three days since he'd been discharged from hospital and his face was still an ugly shade of purple.

Mai smiled as Fleur placed the jam and cream on the table, followed by the steaming hot scones. The usual musketeer meeting had expanded to include Nicholas, Jamie, Ryan and Lincoln. They had gathered together to catch up on everything that had happened over the past few days.

"What's the latest on Shane?" Nicholas asked Lincoln and Ryan.

"The forced detox hit him hard," Lincoln said. "He confessed to breaking into your shed and the empty unit. He'd been angry and wanted to make you suffer and then he ran into the Tiger, who you know as Creepy Guy. He works for the drug cartel that Shane owed money to and they forced him to work for them. Shane gave Gordon the drug that caused the crash, and started both fires at the cafe and bakery."

"No sign of the Tiger yet," Ryan added. "Looks like he's in hiding."

Hannah passed Ryan a scone.

"Where are you with the insurance claim?" Jamie asked Mai.

"They're going to cover me for everything." It had been a long couple of days waiting for the result.

"That's great!" Fleur said.

"But it's going to be six months until you've got a building," Kit pointed out.

Mai grinned, excited to share the news. "Well here's the thing. I've been researching the delivery option Kit suggested. You know, allow people to order and pay for food and have it delivered to their door."

"But where will you bake?" Jamie bit into his scone.

"From my parents' place," she said. "They've got a huge kitchen and I can get a licence to operate from there until the development is finished." She grimaced. "But it does mean I have to move back in with them temporarily." Part of the food licence she'd applied for required her to live at the place where she baked. "I'm going to set up the website for orders and have a cut off time for next day delivery. Then I'll know how much I need to bake each day. It won't be as much as the bakery, but it will ensure people remember me."

"What about your staff?" Fleur asked.

That was the worst part. "There's not a lot I can do for them. I'll need someone to drive the delivery van, but that's all I can offer at the moment." She might be able to do a roster to employ both Jodie and Sylvia part-time. "If it's a success, Penny can bake at her place too."

"You'll make it work," Kit said.

She would. She felt far more optimistic about everything. After surviving Shane and the bush fire she could handle anything that came her way.

They swapped other news until people began to make a move.

"We need to pick Felix up from Jacob's place," Hannah said as she got to her feet.

Nicholas handed Mai her crutches and they went outside. She hugged her friends, ending with Fleur. "Thanks for giving me a place to stay."

"Any time. If you need a break from your parents, you're welcome to drop by." Fleur glanced at Nicholas. "Though I suspect you might have a better option."

Mai smiled. She and Nicholas hadn't spoken any more about the future. It hadn't helped that his parents were still in town and his mother flitted around him like a mother hen. But she was fine with that. Nicholas loved her and they had plenty of time to work something out.

She placed her crutches in the back of her car, and hopped into the driver's side. She'd never been so glad to have an automatic car. Nicholas slid in next to her and she headed towards his place.

"Want to go for a drive?" he asked. "We could go up to the lookout over the beach."

"Sure." She changed directions and headed for the lookout. When she pulled up and turned off the engine, Nicholas said, "I spoke to my father today."

Her heart skipped a beat. He'd been dreading that. "And?"

"I told him I wanted to finish this development, but then I was going to resign, find something else."

"How did he react?"

"Better than I expected. Mum's been talking to him." He sighed. "Can you handle marrying someone who might be unemployed soon?"

Her mouth dropped open. "Marry?"

He reached into his pocket, wincing as he did so, and pulled out a gold ring, with a small clear diamond set into the band. "I want you in my life forever Mai. The thought I could have lost you, you could have died …" He swallowed. "You've shown me how much fun life can be, taught me to live again and I can't imagine my new life without you in it."

She stared at him, joy and love running through her. He wanted to spend his life with her. "Yes," she said, holding out her hand so he could slip the ring on her finger. "Absolutely yes."

"I didn't want to get you a ring which would get dough stuck in it when you were kneading," he said. "But we can change it if you don't like it."

The fact he'd thought of it made her love him even more. "It's perfect."

She kissed him, his taste warming all of the places inside her which had still been sad.

While it had hurt to lose her bakery and all of her possessions, they weren't what truly mattered.

Family and friends mattered.

Nicholas mattered.

They would rebuild.

And they would build a life together.

Thank you for reading!

I hope you enjoyed the book. It would be super awesome if you could leave a review wherever you bought it, because I love to hear what you thought of the story (yes, even if you didn't like it!)

Be sure to check out the next book in the series, Nothing to Hide.

ACKNOWLEDGEMENTS

A big thank you to the people who helped me research this book. First of all to Matt Hartfield who continues to help me with all the policing details. Any mistakes are my own and for the good of the story. Also to Gary and Ted who gave me information about the volunteer bush fire brigade and the volunteer fire and emergency services. The information you gave me was invaluable.

As always I need to thank those people who helped me see this book into print: thanks to Lana Pecherczyk for the awesome cover, Ann Harth for her structural edits, Teena Raffa-Mulligan for her copy-edits and the Blurb Bitch, Carol Eastman for the blurb.

Nothing to Hide

The Blackbridge Series #3

Fleur's story is coming in 2018
http://www.claireboston.com/NothingToHide

About the Author

Claire Boston is a contemporary romance author who enjoys exploring real life issues on her way to the happily-ever-after. She writes heart-warming stories, with resilient heroines and heroes you'll love. In 2014 she was nominated for an Australian Romance Readers Award for Favourite New Romance Author.

When Claire's not writing she can be found creating her own handmade journals, swinging on a sidecar, or in the garden attempting to grow something other than weeds.

Claire lives in Western Australia with her husband, who loves even her most annoying quirks, and her grubby, but adorable Australian bulldog.

You can connect with Claire through Facebook (https://www.facebook.com/clairebostonauthor) and Twitter (https://www.twitter.com/clairebauthor), or join her reader group (http://www.claireboston.com/reader-group/).

Also by Claire Boston

<u>The Texan Quartet</u>
What Goes on Tour
All that Sparkles
Under the Covers
Into the Fire

<u>The Flanagan Sisters</u>
Break the Rules
Change of Heart
Blaze a Trail
Place to Belong

<u>The Blackbridge Series</u>
Nothing to Fear
Nothing to Gain
Nothing to Hide (coming 2018)

<u>The Beginner Writer's Toolkit</u>
Self-Editing